TWIST
OF
FATE

TWIST OF FATE

ALENA MCPHERSON

CRYSTAL CREEK
BOOKS

Published by Crystal Creek Books
La Crosse, Wisconsin

ISBN: 979-8-9928513-1-1 (paperback)

This is a work of fiction. Names, characters, businesses, places, events and incidents are either the products of the author's imagination or used fictitiously. Any resemblance to actual persons, living or dead, events or locales is purely coincidental.

While Lake City, Minnesota is a real and very beautiful place, some details were changed and others added to suit the narrative. Larson's Point and the town of Cascade, Minnesota are fictional.

First edition (August 2025)
10 9 8 7 6 5 4 3 2 1

For those who work in public service,
in gratitude for all the shit they deal with

To Red Wing
and Frontenac

Hok-Si-La Park

61
63

Sunset Motel & Resort

Territorial Rd

Mayo Clinic

Oak St

Grant St

Lakeshore Dr

Ohuta Beach

County 5 Blvd

Monroe St

Madison St

Jewel Ave

Washington St

Doughty St

Walnut St

High St

Wise Ace Hardware

Hidden Meadow Ln

Jewel Ave

9th St

7th St

8th St

Lyon Ave

Marion St

6th St

Irving St

Lakewood Ave

Minnesota St

5

10th St

Lake City Police Department

The Jewel Golf Club

Center St

Ardent Mills

Clubhouse Dr

63

Cross St

Orchard Ln

63

9

Minnesota

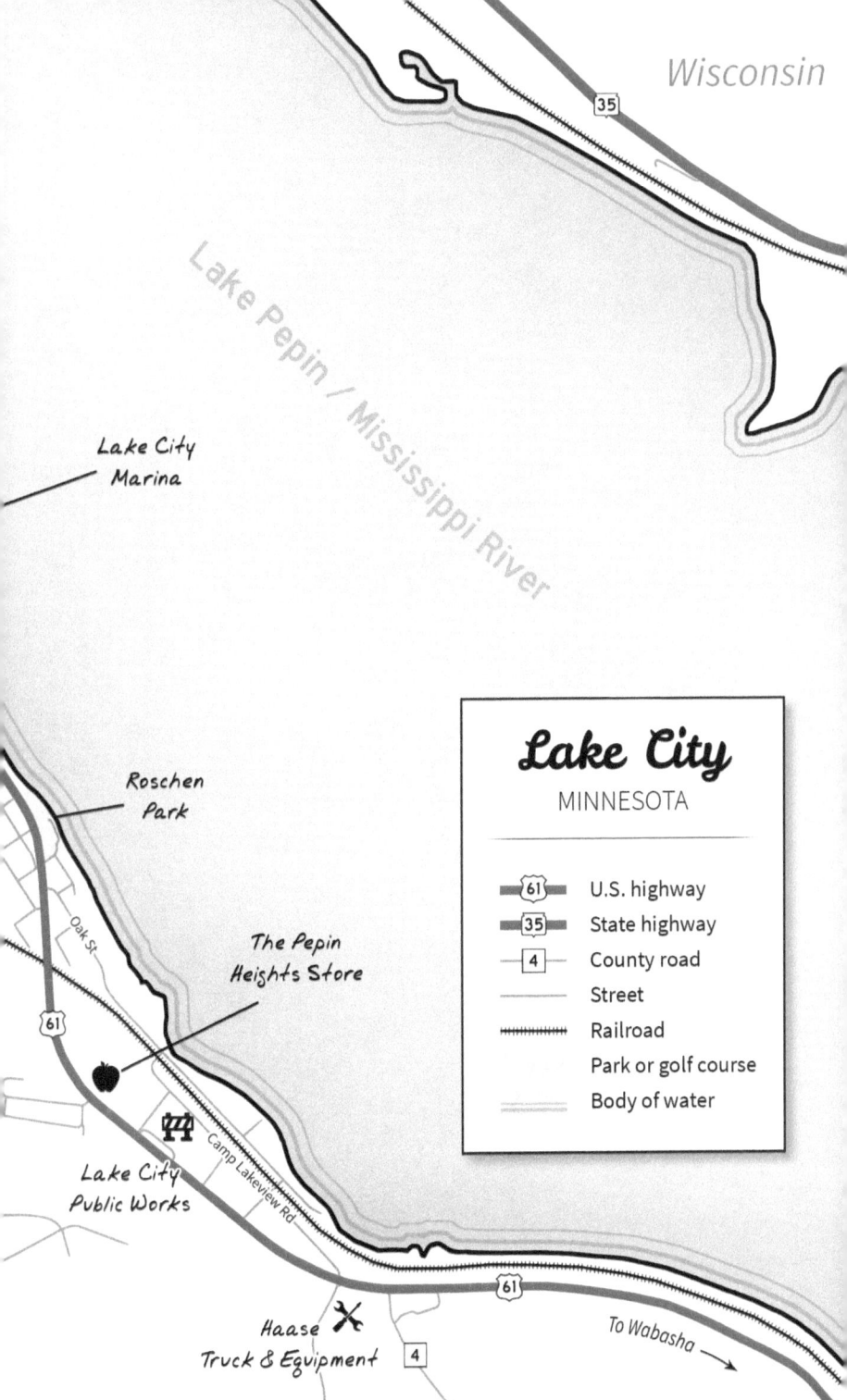

1

CALVIN STRODE to the front door of Paredes Fine Diamonds and rapped on the glass, ignoring the *sorry, we're closed* sign. He'd had to avoid the temptation to speed to get here. A struggle given the circumstances, but he'd gotten pulled over for running a stop sign less than a week ago. The noon traffic had really tested his patience.

Just as he was about to knock on the door a second time the store's broad-shouldered owner peered through the window. Sharply dressed as always, his black suit and dark skin made the gold he wore seem to shine that much brighter. Few people could pull off the look, but his massive watch and sizable rings complimented his burly figure. He unlocked the door and swung it open. "Cal? What are you doing here?"

"What do you think I'm doing here? Trying to talk some sense into you."

"I told you, I've got this."

Calvin stepped in and closed the door behind himself. With a t-shirt and jeans, he was dressed far more casually than Rodney, but apparently he was the only one who was taking this situation seriously. "No, you don't. Why the hell didn't you tell me?"

"I did like twenty minutes ago. Didn't think you'd come right over, though."

Calvin walked past him and to the middle of the small retail space. Shattered glass crunched under his boots as he took in the empty display cases. "You can't do this, Rodney. You've worked too hard to get where you're at."

"See? This is exactly why I didn't say anything earlier. I knew you would've tried to talk me out of it."

"Yeah, because it's gonna blow up in your face! I wouldn't be your friend if I didn't tell you that."

Rodney glanced over at the front door as he straightened the cuffs of his sleeves. "Can we talk about our difference of opinion some other time? A detective is going to be stopping by."

"They're sending a detective?"

"Yeah. She'll be here any minute."

Calvin rubbed his face. "Shit…"

"Settle down, will you? They're not going to figure it out."

"They do this for a living, Rodney. Of course they're gonna figure it out. Why do you think they're sending a detective if the cops were already here?"

He put his hands up reassuringly. "She said on the phone they just needed to tie up a few loose ends."

"Yeah, and if those 'loose ends' happen to be your financial problems or your car you're—"

A firm knock on the glass prompted both of them to turn to

the door. A woman in a dark-colored pantsuit held up her badge for them to see.

Rodney leaned in and put a hand on Calvin's shoulder. "You know I'm only doing this for my family, Cal. Don't sell me out."

Calvin sighed and met his gaze. "You know I wouldn't."

Rodney patted him on the back before he walked over and opened the door. He held it for the detective.

"Mr. Paredes?" she asked.

"That'd be me. Please, come in."

She shook the hand he offered. "I'm Detective Holden. We spoke on the phone."

Calvin gave the detective a quick once-over as she and Rodney exchanged greetings. Blonde hair, pale eyes. She held an air of authority despite her small stature. Calvin's first thought was that a lot of guys probably underestimated her, a mistake Rodney was making right now. A. Huge. Fucking. Mistake.

Calvin had to keep himself from fidgeting. Rodney could end up in prison over this. What the hell would his wife do if that happened? Fuck—

"You said you had a few questions for me?" Rodney asked.

"Yes, only a few," Holden said. She clasped her hands behind her back as she studied the display cases. "You don't have any idea who might've done this?"

"No, none at all. I mean, it could've been anybody."

"And your security cameras weren't functioning?"

"No. I meant to put up new ones, but it got pushed back."

She looked at one of the devices in question. "That's a little too convenient, don't you think?"

"What?"

"I've closed more than my fair share of burglary cases over

the years, Mr. Paredes," Holden said. She ran her hand along the countertop as she continued. "Almost all of them have some indication of forced entry. A broken window, a drilled lock, damage on the doorknob or on the jamb itself. I went over the photographs the responding officer took and double-checked everything myself before I knocked on your door. I didn't see any of those things."

Rodney wrung his hands together. "What are you saying?"

"How many employees currently work for you?"

"None. It's only me," he said. "I'm a sole proprietor."

"Mmm, interesting. Because cases like yours, the ones without any signs of forced entry, almost always end up being an inside job. The owner, an employee, a close friend. Someone who has easy access to the business. And based on what you just said, that's only you. Correct?"

"I—"

"Stop talking, Rodney. You don't gotta answer her questions."

She shot Calvin a stern look before turning her attention back to Rodney. "He's right, you don't. But I could take what I have to the judge. Get a warrant. Make it official." She stepped back to the display cases, pushing some of the glass on the floor aside with her shoe. "Once he sees the paperwork from your insurance company showing you doubled the coverage on your inventory a week before the 'theft', I'm sure he'll be happy to issue one."

He doubled his insurance and didn't think that'd be a huge red flag? What the hell, Rodney?

"I suggested that," Calvin blurted out. "There's been a lot of thefts in the area lately, so I thought it'd be a good idea."

Holden narrowed her eyes. "And who are you, exactly?"

"He's a friend. That's all," Rodney said.

"Well, unless your 'friend' has something case-related to say, I suggest he keeps his mouth shut. As for you, Mr. Paredes, I'm going to give you one more chance to be honest with me before I get a warrant *and* have you charged with lying to the police."

Calvin wasn't the type to pick a fight with law enforcement, but her tone of voice was unnecessary. "Take it easy on Rodney, alright? He's just a family man trying to make ends meet."

"That's another reason Mr. Paredes is our prime…no, our only suspect. I've seen his bank statements and the collection notices. That car of his he reported stolen a few weeks ago? The insurance lapsed on it a month ago due to nonpayment. Clearly that wasn't a setup, but I'd say it was the inspiration for this one."

"That's nothing more than speculation," Rodney said, his voice wavering slightly.

Holden smirked. "Maybe, maybe not. It does make me wonder if the vintage ring you 'forgot' you'd left in the car was a last ditch effort to get some money out of the deal. Why else did you wait to report it until the next day?"

"That was his late grandmother's ring," Calvin said. "And he only reported it because he's hoping you guys can get it back."

Holden tapped her foot impatiently and turned back to Rodney. "I'm not here for whatever trinket you lost, Mr. Paredes. You can tell me about this insurance scheme of yours now, or I think it's time I call the judge. What will it be?"

As Rodney wrung his hands again, Calvin read the expression on his face. Fuck, he was going to cave. Why the hell did Rodney have to pull a stunt like this now? Calvin tried to think of something—*anything*—he could say that might get Rodney out of this mess.

Before he could come up with more than one idea, Rodney started talking. "Alright, Detective. The truth is—"

"Rodney, don't."

She gave Calvin a withering look. "For the last time, unless you have something case-related to say you better—"

"I have something case-related to say, alright."

The room went silent as all eyes turned to Calvin. Rodney stared at him in disbelief while Holden merely crossed her arms.

"Oh? And what would that be?" she asked.

"Rodney didn't do it."

"And who did, then?"

Calvin took a step forward. "I did."

2

CALVIN SHIFTED HIS WEIGHT on the bare metal chair, wondering why the hell interrogation rooms were so damn uncomfortable. Drab, chilly, claustrophobic…Oh, right, because they wanted him to sweat it out. Figuratively at least. What a great way to spend his twenty-seventh birthday.

He ran a hand nervously through his short, straight brown hair. He'd planned on getting it trimmed again while he was on leave, but that didn't matter now. Civilian crime or not, there was no way this wouldn't end up with a less-than-honorable discharge once his superiors found out. With two months left of his eight-year commitment, no less. Wasn't that awesome timing.

His folks would probably disown him when they got wind, too. Maybe even fly up here to yell at him in person. He could already hear their accusatory words. About how he was bringing shame to the family, about how it made them look as parents, about what the neighbors would think. Like any of them cared what went on seven hundred miles away. And even if they did, Calvin didn't give a shit what his dad's golf buddies thought of him. He never fit in with that kind of lifestyle anyway.

There was a knock on the door.

A clean-shaven man of medium build entered. Early forties, probably, with a manila folder in his hand. The button-up shirt he wore was denim blue, the sleeves rolled up as if the chill in the room didn't exist. His belt, watch, and silicone wedding band were all black, the curls of his hair a shade of brown so dark they might as well be.

"Good afternoon," the man greeted, his eyes ice blue but his expression warm. He slid out the chair across from Calvin and sat down. "I'm Detective Kessler with the Minneapolis Police Department. I'll be taking your statement today."

"What happened to Detective Holden?"

At that, Kessler paused, contemplating the accent no doubt. Didn't ask though. Probably just assumed he was from Texas like everyone else did. "She has a more pressing matter to attend to at the moment, so unfortunately you're stuck with me."

Kessler's smile met his eyes at that last bit, and Calvin found himself starting to relax. This was the first time since he'd been brought in that someone was talking to him like he was a decent human being instead of a low-level criminal, someone unworthy of basic kindness.

Kessler opened the folder and pulled out some paperwork. "For the record, could you please state your name?"

"Calvin Haggerty."

"Alright, Calvin. Before we get too deep into this, I need to make sure you understand your rights." Kessler handed him a sheet of paper with his rights listed before he proceeded to read his own copy from a small card he pulled out of his shirt pocket. "You have the right to remain silent. Anything you say can and will be used against you in a court of law. You have the right to an attorney. If you can't afford an attorney, one will be provided for you. Do you understand the rights I have just read to you?"

"Yes."

"With these rights in mind, do you wish to speak with me?"

"Yeah. Like I told Detective Holden, I don't need a lawyer, and I'd like to cut a deal."

Kessler took a minute to skim the file. "Let's start from the beginning. How do you know Rodney Paredes?"

"He's a good friend of mine. We go to the gym together."

"And how long have you two known each other?"

"A little over ten years," Calvin said. "We met at a summer camp when we were in high school."

"You went to high school together?"

"No. I grew up down south, but always spent summers up here with family. He's lived in St. Paul his whole life."

"So you've known each other quite a while, then."

"Yeah."

Kessler took a few notes before continuing. "As you're aware, this past Thursday at 6:27 P.M. police responded to a silent alarm at Paredes Fine Diamonds, after which your friend Rodney stated that merchandise worth approximately $17,000 was missing."

Calvin tensed his jaw. Yeah, he knew. Of course they wanted to spell everything out for the recording, but it was grueling nonetheless.

At his silence, Kessler flipped to the next page. "Detective Holden was assigned the case, and this morning in front of her you freely admitted—without questioning—that you were the one who broke in and stole the merchandise. Is that correct?"

"Yes."

"Why did you do it?"

"I was careful. I thought I'd get away with it."

"But you said he's a good friend of yours."

"That's exactly the point," Calvin said, trying to keep the frustration out of his voice. "I know the location. He'd never think it was me and with the insurance payout it wasn't gonna be money out of his pocket. Theft is up so I figured it'd blend in."

"And you probably would've gotten away with it, so why the spur-of-the-moment confession?"

"It wasn't supposed to go down like this. His wife is due next month, and my conscience won't let me stand idle by while he goes to prison in my place."

That seemed to satisfy Kessler, who flipped to the next page. Good. At least they were almost to the bottom of the stack now. "According to the report, there were no signs of forced entry. How'd you get in?"

"You guys saw the place. It doesn't have the best security. He keeps a spare key under that concrete dog statue by the door."

Kessler twirled the pen in hand. "What kind of dog?"

"A Chihuahua or some shit. Go ahead and ask Rodney if you don't believe me."

He smiled, repeating Calvin's words as he jotted them down. "'A Chihuahua or…some shit'. Got it."

Man, he was going to ask Rodney about that gaudy-ass statue. How thorough. Good thing that hadn't been a lie.

"So you used the spare key, let yourself in after hours, and took the merchandise," Kessler summarized. "Then what?"

"What do you mean 'then what'? Then I went out the way I came, locked the door, and put the key back."

"No, what did you do with the merchandise?"

"I sold it to some dude in a back alley. You know, the kind of guy who's interested in whatever you're selling."

"Where?"

Calvin shrugged. "I don't know, downtown somewhere. It was late and I'm not familiar with that area to begin with."

"Did you get his name?"

"No. He didn't ask questions and neither did I."

Kessler tapped his fingers on the desk, not happy with that answer. Understandable, since they were probably hoping to track the jewelry down. Like that was gonna happen.

"How much did he give you?" Kessler asked.

"A couple grand."

"You sold merchandise worth $17,000 for a couple grand?"

"I was in a bind. You can't really expect market value in those kinds of circumstances."

"So what did you do with the money?"

"I…" Calvin dropped his gaze as he thought about what he should say. "I have a bit of a gambling habit. I lost it all at the casinos."

Kessler set the pen down, his voice surprisingly soft. "Tell me about your habit."

"That's not why I'm here, so I'd rather not."

"Based on what you said, that's exactly why you're here."

"Look, I'm not contesting anything. Why the hell do you want to drag this out any more than necessary?"

"I'm a detective," Kessler said, speaking to him in the same kind of warm, nonjudgmental manner Calvin used with his niece. "It's my job to try to see things from your perspective. Is there a reason you're not willing to talk to me about it?"

Calvin rubbed the back of his neck. Kessler really seemed to be taking a genuine interest in his well-being, something few people—and even fewer strangers—had ever done. It felt wrong to throw that back in his face, but Calvin couldn't risk screwing this up. Not when he was so close to the finish line. "I'd like to be done here, that's all. If I gotta use my right to remain silent to get you to understand, then I will."

Kessler studied him for a minute. "If you'd rather not discuss it, then I won't press further, but since you're sitting across from me you need to understand that your habit has gone too far. The sooner you realize that, the better."

"Yeah, I got it. So is there anything else you guys need or can we wrap this up?"

"No, that about covers it," Kessler said. He squared up the paperwork and tucked everything into the folder. "I appreciate how cooperative you've been, and I'll be sure to write that in my report. However, in the end it's the courts that will decide what your sentence is."

Calvin sighed, not looking forward to that part any more than he'd been looking forward to this. "What happens now?"

Kessler stood and pulled a pair of handcuffs from his back pocket. "Calvin Haggerty, you're under arrest."

3

Five Years Later

BEN KESSLER couldn't pinpoint the exact ladder he'd walked under, but it must've been a pretty damn big one.

Rain pattered on the roof of his squad, melting his view of the outside world as it trickled down the windshield. Traffic was light thanks to the weather, but the occasional sweep of the Explorer's wipers cleared the glass as methodically as he watched the street. Unlike most people he knew, he looked forward to the rain. It was calming, brought him inner peace.

Since his vehicle was stationed perpendicular to the empty thoroughfare, he glanced out the side window. A ghostly mist draped across the tops of the bluffs, obscuring the distinction between earth and sky. He'd always missed the unrivaled beauty of the Driftless Area. He just wished his move had been under different circumstances.

But even if it was somewhat unprestigious to be running

traffic in a town with a population that didn't break five digits, he considered himself lucky to have gotten the job. Turns out a lot of departments weren't interested in hiring a forty-six-year-old "rookie" since they tended to have their own ideas on how things should be done. Overqualified, most had said. The large gap in employment hadn't helped, either.

He looked back at the road, scrutinizing the occasional car as it went past. Another thing he liked about inclement weather was how the low light played with the ghost graphics on his vehicle, the charcoal decals nearly invisible against the jet-black paint until headlights hit it and illuminated the lettering to a blazing white. It was always fun to witness the exact moment when a questionable driver saw it, which was evident by the split-second flash of their brake lights. Nothing like a marked police car to bring out the good driver in anyone.

Which was all Ben had seen in the last hour—good drivers. He was getting restless. The second-shift dispatcher had pulled him aside on his first day to give him a quick rundown of the department, making sure he was aware of its "laid-back" nature. He'd expected as much given the size of the town, but what he hadn't expected was how hardcore she'd sugarcoated it. On any given shift he did at least four times as many traffic stops as any other officer, which hadn't won him a lot of friends in the department.

Movement down the street brought his attention to a crystal-blue sedan approaching noticeably slower than the posted speed limit of twenty-five. While that alone wasn't necessarily enough to pull the car over, the inoperative driver's side headlight sure was. Ben shifted his vehicle into drive and waited for the car to pass by, pulling out the moment it did.

After all, he wasn't here to make friends.

He grabbed the radio and called out his badge number to identify himself to dispatch. "1308, traffic."

A polite female voice responded. "Go ahead."

"Traverse and Oakland with Minnesota seven zero two, Sam Henry Robert. Seven oh two, S-H-R."

"Copy."

At the flip of a switch he bathed the landscape in red and blue. The Hyundai pulled leisurely to the side of the road, misting the Explorer's windshield with spray from its tires before coming to a complete stop. Ben stopped a short distance behind it and shifted into park, leaving his squad running to feed the insatiable draw from the electronics as he punched the license plate into his computer.

It didn't take long for the return to come back, and Ben quickly skimmed it. The plates were valid until January and did belong on a blue Hyundai Sonata. There were two registered owners listed as well, both in their mid-fifties. Richard and Dana Pierson. Household names in this town, but Ben didn't concern himself with that.

He opened the door and stepped out, pressing the power lock button as he took in the fresh, earthy smell that greeted him. The droplets of rain accumulating on the surroundings acted like tiny mirrors, glittering the car in front of him with flashes of red and blue as he approached. He touched the sedan's trunk as he walked by to ensure it was fully latched, a habit that gave him peace of mind for more than one reason.

It was too wet to leave fingerprints behind, but at least he could be relatively certain that no one would be popping out of the trunk without him hearing it. A couple of the department's younger officers had given him shit about how he did it on every vehicle without exception, but he had no intention of changing his behavior to suit anyone's opinion. If they wanted to think of him as overly distrustful then they could go ahead and knock themselves out.

At the driver's side window, Ben couldn't help but notice his reflection in the glass. His image in uniform was a nostalgic reminder of his former self before he'd been promoted to a detective position. But that was fifteen years ago and a few hundred miles away, back when he had a lot more faith in the system than he did now.

He shifted his gaze away from the mirror-like surface and brought his attention back to the present. The Hyundai's window was still up, so he tapped gently on the glass with the back of his hand to encourage the car's operator to intervene. Which he did, after a moment of hesitation. As the window rolled down, the stench of beer rolled out at approximately the same rate.

Ben took a step back from the odorous cloud as he tallied the occupants. College kids, a male driver and three passengers. One male, two female. All in their early twenties and, from the looks of it, all four of them drunk. Ugh, he hated dealing with drunks. But it came with the territory, so might as well get to it. "Good evening," Ben said. "I'm Officer Kessler with the Cas—"

"Can we cut to the chase, Officer?"

Ben tilted his head at the interruption. A feisty one, but sure, he'd play. "Do you know why I pulled you over?"

The kid didn't miss a beat, like he'd been waiting his entire life for that question. "Because you haven't met your quota for brownie points yet?"

Ah, sarcasm. That'll get him far. Ben kept his tone casual,

not giving the kid's comment a hint of recognition. "Your driver's side headlight is out."

"A headlight? Wow. That's really scraping the bottom of the barrel," the kid chastised. The smell of stale booze wafted out of his mouth at every word. "Don't you have better things to do?" He turned to his passengers with a smirk on his face, checking to see how impressed they were with his smart-ass comments. It was the kind of interaction that made Ben truly appreciate his even-tempered nature.

"I'll need to see your license and registration, please."

There was a disgruntled sigh as the kid leaned over into his buddy's lap to fish the paperwork out of the glove box. After he found the correct one, he sat back up and grabbed a wallet from his back pocket, fumbling as he extracted his driver's license. He handed both items out the window. "There. Anything else?"

The first thing Ben did was look at the photo on the license. It was a match to the kid's face, so he looked at the date of birth next. Jack was old enough to drink—barely—but he must've missed the part about not doing so while driving.

Ben looked up and gave Jack a quick nod. "Sit tight and I'll be back in a minute."

He tuned out the snickering from the car as he walked back to his squad, thankful to finally get a break from the unrelenting stink. Hopefully his uniform didn't absorb the smell or he'd be back at the station changing the instant this call was over.

The sound of the rain changed in pitch as he got in his squad and closed the door. He clicked on the map light to take a closer look at the security measures on Jack's license to ensure it wasn't counterfeit. Weird bendy material, check. Holographic loon, check. He flipped it over and grabbed a palm-sized magnifying glass from the console to examine the small red outline of the state on the bottom right corner. Yep, tiny little "Mennesota" hiding in between the correct spellings. Satisfied, he picked up his radio again. "1308, I'll have a Minnesota DL."

"Go ahead."

He held the license above the steering wheel to keep the Hyundai in his peripheral vision as he recited the information in front of him. "Last name Pierson, Paul Ida Edward Robert Sam Ocean Nora. First name Jack, common spelling. Middle H, Henry. Male out of Minnesota."

"Copy, and your vehicle comes back valid as a 2015 Hyundai Sonata, blue in color."

"Copy."

He stayed in the squad, flipping the license absentmindedly as he waited for a return on the driver. The harmonic drumming of the rain intensified, so he increased the speed of the wipers a notch. At least he had plenty of time for a field sobriety test before the light started to fade. Unless of course Jack had a warrant, which would certainly expedite things.

"Dispatch to 1308."

"Go ahead," Ben said.

"Your driver is valid and clear."

"Copy."

So no warrant, but with Jack's stellar attitude and three other subjects to keep an eye on, Ben couldn't shake the nagging feeling that this part of the traffic stop wasn't going to go well. With the radio still in his hand, he called for his sergeant, the only other officer on duty. "1308 to 1302."

This time a resonant male voice came over the radio. "1302, go ahead."

"1308, I need a second unit for fields, Traverse and Oakland."

There was a lengthy pause before the radio crackled back to life. "1302, negative on fields," his sergeant directed. "The... weather could skew the results. If that's all there is, go ahead and cut him loose."

Ben tapped his fingers on the steering wheel, trying to remember what the ten-code was for "you're a fucking idiot". Like no one ever walked a straight line in the rain. He'd heard plenty of bullshit during his career, but he wasn't used to it coming from his side of the line. He slammed the radio in its holder before promptly opening his driver's door. *Cut him loose.*

"Like hell," Ben muttered as he stepped back into the rain.

4

THE SCHEDULE for Ben's position was also complete bullshit. Yesterday he worked a second shift while today he was on a first, with his third shift coming up tomorrow. Well, technically tonight at midnight. Anyone with half a life would've turned on their heels when that came up, which is exactly what everyone who'd interviewed before him had done.

He pulled into the employee lot of the police station and backed into an empty stall. As he got out and walked into the building, it wasn't hard to miss that his Charger, while black, was the only sedan in a lineup of dark-colored pickups.

Always the oddball.

"Morning, Evan," Ben said as he walked up to the lobby's dispatch window. Most departments used a centralized dispatch service, but Ben appreciated the in-house one here. It was nice to be able to put faces to the names for once.

"Good morning, Ben," Evan said. He glided his office chair away from the monitors and over to the glass. "I heard you had a delightful shift yesterday."

"That's an interesting way of putting it. Did you hear that from Sarge?"

"No, Chief. He wants to see you in his office before you go set up your squad."

"Of course he does," Ben said under his breath before he addressed Evan. "Thanks."

Evan was also one of the department's more recent hires, and even if it was the unpopular opinion, Ben liked the guy. He was dependable and he did his job. He could be frank to the point of offense at times, but Ben would take that over fake friendliness any day.

Evan buzzed him in, and Ben rounded the corner, almost getting plowed into by a young officer whose attention had been solely focused on the steaming mug that'd just met his lips. His brown eyes were a shade darker than his skin, his black hair in a buzz cut as tidy as his uniform. He shook a few drops of spilled coffee off his hand before offering his usual radiant smile. "Shoot, my bad. Morning, Ben."

"Hey, Alex. Weren't you supposed to be off today?"

"I was, but Jonathan called in sick."

"What about Harper's recital? You've been talking about it the entire time I've worked here."

"I know, I'm lucky they hired someone or they wouldn't be giving me any time off," Alex said. "It starts at two, so I'll be out of here at noon. You'll be on your own until four, I think."

"I'm done at four, anyway. But wasn't there talk about going to ten-hour shifts?"

Alex laughed. "They've been saying that for months. Eights are tough, but I'd just be happy if I didn't have to work on half of my scheduled days off."

Ben lowered his voice. "I'm speaking from experience here, but the only reason they call you every time is because you're the only one who never refuses. It doesn't take long for them to figure that out, and then you end up at the top of the call-in list."

"Yeah I know, but I always feel bad about leaving someone else high and dry. I mean I don't want to miss her first recital, but with Jon gone you're—"

"Don't worry about me," Ben said. "I'll manage. Enjoy your time off."

Dispatch called over his radio, so Alex lifted a hand to bid farewell. Ben nodded in return, then walked the rest of the way down the hall and to the large office on the left. The door was partially open, so he knocked on the frame. "Good morning, Chief. You wanted to see me?"

Chief looked up from the double monitors of his computer before swiveling to the center of the desk. He gestured to the two vacant chairs in front of it. "Ben, please. Have a seat."

Ben closed the door and sat down, crossing his legs comfortably. Framed certificates adorned all four walls, interrupted only by the occasional piece of police-themed décor. Despite the number of trinkets the bookcase held, it was the large L-shaped desk that dominated the room, the organized stacks of papers on its fringes complimented by family photos, honorary medals, and a navel orange.

His younger self might've been nervous at being called into a superior's office like this, but experience had long since given Ben a reassuring confidence in his ability to make the right call, and thus not fear the consequences. But as much as he wanted to tell Chief that he shouldn't keep his login credentials on a bright blue sticky-note on his monitor, now didn't seem like the best time.

Chief straightened his dress shirt before leaning forward to rest his arms on the smooth mahogany surface in front of him. "I take it you know what this is about."

"I would assume last night's DWI."

"You've worked in law enforcement for over twenty years," Chief said, glancing at a stack of papers Ben recognized as his employment application. "Your record is exemplary. Every former supervisor of yours I that spoke to had nothing but good things to say about your attitude, your performance, and your professionalism. I know Sergeant Vaughn expressed concerns that our position might not be a good fit for you, but since you'd specifically mentioned that you were looking for a change of pace, I decided to take the chance."

Ben wasn't sure if he was supposed to say something or not given the pause, but in the end it was a statement and not a question, so he opted not to.

Chief slid the papers aside before he continued. "You haven't had a single disciplinary action over your entire career. I realize this isn't the large metropolitan area you're used to working in, but I'm sure at some point you must've heard of this little thing called the 'chain of command'. Am I correct?"

"You are," Ben agreed, keeping his tone respectful. "But I'm also aware of my right to use discretion, which means I have the freedom to make decisions through my own personal judgment. In this case I made the decision to continue with fields."

"Jack left in an ambulance thanks to a broken ankle."

"He shouldn't have run," Ben stated.

Well, bolted was probably a better way of describing it. And drunks don't bolt well, especially when there's a curb involved. The most ironic part of it all was that Ben hadn't even chased him. No reason to, since he still had the kid's license with his home address in the palm of his hand.

"And when you found out whose vehicle it was you didn't stop to think that maybe you should yield to your superior on this one?"

"No, I didn't."

"The mayor is literally fuming over this."

"Then maybe he should tell his son not to drink and drive," Ben shot back. Blunt honesty probably wasn't the best approach in this situation, but he wasn't willing to back down. He'd made the right call, consequences be damned.

Surprisingly, Chief softened his tone. "Listen, I know things have been difficult for you since your wife passed away, but—"

"That has nothing to do with this, so let's leave it out of the conversation."

Chief shot him a pointed look but let the interruption slide. "My point is, you can't let your personal problems interfere with your job. You need to tone it down."

Ben thought about what his reply should be. Nothing was interfering with his job. He'd been well within his legal bounds to do a field sobriety test, but Chief wasn't going to budge one inch from his stance, either. Ben's own tenacity made it easy to spot the trait in others.

Might as well try deflection. "If there's nothing else, I'd like to get back to work."

"Look, here's how this is going to go," Chief said, steepling his fingers. "Lake City is short-staffed and one of their full-timers is going on maternity leave. I owe them a favor, so you'll be filling in down there until she's back and this whole goddamn mess blows over."

"With all due respect, I wasn't hired as a vacation relief."

Chief slammed his fist on the desk as he stood. "You were hired to do whatever the hell I tell you, and if that involves washing your squad in nothing more than a blue line bikini then that's what you'll do!"

Ben stayed quiet, going with his usual tactic of dealing with an angry person by not reacting. Not immediately, anyway, since the only thing haste led to was bad decisions. He knew beyond a shadow of a doubt he'd be quitting over Chief's remark, but that still left him with two choices—now or later?

Now was by far the more appealing one, but he had to think about collateral damage. If he walked out this instant, Alex would have to stay to cover his shift. He was a great cop, but he needed to learn to stand up for himself.

No, it had to be later.

"Listen," Chief said, bringing the volume down to a more acceptable level as he lowered himself into his chair. "I'll give you tonight to think it over and get your head on straight. Tomorrow, I'll expect the right answer."

It'd been a rough shift, rougher than most. When Ben got home he went to the fridge to grab a pop before sitting down on the sofa to think things over. After cracking the can open and taking a sip he glared at the window, debating with himself for all of five seconds before he got up and closed the blinds. He didn't share the enthusiasm the sun had for the day.

He'd assumed that the rest of his shift couldn't possibly be worse than his morning pep talk with Chief, but apparently he'd made the mistake of underestimating fate again. When he'd gone to set up Police Squad 10, his assigned ride, it had a dead battery, so he'd switched over to PS12. Halfway through that squad check he found out PS12's cameras weren't working, so he had to find the booster pack to jump-start PS10. He managed to get it going, only to find out on his first traffic stop that the battery in his handheld radio was also dead because whoever had it before him forgot to charge it after their shift.

And last but not least was the drunk who puked all over his backseat. Which was cloth, because the department was too damn cheap to spring for the plastic replacement ones even though there was plenty of funding to cover inspirational posters and ridiculous training that wasn't related to the job. He didn't know what his next move was, but he'd never been more relieved to leave a job than this one. Speaking of which, he should probably start crafting his letter of resignation.

He walked over to the desk and turned on his laptop, setting his Sprite to the side as he sat down and waited for the machine to boot up. Once it did, he skimmed a few examples before he began to draft his own document.

By the time Ben's pop had warmed to room temperature, his letter of resignation was equally unsatisfying. Everything he'd written by following the examples seemed too damn nice, but if he put down his honest opinions it came across like he was the unreasonable one. He reread his work, and after deleting every sentence that didn't seem quite right, his document looked the same as it did when he started. Blank. As much as he hated to admit it, he started to think that maybe he should suck it up and stay on until he found a better position. After all, his badge was all he had left.

Still, he wasn't going on some random assignment in Lake City. If Chief owed them a favor then he could go down there and do it himself. Ben was hired here, and he intended to work here, not be sent all over the county on a whim because someone owed somebody else a favor. He'd have to word that a little more elegantly tomorrow, but it hadn't been particularly difficult to see through Chief's bluff. While Ben would certainly get a stern reprimand for refusing to go, when push came to shove the department was too short-staffed to seriously consider firing him. Not for something that minor, anyway. Even if they were to hire a brand-new officer tomorrow it'd be at least two months for them to be trained in and ready to fly solo, and that was only if they'd already gone through the academy.

Ben drank the last of his tepid Sprite, not caring that it was also half-flat. Next to the ring of condensation on the desk sat his phone, and he picked it up to check the time, frowning when he saw it was later than he'd expected. If he was going back in at midnight he should probably try to get some sleep, but he wasn't really in the mood for that. He got up and opened the blinds to take in the fading light.

He was tired, physically and mentally. Tired of criminals getting off to reoffend the next day. Tired of running into the same ones over and over, on or off duty. It was like fate kept bringing around people he didn't want to see, and never someone who was simply a decent human being. It didn't matter how obscure of an aisle he wandered through at whatever store he happened to be at. No matter what, Ben was always running into someone he'd rather not run into. He didn't know why it kept happening. It hadn't always been like that.

Or was it simply his perspective that'd changed?

Ben's thoughts drifted back to a year ago, when everything around him had shattered into pieces. The empty can crunched in his hand. He'd dealt with his fair share of criminals over the years, but he'd never taken a personal interest in any of them outside of work. Until a man named Andrew Dixon came along, that is.

And all over a case Ben hadn't even worked.

He sat back down in front of his computer and pulled up the Minnesota Court Records Online, entering Dixon's name to run a case search. It was probably borderline stalking, but he wasn't about to use his law enforcement credentials to look Dixon up illegally. The man had long since left the address he'd had a year ago and nothing else had surfaced on MCRO since, but it'd been a while since Ben checked. Maybe there'd be something now.

Lo and behold, there was a new entry. A seat belt violation from two months ago. Ben clicked *View Case Details* and scrolled down, stopping short when he read the location.

Lake City, MN.

Without hesitation he dialed and put the phone to his ear. "Hey, Felicia. It's Ben. Tell Chief I'll take the assignment."

5

GARTH BROOKS PLAYED on the radio as Calvin steered his silver F-150 right, turning south onto Lakeshore Drive. Perfectly landscaped houses and condominiums flanked the right side of the road, but the view to the left was what truly made this part of the drive spectacular. He rolled down the window and put his hand out, the wind tossing his shoulder-length hair as he took in the endless expanse of Lake Pepin. Warmth swirled around him as the sun glittered off the water's surface. He'd only been out of prison for a few months, but damn it felt good.

He put his hand back on the wheel and drove the next mile and a half to Chestnut Street before taking the next right onto Washington. A cluster of small boats monopolized the corner lot, the sweeping blue sky bright and inviting as it overlooked this particular classic American Main Street. Calvin had seen plenty of them during his travels, and hands-down there was nothing as reinvigorating as that small town feel. Everything was slower, more relaxed.

He caught one more view of the lake as he arrived at his destination a few blocks down, pulling right to park in one of the angled stalls in front of the glass entry doors of Wise Ace Hardware. There were a few other stores in Lake City that were closer to his place, but he always made a point of taking the extra time to stop at this one. Sparrows under the awning protested his arrival as he walked past the palleted stacks of mulch and topsoil that lined the quaint brick building. God what a beautiful day.

The familiar sea of merchandise greeted him as he entered, but the expectant smile he carried was for the redhead behind the counter. Marissa didn't seem to have noticed the door, all of her attention focused on the thick pad of paper in front of her.

"Hey, darlin'," he greeted.

"Hey, cowboy," she said as she looked up. Her flustered expression lightened as she brushed away an unruly lock of hair that had escaped her ponytail.

"New sketch?"

"Not today," she said, lifting up the pad for him to see. "It's inventory week."

"Your drawings are good, Marissa. You should quit trying to find reasons to hide them."

She blushed. "Didn't we have this conversation last time?"

"Alright, maybe we did," he conceded, taking in the extensive list of handwritten notes cluttering the page. Organized chaos if anything was. "As long as you're having fun."

She set the pad down and glared at him. "I hate math."

"Well I had to at least try to make you feel better."

"You did, don't worry. Now that there's a customer in the

store I can take a break from it." She leaned over to the side to get a better look at his truck through the front doors. "Aww. Where's Greta?"

"Sleeping in. The kids next door were lighting off firecrackers again so she was up most of the night," Calvin said. He thumbed to the back of the building. "Thought I'd grab her favorite treat to cheer her up."

"Man, I'd be thrilled if my boyfriend was half as thoughtful. Luckily for you we restocked everything this morning."

He tipped an imaginary hat. "You're the best."

As Marissa went back to her work, Calvin skirted through narrow aisles, the dark wood planks under his boots worn and uneven from decades of use. It may not have the grand entrance and polished floors of the big box stores, but the one thing a place like this did have was character. Calvin would take that over glitz any day.

He went past the pool noodles and bags of charcoal before disappearing into the snack aisle, which was as empty as the rest of the store. Understandable given how nice it was outside. Maybe once Greta was up, he'd see if she wanted to hit the trails. Probably, but she was always more receptive if he brought food.

Calvin started scanning the shelves in earnest. All the usual crap. Candy, fruit snacks, pretzels, and…wait, seriously? Who the hell thought deep-dish-pizza-flavored potato chips were a good idea? Like either one wasn't unhealthy enough on its own.

He shook his head before moving on. Popcorn, chocolate bars…ah, there they were. He reached for the bottom shelf, the bright yellow package of vanilla Oreos crunching as he picked it up. He may not care for junk food himself, but whatever his girl wanted, she got.

The sound of the front door announced the entry of another shopper, followed by Marissa's cheerful tone. "Good morning, sir," she greeted. Her voice carried over from the register a second time. "Will that be all?"

That was quick. Must not've needed much.

"Yeah, just this," the man said.

Calvin headed back toward the register, getting a vague sense of familiarity at the sound of the customer's voice. Couldn't place him, though. Not until he got closer and his footsteps caught the other man's attention and he turned around, causing Calvin to stop short the moment they locked eyes. Suddenly he was very aware of how he knew him.

Minneapolis, five years ago. The detective who had arrested him.

Streaks of silver now graced his hair, and his wedding band was gone. The black suit jacket he wore was unbuttoned, the navy button-up shirt under it tucked neatly into his black slacks. How the hell was he not roasting? Detectives liked to look sharp, sure, but if he was here shopping then he was almost certainly off-duty. Why anyone would want to wear black—or anything with long sleeves, for that matter—this time of year was beyond him. It was almost the middle of August for Christ's sake.

But despite the detective's unseasonably warm outfit, it was the expression on his face that really caught Calvin's attention. Recognition for sure, and something else he couldn't quite put his finger on. Disbelief, maybe?

Marissa's curious voice broke him out of his thoughts before he could analyze the look any further. "You two know each other or something?"

Both men redirected their gaze to her, but it was Calvin who broke the silence. "It's been a few years but yeah," he explained, before kindly addressing the older man. "Wasn't expecting to run into you in my neck of the woods, Detective."

"Officer," he corrected, his face taking on a more neutral expression. "And I'm only here for a short-term assignment."

At that he turned his attention back to Marissa, thanking her quietly as she handed him his receipt. He tucked it and the map he'd bought into the inside pocket of his jacket, the butt of a gun in a shoulder holster visible as he did so. Once everything was stashed away, he shot one last glance at Calvin before turning wordlessly to leave.

Well, that explained the jacket at least.

Calvin walked up to the empty counter and set his Oreos down, looking out the front doors to feed his curiosity about whether or not the former detective was driving a squad car. The audible beep from the register's scanner pulled his attention back to the counter before he got a chance to find out.

"Nothing else for you today?" she asked.

"Nah, that's it," Calvin said, thankful that Marissa had the common courtesy not to pry. It was never fun having to explain his felony conviction, and he was hoping to leave that as far in the past as he could. He handed her a five-dollar bill as she totaled the purchase. "Can't buy everything all at once or I won't have an excuse to come back."

"Good one," she said as she gave him his change. "And don't forget to tell Greta I said hi."

"You know I will. Thank you, sweetheart."

She smiled back. "Anytime, Cal."

He walked out of the store and opened the door to his truck, setting the Oreos on the passenger seat. After backing out and heading down Washington Street he took two right turns to get himself northbound on Lakeshore Drive. As the blocks passed his eyes were on the road, but his thoughts lingered on the former detective.

Calvin had only interacted with the man once, but something had changed. He was a lot friendlier back then, while today he seemed distant and reserved. Suspicious, almost. Being demoted could explain the shift in demeanor, but given his professionalism, at least from what Calvin had seen, that theory didn't quite seem to fit. He'd probably ended up hating a desk job and went back to his old position. That left the divorce. Those could really do a number on people. Kessler, that was his name.

Still, he couldn't think of any good reasons why they'd send a cop from Minneapolis all the way down here.

*   *   *

Calvin turned into his driveway and parked, turning off the ignition but not taking any further action to get out. Home already. He'd been so absorbed in his thoughts he hadn't even noticed the minutes tick by. The encounter at Ace was brief and they'd barely said a single sentence to each other, so why the hell did he care about it so much?

Was it an unwelcome reminder of a part of his life he wanted to leave behind? Possibly, but that didn't seem quite right. His friendly greeting had been more or less dismissed. Is that what bothered him? Maybe, but he'd long since broken his childhood habit of caring what other people thought of him.

Or had he?

Five years ago, Kessler afforded him a level of kindness no one else had, something that had really resonated with Calvin during a vulnerable time in his life. But today Kessler had looked at him with the same level of distrust that everyone else had back then. What Calvin didn't understand was why. He'd addressed Kessler respectfully, and since they hadn't crossed paths since the arrest, Calvin hadn't given him any reason to be standoffish.

Yeah, that could very well be it. Maybe he did still care what people thought of him. Certain people, anyway. It was a short list, but apparently Kessler had made it on there. Kind of unusual for someone he barely knew, though. Maybe it really was nothing more than the mystery of Kessler's change in demeanor.

Calvin sighed and unbuckled, grabbing the package of Oreos before opening the driver's door and getting out. In the end none of it mattered, since he'd probably never see Kessler again.

AS SOON AS BEN LEFT the hardware store he circled around the block, pulling his car into the bank's lot across the street so he could find out what Calvin Haggerty was driving. He backed into a stall with a clear line of sight of the store and pressed the start/stop button on his dashboard to shut off the engine.

Running into Haggerty had caught him off-guard, but even with the long hair Ben had recognized him immediately. In his line of work people were rarely cooperative, and even among those, Haggerty had stood out. He could count on one hand the number of interviews he'd done that had gone that smoothly.

The fact that Haggerty *and* Dixon were in Lake City was too much of a coincidence for Ben's taste, especially considering that his former dealings with both were in the Twin Cities within a few years of each other. It'd been a little over five years since Haggerty's arrest, so he must have received a lenient sentence in exchange for his plea bargain. Dixon, on the other hand, hadn't done any time.

A possible connection between the two had never crossed his mind until now, and if Ben hadn't been so preoccupied with that thought when he'd left the store, he would've looked over the vehicles parked in front of it then so he wouldn't have to be doing it now from across the street. Blindsided or not, he needed to get back on his game. That was the second time today he'd blundered because of a distraction, and in his line of work he couldn't afford to be making those kinds of mistakes. He never used to, after all.

It took less than a minute for the front door of Ace to swing open, the glass flashing with the sun's glare as Haggerty exited. Only a handful of cars were parked reasonably close, and he took a few steps to the most likely, the silver pickup out front. Ben was too far to read the license plate, so he looked over the vehicle for identifying features instead.

F-150s were a dime a dozen, especially in that color, and his looked to be relatively stock. Original wheels, standard ride height, no aftermarket trim or fender flares. The vehicle's reverse lights came on and Haggerty backed out, turning the wheel right to align his truck with the road. That gave Ben a good view of the vehicle's front end, which was also stock except for one minor modification. Cab lights. Those weren't particularly common on half-ton trucks.

Haggerty shifted into drive and headed south. Once he was out of sight, Ben let another minute pass before he pressed the brake pedal and pushed his car's start/stop button, the gauges lighting up as the engine hummed to life. He shifted into gear and took a left as he exited the lot.

*　　*　　*

It only took about five minutes for Ben to drive back. As soon as he left the bank's lot he'd gotten back onto Lakeshore Drive and headed north, passing a couple rows of luxury condos and a manicured storm-gray house before making a left turn into the parking lot of the Sunset Motel.

His department had unquestionably gone all out to get rid of him, going as far as covering the cost of booking a small motel room for him for the month and a half or so he'd be here, even though he lived well within the Lake City Police Department's one-hour distance requirement for officers. It would've almost been flattering if it wasn't so gracefully insulting, considering that something as simple as getting a properly sized uniform shirt for the third-shift dispatcher "wasn't in the budget right now". Once he was done here and Dixon was behind bars, he would make a point of putting his resignation back on the front burner, but for now the arrangement suited everyone.

Ben drove past the motel pool and parked in a stall at the back of the lot. When he got out he pressed the tiny black button on the outside door handle and the car locked automatically. The passive keyless entry system was a nice feature, and he was glad he'd taken the time to read the owner's manual instead of actually listening to that last ridiculous training video the department had insisted he watch. Hurricane Preparedness Planning. Like he needed that. Finding out his keys never had to leave his pocket had been far more useful information.

The motel's white doors and matching white numerals stood out against the dark gray color of the exterior while the large planters and teal beach chairs on the veranda gave off a subtle tropical vibe. Instead of heading straight for his room, Ben paused to lean over his car's roof, feeling the heat radiating from its surface as he took in the view across Lakeshore Drive.

The body of water was impressive, but he still didn't fully understand why they called it a lake. In all reality it was one of the wider areas of the Mississippi River—not landlocked in any way, shape, or form—and it wasn't like the state of Minnesota had a shortage of lakes it needed to worry about. The thought percolated in his mind as he walked up to the door of Room 7 and fished the keys out of his pocket. Maybe if it wasn't for Pepin, his car's license plate would read *9,999 Lakes*.

The icy scent of air conditioning leaked out as he entered. The room was basic but clean, and a lot nicer than similarly sized motels he'd stayed at in the past. Recently remodeled, if he had to guess. Other than a veneer entertainment center, a black mini-fridge, and a retro-style blue microwave, it was mostly white. TV on the left and bed on the right, sandwiched in a little nook between the room's windowed outer wall and the inner wall that separated the bathroom from the rest of the space. There was only about twenty-four inches of space on either side of the bed, but for some reason they'd still opted for two end tables, each barely larger than the lamp that adorned it. Probably for the sake of symmetry.

He threw his room keys on the entertainment center and closed the door. He'd traveled light, only bringing a few changes of clothes, his uniforms, shaving supplies, and a backpack with his gear for the shooting range. Whatever else he needed he'd buy locally, but that'd be later. Right now he wanted to get the lay of the land.

The oval breakfast table was white like everything else, and smaller than the map he'd purchased, which draped over it like a tablecloth once it was unfolded. He sat down and oriented it to the small subsection showing Lake City, then grabbed a pen, marking Dixon's residence and the police station before using his phone to look up other points of interest. Everyone had to eat and most had to buy fuel for their vehicle, so he drew icons for grocery stores, restaurants, and gas stations. Next up he outlined parks and any other locations someone with nefarious intent might use for a meeting place.

The map feature on his phone worked well for navigation, but Ben found it much easier to study the main thoroughfares and look for efficient ways to travel between points of interest if he could see everything all at once. With a town the size of this one it was a relatively easy task. He wasn't sure what his plan was yet, but he was going to see to it that Dixon got caught if he so much as thought about committing a crime.

Ben didn't bother going over each and every street, but the overall naming conventions weren't surprising. Half of them were presidents, numerals, or trees. Chestnut, Walnut, Oak. Maybe if he got bored enough he'd drive around and see if said species lined their namesake thoroughfares.

With nothing left to mark down, Ben folded the unwieldy piece of paper and made a mental note to bring a pair of scissors the next time he traveled. For fun, he ran Haggerty through MCRO as well, but other than his conviction five years ago and a minor traffic violation shortly before, it was unremarkable.

He tucked the map back into his jacket. The next time he went out he'd put it in the glove box of his car so he could mark down any additional points of interest or routes Dixon liked to use as Ben came across them, which would likely be when he was behind the wheel. Finished with the task at hand, he found his thoughts back on the chance encounter at Ace.

He'd always been a numbers person, and right now he was thinking about how slim the odds were that he and Haggerty were both in the same small town, at the same store, on the same day, within the same short time span of a few minutes. About how many inconsequential things had to fall into place for that to happen. If either of them had hit an additional red light or two the entire encounter wouldn't have happened, which wasn't much of a stretch considering Ace was Ben's third stop of the day and the only one he hadn't planned on making.

The first had been Kwik Trip to fill up his car and grab a map of Lake City. Next he'd decided to stop at an art gallery for old times' sake, but halfway through Willow Gentile he realized he'd forgotten the map. That'd been his first blunder of the day, which wouldn't have happened if he hadn't been distracted by the lady in kitten-print pajamas who didn't realize that it was customary to pay before you ate the merchandise.

Since Ben's pride had insisted that he couldn't go back to Kwik Trip for a map, he'd asked the lady running the watercolor class where he could find one. She'd suggested Ace Hardware, since it was right around the corner. Two minutes later there he was, walking through the door and into Haggerty.

Ben shook his head. Sometimes it was really, really hard to believe it was all a coincidence.

7

FOR THE NEXT FEW DAYS Ben did everything he could to keep his interest in Dixon under the radar. He wasn't about to misuse his police resources to accomplish his goal, but he did as much surveillance on the man as he legally could. He'd already checked the public court records for Dixon's location by running him through MCRO, and he did the same for Dixon's flighty friend, the only accomplice of his Ben knew the name of. No luck there, so one starting point was going to have to be good enough.

During his shifts, Ben always took the unmarked Explorer if it was available and drove by Dixon's place at various times as he did his rounds. He also spent a decent amount of time running traffic nearby to see which vehicles were typically in the area and which weren't. His only interest at this point was finding patterns in Dixon's behavior.

It was cloudy and cooler today, which Ben appreciated, since all his uniforms were long-sleeved. He'd positioned his squad four cars behind the black Audi A8 in traffic, the shift in weather not nearly as interesting to him as the change of habit. Dixon wasn't usually out during the afternoon rush hour.

The Audi turned south onto Lyon Avenue and Ben followed, two of the cars between them doing the same. Shops gave way to houses as the blocks passed and Ben hoped wherever Dixon was going was nearby. Lyon was one of the main roads leading out of Lake City, and he wouldn't be able to follow him past the city limits unless he committed an infraction. So far it seemed that whatever illicit activity he was involved in took place out of town. Not unusual, since criminals often knew they were more likely to be recognized in their own neighborhood.

Halfway through town, Dixon took a left on Eighth Street. It wasn't a common thoroughfare, so Ben decided to take a chance and went straight before turning into the parking lot of Gerken's country store on the corner instead. He drove his Explorer along the far side of the building and into the gravel area between the mill and the train sitting behind it, using the grain bins for cover and the black tank cars for camouflage. He parked behind two of the bins, the gap between them giving him a decent view of the storage units across the street while leaving only a small portion of his squad visible.

His guess was spot-on. Dixon parked between two of the storage buildings and got out, his suit combined with the Audi making the scene look like something out of *The Transporter*—if Jason Statham had shoulder-length blonde hair, that is. But even if Dixon had expensive taste in cars, Ben hadn't seen him in a suit before. Must be an important meeting.

The pearl-white Lexus that pulled up seemed to confirm it. Late model and spotless, it parked in front of the storage units as Dixon walked up to the driver's side window. With the vehicle's right rear corner facing Ben, he couldn't get a visual on the driver, but he could see that the vehicle had Wisconsin plates, even if he wasn't close enough to read them. He watched intently, hoping to see something he could use as probable cause.

Unfortunately, the interaction was brief. It looked like the driver might've handed Dixon something, but from Ben's angle he couldn't be sure. They could've merely been shaking hands, and after that, they quickly parted ways.

As the Lexus exited, Ben thought about pulling it over to find out who the driver was, but he didn't have sufficient legal grounds to do so. He also didn't want to risk spooking the person with his presence, at least not until he found out who he was dealing with. At any rate, knowing the date and time of the meeting was potentially useful information, and now Ben had seen another vehicle worthy of keeping an eye out for.

Dixon got back in his car and pulled out after the Lexus, taking a left onto Eighth Street instead of heading back toward Lyon Avenue. As much as Ben would've liked to follow him, he decided to let Dixon move on rather than give away his hiding spot. Hopefully there'd be some regularity to their interactions, and if so, he'd be using the location again.

As he waited for the Audi to move from view, Ben started to wonder if that was part of what bothered him about Haggerty. Both he and Dixon had a muscular build, light stubble, and long hair. Brown hair versus blonde and distinctly different tastes in clothing, but still. The superficial resemblance was enough to rub him the wrong way.

It didn't take long until both the Lexus and Audi were out of sight. Ben shifted into drive, but before he had a chance to pull out, something caught his eye. A vehicle was exiting the parking lot shared by the liquor store and the unmarked white building adjacent to the storage units. With his focus on Dixon and the Lexus he hadn't even noticed it until now, and under any other circumstances he wouldn't have given it a second thought.

A silver pickup. Haggerty's F-150 to be exact, and turning left like Dixon had. How interesting. And as useful as they were for identification, those damn cab lights were another thing about Haggerty that Ben couldn't stand. Half-tons didn't need to be parading around like fucking semi-trucks.

This was the second time Ben had seen Haggerty in the area while he was doing surveillance on Dixon, and right now he valued answers over stealth. He pulled out the moment Haggerty went past, positioning his squad behind the F-150 as he picked up his radio. "1308 to dispatch, can you run a plate for me?"

"Go ahead," she promptly replied.

"Minnesota three six zero, Edward Charles Zebra. Three sixty, E-C-Z. Tell me who the registered owner is as well."

"Copy."

Ben followed the pickup's every move, making a point of being obvious as he waited for a return from dispatch. He needed a reason to pull Haggerty over, and if he was lucky enough, the return would give him one. Haggerty took a left turn on Irving Street past the auto repair shop and then another left the very next block onto Seventh, almost certainly trying to find out if he was being tailed.

Ben stayed right on his bumper. This time, Haggerty went two blocks before taking another left, now southbound on Lyon

Avenue. Ben stopped as briefly as possible at the stop sign before making a quick left behind him.

Blocks passed with no other turns. Haggerty kept it under the speed limit and had been using his turn signals religiously, but Ben knew if he stayed behind him long enough, he'd make a mistake. Everyone did. Hopefully it'd be soon, since there was only about a quarter of a mile left until they were out of the city limits. Houses became sparser as the landscape opened up.

Finally Ben got what he was looking for. Haggerty drifted over in his lane enough for the edge of his tires to skirt the far side of the white line before he quickly corrected. It was paper thin even by Ben's standards, but that combined with the fact that Haggerty had left a parking lot next to a liquor store was enough for him to feel he could safely justify a stop. Thin was better than nonexistent, after all.

"Dispatch to 1308."

About damn time. "Go ahead."

"Your vehicle comes back valid as a 2011 Ford F-150, silver in color. Your RO is Calvin Haggerty, also valid, I'm showing he's on supervised release. No wants or bonds."

Supervised release, perfect. That'd give Ben more latitude during their interaction. "1308, I'm gonna be doing a traffic stop on that vehicle, Lyon south of Orchard. I'll be out with the RO."

"Copy."

Ben lit him up but kept the siren off. Haggerty knew damn well he was there, so it shouldn't take much. Right on cue, the pickup's turn signal came on and he pulled onto the shoulder, nothing but grass and trees fading toward the bluffs in front of them. Ben parked behind him and angled his squad left so any passing traffic would be forced to go around.

On a highway like this he would normally walk up from the passenger side, but Haggerty had parked right up to the edge of the shoulder. Not wanting the disadvantage of unsure footing on the embankment, Ben waited for traffic to clear before getting out and approaching from the driver's side.

As he went past the back of the truck, he pressed his hand against the tail light to leave fingerprints behind in case Haggerty decided to do anything stupid. He also glanced into the bed of the truck before resting a hand on his gun as he approached the open driver's side window.

The keys were on the dashboard and Haggerty had his hands on the wheel. His light blue plaid shirt was the same color as his eyes, but even with the cooler weather, he'd rolled the sleeves up and left it unbuttoned. An unobtrusive silver necklace rested on the white tank underneath it.

"Is there something I can help you with, Officer?"

Ben chose to skip the pleasantries. "I stopped you because your vehicle crossed the white line back there. I'm going to need to see your license and registration."

Haggerty reached into his back pocket to retrieve his wallet, pulling out the license before grabbing the registration from the driver's side visor. He handed both items out the window.

Ben flipped through the documents, pleasantly surprised that Haggerty didn't offer him some kind of ridiculous excuse about why he drifted over. "Where are you coming from?"

"Eighth Street," Haggerty said. "Just pulled over to answer a phone call."

"You didn't stop to make a purchase at the liquor store by chance, did you?"

"No, sir."

Ben looked at him for a second before handing the license and registration back. "Step out of the vehicle, please."

Haggerty eyed him distrustfully but complied, setting his things on the dashboard before he unbuckled and got out. "Any specific reason you want me out of the vehicle?"

"You're on supervised release. I don't need a reason to search you." Ben shoved him toward the front of the Explorer. "Hands on the hood."

Haggerty glared at him, but again did as he was told. "You know, I don't remember you being such a hard ass last time."

Ben tilted his head. Haggerty was brutally honest, calling it as he saw it even in the face of authority. He saw himself in that.

Too bad that's where their similarities ended.

"Any weapons I should know about?" Ben asked as he started to pat Haggerty down. He'd definitely made good use of the gym while he was in prison.

"A pocket knife," he said, nodding toward the right side of his jeans.

Ben quickly retrieved the item, glancing at it briefly before pocketing it. Legal, since it wasn't a switchblade, so he'd get it back later. He moved on to Haggerty's sides. "Any guns?"

"Felons can't have guns," Haggerty replied, more than a hint of contempt in his voice.

"Oh, is that what I asked?" Ben shot back, doubling the force of his hands.

That brought Haggerty's tone back in line. "No, no guns."

Ben finished patting him down and stepped to the side to make eye contact. "I haven't been in town very long, but it seems like every time I turn around, I'm running into you. Care to explain?"

"It ain't a big city, as you likely noticed. Since I live here, I imagine you see me a lot."

"How long have you lived here?"

"A few months."

"Not long. Why here?" Ben asked. At the time of Haggerty's arrest his address hadn't been in-state, and even if he had decided to take up residence in Minnesota, it seemed more likely that he would've chosen something near Minneapolis. During his interview he'd mentioned having at least one close friend up there, after all.

"I just got released and wanted a fresh start," Haggerty said. "My cousin lives in the area so it seemed like as good a place as any."

Ben considered his answer. It was plausible, but if there was so much as a single frayed strand of a thread connecting him to Dixon, he was sure as hell going to find out. "I take it you were explained the conditions of supervision prior to your release?"

Haggerty pursed his lips. "Yes I was."

"Good, that'll make this easy, then." Ben picked up his radio, shooting Haggerty a glare as he spoke into it. "1308, I'm gonna be searching the vehicle."

"Copy."

IT WAS PROBABLY A BIT undignifying to leave Haggerty handcuffed to the push bumper of his squad while he searched the truck, but in the end, Ben felt it was justified. He had no interest in dealing with another runner, since it'd gone so well for him last time. Haggerty had offered to take a breathalyzer test to save both of them time, so Ben had given him one for the sake of appearances. He'd passed, no surprise there.

The truck's interior was clean and clutter-free, not unlike the outside of the vehicle. The first thing to catch Ben's eye when he got in was the small black box mounted unobtrusively below the dashboard. A scanner. He clicked it on, not at all surprised to find it set to the police frequency.

In Minnesota only police officers, state troopers, and civilians with an amateur radio license could legally have such a device in their vehicle. Since there was no way in hell Haggerty qualified for the first two, Ben reached over and clicked open the glove box to check for the appropriate paperwork. On the off chance he had it, that is.

The small storage compartment was a bit messier than the rest of the vehicle, so Ben pulled everything out and laid it on the passenger seat to separate the paperwork from the odds and ends. Napkins, a pen light, some twine, and a creased old map showing the local hiking trails and fishing areas went on one side. He also found a pair of Z87 safety glasses, not unlike the kind Ben would wear at the shooting range. Once that stuff was out of the way, he turned his attention to the paperwork.

Normally he'd be most interested in the registration and insurance documents, but Ben scrutinized every single piece of paper in front of him. Most of them were parts and maintenance receipts for the truck, and there were a few outdated copies of his insurance cards next to the current one. Nothing hinting at a possible connection. To further his disappointment, it turned out Haggerty did indeed have a valid amateur radio license. He'd still be questioning him about that regardless.

Unsatisfied but finished, he put everything back in the glove box. Other than the scanner and a half-eaten vanilla sandwich cookie, the truck had checked out. He didn't find any liquor or dog food in the truck, which told him Haggerty hadn't stopped on Eighth Street to patronize one of the businesses there.

Grass by the road whispered in the wind as Ben got out. He closed the door and walked back to Haggerty, leaving him cuffed to the bumper as he started his next round of questioning.

"Care to tell me what the scanner is for?" Ben asked. Based on the frequency it was obvious, but he wanted to see what his answer would be.

"It's just a hobby of mine. I've got a license for it in the glove box if you'd like to see it."

"Your truck can't be that comfortable. Why a mobile unit?"

"Reception is crap at my place," he said, keeping his tone respectful. "I know the laws. I don't use it when I'm driving."

Unlikely, Ben thought, but since it was off and he did indeed have the paperwork for it, there wasn't anything he could charge him with at the moment. "Keep it that way."

"Yes, sir."

Ben picked up his radio. "1308."

"Go ahead."

"I didn't find anything on my stop, so Calvin will be on his way, and I'll be clear."

Even if it was common practice to use a subject's first name when communicating with dispatch, Ben hated doing it lately. He had no desire to be on a first-name basis with any criminal.

"Copy," she said.

Ben unlocked the cuffs and handed Haggerty his knife back. "You're free to go."

Haggerty muttered a quiet *thank you* and walked to his truck. Ben got back in his squad and watched Haggerty pull out, his suspicions unconfirmed but no worse for wear. He knew beyond a shadow of a doubt that there was a connection between him and Dixon, even if nothing more than Haggerty's presence in Lake City supported it.

*　　*　　*

The rest of Ben's shift was uneventful. A handful of speeding tickets. A busted tail light. And in one of the more affluent areas of town, two houses that might not have a burn permit and a guy that needed to get a life.

As he waited for the small coffee maker in his room to finish brewing, Ben walked over to the bed and looked out the window. It seemed later than it was, the fading light struggling to force its way through the cloud cover still blanketing the sky. The forecast said sun tomorrow, but at least he wouldn't have to spend most of the day in it. Being on the day shift today had certainly worked out in his favor, but the night shift had its advantages, too.

Before the coffee maker finished sputtering Ben's phone rang. He pulled it out of his pocket and looked at the caller ID, his brother's name flashing on the screen.

"Evening, Miles," he answered.

"Hey. How's the new assignment going?"

Ben sat down on the bed, switching the phone to his other ear. "Alright. The town's charming for how small it is, but there's not exactly a lot going on."

"No bustling nightlife?"

"You know how I meant that."

"Yeah, yeah, just had to razz you. Everyone knows you wouldn't be caught dead in a bar unless you were there to arrest someone," Miles said. "Speaking of which, did the printer in your squad break or something?"

"What kind of question is that?"

"I couldn't help but notice that traffic stop you did earlier without giving so much as a written warning. That's not exactly your style as of late."

"There wasn't anything I could cite him for," Ben defended.

"Then you didn't look hard enough."

"Is that constructive criticism or are you trying to one up me as usual?"

"Trying? Boldly succeeding is more like it."

Ben rubbed his eyes. He couldn't argue with that. "If you could stop using your position to keep tabs on me, that would be great."

"I worry, that's all. That time of year's coming up and—"

"I don't need the reminder, but thanks."

"What I was going to say," Miles continued, "is maybe you should get a hobby or something. You know, help take your mind off of things."

"Yeah, I'll take that into consideration," he said dismissively. Like learning how to fish was going to do him any good. But as irritating as Miles's suggestions were, at least he'd quit pitching counseling. Talking about things that bothered him meant thinking about things that bothered him, and Ben preferred to keep his mind otherwise engaged.

Thankfully Miles had also gotten better at taking a hint, and promptly changed the subject. "Listen, I'll be spending the week upstate on a manhunt. Try not to do anything rash while I'm gone, will you?"

If he was referring to the DWI that landed him here, Ben hardly considered that rash. He'd simply been doing his job. Miles needed to quit worrying so much and focus on his own problems, which he obviously had if he was going upstate again.

"Still haven't closed the Vince Leighton case, I take it?" Ben asked.

A lengthy pause. "We've hit a couple of snags, but we're close to making an arrest."

"Close? What's it been, six months so far?"

"Leighton's cunning, I can tell you that," Miles said. "Always moving, constantly using new aliases. He's got people working for him in every corner of the state."

"Cunning or not, you've always caught them in half that time. Less, usually."

"Your point?"

"Makes this one a new record if I remember correctly."

"Is that your version of constructive criticism, Ben?"

"No. Just a friendly reminder that things don't always work out the way we'd like them to."

"This time everything will go according to plan," Miles said. "Assuming I leave on time."

Oh, time to go because Miles could dish it out but he couldn't take it? Hint taken. "Have fun," Ben said.

"I'm sure I won't, but thanks."

Click.

9

HEADLIGHTS PASSED on the road in front of him as Ben kept an eye on his radar. The residents of Lake City were taking it easy tonight.

This time he was parked by the Pepin Heights Store, which was more of a barn-turned-business that—according to the sign, anyway—sold apples at the very least. Nightfall and three mature trees helped obscure the white doors of his Explorer as he waited to snag someone who thought forty-five was too slow for a sparsely populated highway at the edge of town.

The chime of an incoming message brought his attention to the laptop mounted on the center console. He reached over and flipped open the lid, squinting from the brightness of the screen as he looked at it. It was a BOLO from the Goodhue County Sheriff's Office.

(HRENAKER 21:19:46→) ∗∗∗BOLO/WARRANT PER GCSO∗∗∗ FOR A SILVER FORD TRUCK 360ECZ/MN. THE RO IS CALVIN LYNN HAGGERTY, W/M AGE 32, SUSPECTED OF PROPERTY THEFT. LAST SEEN SOUTHBOUND ON HIGHWAY 61/63 FROM HANSEN'S HARBOR. IF LOCATED PLEASE STOP, HOLD, AND CONTACT GCSO. REFERENCE #25-CR-21-627.

Ben closed the lid and flipped his headlights on. *They always repeat, don't they?*

He pulled out of the gravel parking area, taking a right to head back toward town. The first stop he intended to make was Haggerty's residence, which was likely where he was going since he lived on the north end of Lake City, and that's where Highway 61 and 63 ran concurrently. Given the time of night, if he struck out there, he'd check the bars next. He wanted to be the one to bring Haggerty in.

As he reached the southern end of town, a pair of oncoming headlights came into view, the orange auxiliary lights dotting the roof prompting Ben to slow down and nudge his Explorer away from the center line. As the vehicle passed him, his squad's headlights flashed across the silver body of an F-150.

Ben swung a U-turn. He hit the gas to catch up and pulled close enough to verify the truck's license plate. It was Haggerty's, alright. He fell back to a more reasonable following distance as he picked up his radio. "1308 to dispatch."

"Go ahead."

"I'm behind Calvin Haggerty's vehicle, and I'll be picking him up for Goodhue's warrant. Highway 61 and Indiana Street with Minnesota three six zero, Edward Charles Zebra."

"Copy."

They started heading up the bridge that took Highway 61

over the railroad tracks, but Ben flipped on his lights and siren anyway. It'd be tight with the guardrail, but the southbound lane had enough of a shoulder for Haggerty to use. Ben slowed down in anticipation of Haggerty doing the same.

The truck pulled away as it gained speed.

Ben hit the gas. "1308, he's running, southbound on 61. I'll be in pursuit."

"Copy," she replied. "Dispatch to all available units, respond to Highway 61 south of Indiana Street to assist 1308 with a vehicle pursuit. It's a silver Ford pickup heading south."

A male voice came over the radio. "229, I'm en route from Territorial Road."

Really, Taylor? Could you be any farther?

Ben stayed on Haggerty's bumper as they headed out of town. Traffic was light and Ben hoped it'd stay that way. He'd have to terminate the chase if it got too risky, and the nature of the warrant didn't justify the use of a PIT maneuver.

Based on his driving, Haggerty wasn't aware of either. He wasn't stopping, but he had yet to break sixty miles an hour, and whenever Ben's squad moved to the side, Haggerty swung over to block him. They left the last of the businesses behind and hit the open highway when Haggerty took an abrupt right.

Ben yanked the wheel to stay with him. "1308, he's turning onto County 4."

"Copy."

As soon as Ben hit the gas Haggerty swung an even harder left onto a blind drive Ben hadn't even seen. He slammed on the brakes and looked for a street or fire sign, but none were present. He had to back up to make the turn.

"1308, eastbound on the first left. Unmarked blind drive."

"229, there's a freight train sitting across Grant Street. I'll be looking for an alternate route."

"Copy," Ben said.

The so-called drive was paved, but not quite wide enough for his squad. Foliage brushed along the sides of the Explorer as he looked ahead for Haggerty's tail lights, which had disappeared when the uphill path snaked around the first blind turn. Ben nudged the squad as fast as he felt he safely could, when a figure darted into the path of his headlights.

Ben slammed on the brakes and jerked the steering wheel to avoid the hit, one set of tires going off what little pavement had been underneath them. As the squad lurched to a stop, Ben saw two more figures move out of the brush, stopping at the fringe of the light to study him with distrustful curiosity.

Deer.

He took a shaky breath. As much as he would've liked to stop and recompose himself after the near miss, he didn't have the time. He laid on the horn and all three of his woodland friends scattered into the underbrush. After turning the steering wheel back he hit the gas, dirt spraying out from behind the rear wheels as he forced the squad back onto the road. He went slower on the next blind turn, a left that brought him to where the drive ended in a t-intersection with Highway 61.

Ben looked both directions, cursing under his breath when he didn't see tail lights in either. What the hell was that road even for? He picked up his radio. "1308, I lost him on 61 south of 4. Advise County that he was last seen heading south and I'll be checking the area to the north."

"Copy."

Ben turned off his siren and emergency lights before taking a left. Anything to the south was County's jurisdiction anyway, but if he was Haggerty, he would've gone north to head back into town. He'd probably figure that backtracking was a good way to lose his tail. As Ben drove, he scrutinized every possible turn, looking at the situation as if he was the one being hunted. With the bluffs on one side and the river on the other, Highway 61 didn't offer a lot of places for someone to hide.

Residences were out. No real cover for a vehicle, and they carried a high risk of someone calling 911 to report trespassing. Haggerty could try taking the back roads to get to his place, but going home would be an amateur move, so Ben didn't see it as particularly likely. That left businesses. Most were closed by this time of night, plenty had limited lighting, and some offered buildings or sheds large enough to conceal a vehicle.

In less than half a mile, Ben approached the handful of businesses south of town and slowed down. From the perspective of a fugitive, this area looked attractive. Multiple buildings, roads in and out, limited lighting. Ben took a right onto Sportsman's Drive to head behind Wild Wings Plaza, sweeping the landscape with his squad's spotlight. The road ended in a t-intersection with Camp Lakeview Road shortly after it began, leaving Ben at another stop sign and two choices. Left or right.

He turned off the spotlight and looked both ways. More commercial buildings to the left and nothing but trees lining the road to the right. It was a fifty-fifty shot, but his gut instinct was to go left, so he went with that. The few residences he saw were all on the other side of the train tracks to his right, but a pair of cantilever gates blocked the crossing on both sides. No way Haggerty had gone through there.

With only the ditch and train tracks on the right, Ben kept

his attention on the left. The pale green manufacturing building and grassy plot to the north of it didn't provide any cover, but the area coming up looked far more promising—the fenced property belonging to Lake City's public works.

Multiple buildings edged a large gravel lot interspersed with piles of containers, pipes, spools, utility boxes, and various other groupings of random clunk. The chain link surrounding the property was a standard four-foot height that could easily be scaled. The section of fence running parallel to Camp Lakeview Road was fitted with black privacy slats that provided additional cover. As Ben approached the southeast corner of the property, he didn't even need his spotlight to see the glint of the silver F-150 pulled forward into the open-front shed inside.

Ben slowed down and turned off his headlights. This area should've been locked up for the night, but if Haggerty's pickup was inside, then he must've found a way in. Sure enough, as Ben drove up to the rear entry gate, he found it open.

"1308, I see the vehicle parked in a shed behind the public works. I'm going to park on Camp Lakeview Road and approach on foot."

"Copy," the dispatcher said. "Camp Lakeview Road north of Terrace."

"229, the train's starting to move," Taylor radioed. "I'll be en route shortly."

"Copy," Ben said. He parked in the grass just shy of the entry gate. Haggerty might've seen his headlights as he approached, but there was nothing Ben could do about it now. If he hadn't, the fence's privacy slats would help keep his squad out of sight.

Ben lowered the volume on his handheld radio before he got out, pressed the lock button, and closed the door quietly. As he approached the gate he drew his weapon, keeping his finger off the trigger and the muzzle angled toward the ground.

Once inside, he kept to the fence line. Walking on gravel was never ideal from a stealth standpoint, so Ben moved carefully. Tall stacks of black plastic crates shielded him now, but there was an open area between here and the shed. He'd have to break cover to find out if Haggerty was still in the truck. He considered waiting for backup, but Taylor would be in the area soon enough and he wasn't about to let Haggerty slip away twice in one night. He listened for any kind of sound, but heard nothing.

He stayed low and darted to the shed, taking cover against the outside wall as he kept his gun in a low-ready position. After stopping to listen one more time, he leaned into the doorway and peered inside.

The cab was empty.

Ben grabbed the flashlight from his duty belt and clicked it on. Light in his left hand and gun in his right, he crossed his wrists to stabilize the weapon as he checked the back of the truck for possible stolen equipment. Several two-by-fours littered the bed, clearly the remnants of a project someone hadn't had the time or ambition to finish. Not a sight he'd expected. When he'd pulled Haggerty over, his bed had been empty, prompting Ben to shine his flashlight at the rear plate.

512-FCB.

Really? How many silver F-150s could there possibly be out here in the middle of—

Stars exploded into his vision as the force of a blow sent him to the ground. The gravel biting into his hands was almost imperceptible compared to the overwhelming pain in the back of his head. The flashlight cast a dim glow along the ground from wherever it had landed, but Ben had kept a firm hold on his gun. All he could hear was the ringing in his head.

Everything spun as he pushed himself into a sitting position. A figure knelt beside him, but long hair obscured his assailant's face. A hand reached down and into the path of the flashlight, which cast enough light to illuminate the spiked dog collar tattoo on the man's wrist. Ben's blood ran cold at the sight.

He'd seen Haggerty in short sleeves twice this week. He didn't have any tattoos. Not that specific one, at least. Dixon did.

And he was reaching for Ben's gun.

His adrenaline kicked in. If Dixon got his gun, it was game over. Ben pushed himself to the right to throw Dixon off balance, gravel grating beneath him as he tried to maintain control of his weapon. Where the hell was his backup? Two hands on top of his gripped tighter, so Ben did what he could, putting all of his effort into keeping the muzzle aimed at the ground. Dixon doubled his efforts in return and managed to force a finger over the trigger. Dust burst in front of them as a round split the air. The noise sent a fresh wave of pain shooting through Ben's head and he felt his strength starting to wane.

Plan B. Empty the magazine while he still had control of the weapon.

The ringing in his head intensified with every shot, but Ben kept pulling the trigger. He'd gotten eight shots off so far, maybe. The smell of burnt gunpowder leaching into the air worsened his dizziness. He couldn't focus. Dixon repositioned to get a better stance when the scene brightened to searing levels.

Panic took over as the headlights blinded him. A car door snapped open before Ben felt a third set of hands enter the fray and force Dixon off of him. He heard the muffled sounds of a fight, stumbling as he tried unsuccessfully to regain his balance. Gravel bit into his hands again but this time he stayed down, trembling as he tried to slow his ragged breathing. He'd have to trust that Taylor could handle this without his help.

The slam of a car door was followed by what sounded like a car speeding off from behind the shed, but he couldn't have heard that right. The ringing in his ears was too loud. The throbbing in his head had started to ease and the dizziness was subsiding, but the light's assault was unrelenting. He needed to get up.

"Are you alright?"

Fuck. That wasn't Taylor.

A second wave of adrenaline surged through him. Ben forced himself to stand and staggered out of the path of the headlights, immediately training his gun on the voice. His balance improved quickly, but his eyes took longer to adjust. Once they did, he wasn't sure if he believed them.

Haggerty stood in front of his truck, amber lights dotting the roof and headlights flanking him as the vehicle idled softly in the background. He kept the rest of his body completely still as he raised his hands to chest level. "Easy," he said, his southern twang giving the impression of someone trying to calm a skittish horse. "Take it easy."

So he had seen it right. Time for answers.

Ben evened his voice and kept his weapon steady. "I'm pretty sure you weren't telling me the whole truth before, so I expect it now. Talk."

"Alright," Haggerty said, keeping his hands up. "That guy you just danced with, I've been following him for a few months. Didn't expect to run into him out here though, I swear."

Ben suppressed a smile. "You know him?"

"I don't know who he actually is, but yeah, I know of him. Career criminal, goes by the name of Rude Dog. He has a knack for getting away with things."

He sure as hell does, Ben thought, but he kept his face neutral. "And what's your interest in him?"

"He screwed over a friend of mine," Haggerty said. "I'd like to right that wrong."

A mutual goal, and an interesting one. Ben paused as he contemplated what he should do with that. When he came to Lake City looking for Dixon, he hadn't expected someone else to be doing the same.

His gaze went to Haggerty's truck. He also hadn't expected a vehicle pursuit. "You were using the scanner, weren't you?"

"You're right, I was. And I know how it might look given my prior, but whatever warrant they issued is mistaken. I haven't done anything illegal."

"Then why'd you run?"

"Because everywhere Rude Dog goes I've been tailing him, so chances are someone got my plate or a description of my truck somewhere along the line." Haggerty paused for a few seconds before continuing. "I know I shouldn't have run, but I just got out of prison. I don't want to take the fall for whatever shit he's gonna get away with next."

Ben took a long, hard look at Haggerty. He seemed to be telling the truth, but Ben knew beyond a shadow of a doubt that the only legal option right now was to put him in handcuffs and take him in. Let him plead his case with the courts. Still, Haggerty had everything to lose and absolutely nothing to gain from getting involved in the fight, a choice that in all honesty had probably saved Ben's life. Intuition screamed at him to let Haggerty go, but he couldn't do that. Or was it "shouldn't" do that? He struggled to hold his position as the line between what was legal and what was right seemed to blur in front of him.

A smooth female voice broke the silence. "Dispatch to 1308, we have a report of possible shots fired in your area. What's your status?"

10

BEN HAD ASSUMED there were more houses on the far side of the tracks, but the tree line here was far too dense for any of them to have a visual on his location. He reached for his radio, deciding to play intuition over protocol since fate was giving him the opportunity to do so. "1308, it seems that Calvin got away. The vehicle I'm out with isn't his. There are some spent fireworks casings out here as well but it looks like the perpetrators are long gone. You can cancel the other units."

"Copy," she replied. "All other units can clear."

"229, I copy."

"1308, I'll be clear as well," Ben said. He put the radio away but kept his weapon up, uncertainty creeping up on Haggerty's face as his eyes flicked to the gun. What was most likely a painful sixty seconds for him was a comfortable silence for Ben as he decided on his next move. This was an interesting opportunity to say the least, and having someone like Haggerty on his side could be advantageous. "If you're innocent, prove it. Help me take him down."

Haggerty didn't lower his hands. "You're the law. What can I possibly do that you and the rest of your department can't?"

It wasn't an unreasonable question, but Ben didn't want the rest of the department involved. Not yet, and most certainly not like this. "If you've been following him, then you have intel I can use. Locations, habits, accomplices. I want everything you have on him."

The truck's idle was the only sound as Haggerty appeared to be debating the request, his expression showing that he was far more inclined to say no than yes.

Ben pressed further. "The warrant they issued is for theft at Hansen's Harbor. With your record, and your truck being seen in the area at the time, that'll be a tough case for you to win. The prosecution only has to prove your guilt beyond a reasonable doubt. Not beyond all doubt."

"I didn't commit any crimes—"

"And if I take you in, that'll be for the courts to decide."

Haggerty shifted his weight. "I don't have any proof, but that was Rude Dog at Hansen's last night. I was following him and I parked nearby, but like I said...I didn't commit any crimes."

"And it looks like your vehicle stood out more than his," Ben replied. "So, I'll ask one last time. Do you really want me to take you to jail over a case of mistaken identity?"

Haggerty's jaw tensed at the ultimatum and Ben gave him a minute to think it over. This time he couldn't tell which way Haggerty was leaning. If he decided to help him, great. If not, Ben would respect that and bring out the cuffs. Either scenario was acceptable. He fully intended on catching Dixon, and he'd do it with or without Haggerty's assistance.

"That's not exactly my idea of a good night," Haggerty said.

Ben lowered his gun. It was close enough to an agreement. "Roschen Park, tomorrow. Meet me at eight A.M." He holstered the weapon and gestured toward Haggerty's truck. "And go find yourself a different set of wheels."

*   *   *

The emergency room hadn't been particularly busy, so Ben pulled his car into the motel's parking lot only a few hours later than he otherwise would've. The back of his head had hurt like a son-of-a-bitch, but he'd still opted to finish his shift before being seen. Probably not the smartest thing he'd ever done, but that was the only way he could avoid having to explain the night's occurrences to the department. Even though he'd patted off as much gravel dust as he could before he went to the station to change, the custodian had raised an eyebrow at the state of his uniform.

Ben grabbed the soiled garment and his discharge papers from the ER off the passenger seat and got out. The security light on the other side of the lot seemed to cast an unreasonable number of lumens given its distance, so he shielded his eyes. Did they replace the bulb or—

Light sensitivity, of course. He should've remembered that.

He unlocked the door to his room, keeping the lights off as he walked in. He could see well enough thanks to the window. Light from outside filtered through the open blinds, casting lines across the wall.

Ben's gaze came to rest on the large color-block painting that hung above the bed. It was far from the style of art he normally gravitated to, but for some reason he found its simple shapes and basic palette unexpectedly comforting tonight. Shades of pink, yellow, orange, and light blue depicted a crescent moon, clouds, and a setting sun over distant hills, beneath it a streak of pale blue that could easily pass for the Mississippi River. The white backdrop of the sky took up the majority of the canvas, and he chalked up his like of the design to that. It had a dream-like feel to it.

After setting the paperwork aside, Ben grabbed his uniform shirt and unpinned the badge, setting it on the breakfast table before slinging the shirt and pants over one of the chairs. He wouldn't have to worry about washing the outfit right away as he had the next couple of days off, but he did want to clean his gun before trying to get some rest.

The task took longer than usual thanks to the gravel. Once he was satisfied that the Glock was spotless, he reloaded the magazine and palmed it in. He racked the slide to load a round into the chamber, then grabbed a small gun safe from under his bed and used the fingerprint scanner to open it before placing the weapon inside.

Other than getting hit by a two-by-four or whatever the hell it'd been, he felt fortunate about how the rest of the incident had played out. Losing a suspect during a pursuit meant an automatic review of the dash cam footage by his superiors, but thankfully his interactions with Dixon and Haggerty had both occurred out of view of the camera. He'd also been driving the oldest squad in the fleet, which happened to be the only one equipped with a dash cam that didn't record sound.

The last thing he needed to explain his way out of was the amount of time he'd spent behind the public works after telling dispatch that Haggerty had gotten away. Thankfully, Ben only needed to stick with the narrative he'd already written for the report—that he'd walked the property to look for any more spent fireworks casings. It was a reasonable cover story, and he couldn't think of any reason why it might be questioned. Even so, he still couldn't shake the guilt over his actions.

Actions that didn't seem like his own.

Ben sat down on the mattress and gingerly laid back, thinking about all the laws he'd broken that night. Aiding and abetting a fugitive, blackmailing said fugitive—at *gunpoint*, no less—falsifying a report, and failing to report the discharge of his firearm. He wondered if the courts gave out longer sentences for any of those if the offending party happened to be a police officer who was on duty when said crimes were committed.

He had no idea. He'd never broken a single law before.

Restlessness got the better of him. He got up and grabbed his badge off the table, holding it in his hand as he observed how the light from the window glinted off of it. He ran his thumb across it, the ridges and valleys of its silver surface cool against his skin. Word for word, his thoughts ran through the oath of honor, the one he'd taken the day he'd become a sworn officer. That was a far cry from his actions today, from the decisions he'd made mere hours ago. Teetering on the edge of legality didn't quite seem to describe the scenario he found himself in right now.

What the hell was he doing?

11

OTHER THAN A COUPLE of late-model SUVs and a few pickups hitched to empty boat trailers, the lot at Roschen Park was empty.

Ben lounged at one of the picnic tables nested between the silver maples, his Charger parked a few stalls down. Even with sunglasses, the morning glare over the water was painfully bright, which reminded him that he should probably take his next dose of Tylenol. Thanks to unwelcome thoughts and the symptoms of his so-called "mild" concussion, he'd slept worse than usual. Damn headache. He should've said ten A.M.

The park itself was about as quiet as the lot was empty. The soft plodding of jogger shoes occasionally joined the chorus of rustling leaves, and somewhere in the distance a pair of gulls argued over what was most likely a discarded French fry. Even if the sun was trying to murder his eyes, Ben was thankful that at least it was quiet here. All noise did for him at the moment was make his head hurt.

Ben reached into the pocket of his jacket and pulled out the small bottle of pills, twisting the cap off and dumping two of them into the palm of his hand. He took them dry before putting the lid back on, exchanging the container for his phone to check the time. Ten minutes before eight.

He put the device back in his pocket, figuring there was about a fifty-fifty chance Haggerty would show. Not that it really mattered, because if he didn't show then Ben would make it his personal mission in life to bring him in for Goodhue's warrant. But he'd worry about that in ten minutes. He closed his eyes and focused on the sound of waves lapping gently against the rocky shoreline.

The obtrusive growl of a diesel engine and the clanking of metal brought his attention to the entrance of the park, where a large flatbed tow truck was pulling into the lot. It looked like something straight out of the '90s—its oversized front-end was bulky and angular, its dull white paint had probably lost its shine over a decade ago. As it rumbled closer, he was able to make out the faded *Haase Truck & Equipment* lettering on its door. None of the vehicles parked here seemed to be in need of a tow, but he hoped that rig wasn't Haggerty's. Ben grimaced as the machine screeched to a halt lengthwise in front of him.

Well, there was his answer.

"Morning, Kessler," Haggerty said as he rolled the window down by hand. This time he was wearing a gray short-sleeved mechanic's shirt and pair of safety glasses, his hair pulled back into a neat ponytail.

Ben grudgingly stood and walked up to the truck's driver

door. "Isn't that a bit conspicuous?" he asked. And craptastically loud.

"It ain't in my name," Haggerty replied. "And besides, when's the last time you saw a tow truck get pulled over?"

"Fair enough," Ben said. He gestured to the lettering on the door. "Does your boss know you're borrowing it?"

"He's fly fishing up in Canada, and right now I'm his only employee, so chances are he won't notice." He gestured toward the passenger side. "Hop in."

Ben hesitated, debating whether he should ride along or follow in his own car. He didn't exactly revel at the thought of someone else driving.

"You comin' or what?"

He rubbed his forehead and let out a tense breath. "Yeah."

Not caring how it looked, Ben opted to walk around the back of the truck instead of the front. He ignored his reflection in the large side mirror as he approached, reaching up to open the door before using the chrome handle on the back of the cab to pull himself up. Just as he got one foot inside the vehicle he stopped short, finding himself face to face with the unreasonably large mouth of a pit bull.

The dog was stocky and fawn-colored, his white chest and toes giving the impression of a tuxedo. His eyes were the same hue as his fur, but Ben couldn't look past those milky-white teeth as his tongue lolled in and out between them.

God this kept getting better.

Haggerty raised an eyebrow. "Not a dog person?"

"No, it's not that. I mean I never had one but..." He paused, not really sure how to word it. Damn that was a big mouth.

"Ah. Not a pit bull person, then," Haggerty said. He gave the dog a vanilla sandwich cookie before continuing. "You know, you shouldn't judge a book by its cover. Greta's the sweetest dog you'll ever meet."

Greta, damn. He was a she.

Without prompting, Haggerty scooted Greta away from the door and cued her to sit in the middle of the bench seat. Ben debated with himself for a moment longer before getting in and buckling, going with the more likely scenario that Haggerty was being truthful about her demeanor. Breed aside, she seemed friendly enough.

Once he closed the door, Haggerty shifted into first gear and swung the rig around. Ben imagined that the view of the lake must be more impressive from the higher vantage point, but even with sunglasses on he opted to avoid the water's glare and kept his gaze inside.

From top to bottom the truck's interior was a drab, dusty gray, and as angular as the exterior. It made the oversized red button on the side of the shift lever seem out of place, and Ben wondered what it was for. Self-destruct, hopefully.

Haggerty spoke before he had a chance to ask. "I take it you got a database of street names or something. Did you look up who our guy is?"

"His name's Dixon. Andrew Dixon," Ben said. He hadn't needed to look up anything, but decided to keep that to himself.

Meanwhile, Greta kept her face mere inches from his, her hot breath puffing against his cheek as her tongue bounced around. Ben leaned away a bit, hoping to avoid at least some of the flying droplets of spit.

Haggerty gave a sharp whistle as he pointed to the seat, and Greta immediately laid down. Since her dander was probably on everything, Ben reminded himself not to touch his eyes or they'd be itching for the rest of the day.

As they headed out of town, Lakeshore Drive became Highway 61, and the truck picked up speed. Ben kept his gaze off the road, something that wasn't as hard as he'd expected it to be. This was the first time in almost a year that he found himself in the passenger seat. With a stranger behind the wheel, no less. He wasn't sure why he felt inclined to trust Haggerty to that level, but it had to be because of what happened behind the public works. If Haggerty bore any ill will toward him, he wouldn't have intervened.

"So is this some kind of undercover operation or something?" Haggerty asked.

"No. This is completely off the books."

He paused for a moment. "You realize that you're aiding and abetting a fugitive, right?"

Ben looked out the side window. "I'm aware of that, yes."

Another pause, this one twice as long as the last. "You're not going to shoot him or something, are you?"

Haggerty wasn't the type to beat around the bush, that was for sure. "No," Ben said. "I just want him to face justice the way the system intended."

The way he hadn't last time. Justice may be blind, but she really dropped the ball on that one.

"So, last night. You really thought that was my truck parked out there?"

"It was the same body style and color as yours, so yeah. I mistook it."

"For starters, my truck has aluminum rims instead of steel," Haggerty said. "It's also a Lariat. That one was an XL."

"In the heat of the moment, checking the trim package wasn't exactly my first thought," Ben said. In hindsight he knew that his first thought should've been checking the plate, a mistake he was still chastising himself for.

Ben started to wonder if Haggerty was chastising himself for his own mistake, too. He'd ended up with a warrant over the deal. Whatever motivation he had for following Dixon must be important to him if he was willing to risk his freedom over it.

The truck slowed and Haggerty set his turn signal, prompting Ben to glance out the window. Ahead on the right stood a few pole buildings, a hodgepodge of dated vehicles scattered around them. Haggerty swung a wide right and then a near-immediate left to pull into the gravel parking area next to the predominantly placed white building up front. The truck swayed to a stop as the inertia faded, and with the turn of a key, the engine's growl puttered out.

As soon as Ben opened the door, Greta jumped across his lap, all forty pounds of her crushing his manhood as she launched herself into the grass. He gave himself a minute to recover before he climbed out and joined Haggerty, who was swinging a set of keys in his hand as he waited next to the building's front door. Greta had no interest in following them in and went straight to plunging her face into a cluster of dandelion puffs.

Once inside Haggerty turned on the fluorescent lights, which slowly hummed to life. "My place of employment."

Ben took his sunglasses off and looked around. The semidarkness of in here was far easier on his eyes than the intense brightness of outside had been. The smell of grease and rust hung in the air, the concrete floors darkened with grime. Tools and toolboxes lined the walls, but the only item of color was the hoist in front of them, its faded red columns flanking an open-hooded sedan missing its front wheels. It looked as old as Haggerty's pickup, but unlike the omnipresent silver of his vehicle, this one was black. Not exactly rare in the grand scheme of things, but definitely one of the less common colors for a Camry of that age.

"Why are we here?" Ben asked.

"Like you said, I'm on parole. They can search my residence, phone, and my truck at any time if they so please."

"It's supervised release, not parole."

Haggerty glared at him. "Same difference. And since I'm sure stalking would be frowned upon for someone in my position, I keep everything I have on him here."

He walked over to one of the toolboxes next to the Camry and unlocked it with a small key. After grabbing a folder from the bottom drawer, he turned and closed the sedan's hood. As it slammed shut the piercing sound of metal on metal reverberated through the building's interior.

Ben winced and closed his eyes, taking a controlled breath as he rubbed his temple.

"You alright, Kessler?"

"I'm fine. Just a headache."

Haggerty studied him for a second. "Well if those pills you got on you are Tylenol, then you should probably take some."

Ben tilted his head. "What makes you think they're Tylenol?"

"The sunglasses, the headache, the way you were staggering last night. I'd say you got a concussion. They're obviously not sleeping pills, or you wouldn't look so dead tired."

Perceptive and blunt. What a fun combination. "I already took some, but thanks for the suggestion."

Haggerty looked at him for another second before turning his attention to the folder. He pulled out a stack of photographs and laid them on the Camry's hood. Dixon's residence, his car at various locations, and a few of him meeting people who couldn't be identified because of the distance at which the photos were taken. All of the night shots were worthless as well, too dark to show anything more than a pair of red or white lights that identified a vehicle by nothing more than 'front' or 'back'.

Overall, nothing incriminating.

"What's his game?" Ben asked.

"Theft. Vehicles, mostly, but if the right opportunity presents itself he'll diversify."

"Any habits worth noting?"

"He tends to take a late-night phone call outside his house, if that's something you can use. He's either trying not to wake people or he doesn't want anyone inside to hear what he's talking about."

"Every night?"

"Most nights. Never before eleven or midnight, though."

"Do you know who he's talking to?"

"No idea. I've just seen him out there when I'm driving by," Haggerty said. "If I had to guess I'd say his fence, but I don't go around lurking in the bushes at night. Hate for the cops to see me doing that."

"Then don't be seen."

"Easy for you to say. You're not the one with a record."

"Your actions are the only reason you have a record."

Haggerty glared at him. "Not everything's as black and white as the paint job on your squad car, Kessler."

Ben ignored him and went back to the photos, picking up

the one of Dixon with his latest girlfriend in tow. He looked it over, wanting nothing more than to wipe that smug smile off Dixon's face.

"I hope you don't have any plans later," Ben said. "Because tonight we're going to find out who he's talking to."

12

CALVIN FIDGETED in his seat, trying to keep his other leg from falling asleep. At least being on the passenger side meant he had a bit more room to stretch out as the night dragged on.

And on.

And on some more.

He glanced at Kessler, whose attention on the house one property down hadn't faded one iota since they'd parked two hours ago. Not only had he demanded they come early, but he'd insisted on driving, saying the flatbed was too conspicuous for a stakeout. Like his ride was any better. Personal vehicle or not, it had "cop" written all over it. Freaking black Dodge Charger.

And as if that wasn't enough, Kessler's black hoodie, black beanie, and black gloves really rounded out the whole blatantly obvious undercover look. Setting up in a hunting blind in the neighbor's yard would've been more subtle.

Calvin would rather be in a blind somewhere right now, that was for sure. Hunting also required its fair share of waiting, but at least on a hunt the wait itself was enjoyable. Taking in the crisp fall air, listening to the quiet sounds of nature. Sitting here on the side of the street as an empty soda can clanked its way along the gutter was nothing short of soul-sucking.

Still, teaming up with Kessler seemed to be working out in Calvin's favor. The police in Minneapolis hadn't been interested in finding Rodney's late grandmother's ring, but from what Calvin had managed to find out in prison, Andrew—whose real name he only knew thanks to Kessler—had a thing for keeping souvenirs. Rodney's car had been his first vehicle theft, something else he'd found out in prison. Calvin would've taken that knowledge to the police if he'd had any evidence for it, but in the end Rodney didn't care about the car. It was replaceable. The ring, on the other hand, had been in Rodney's family for three generations. Five years had passed, but if there was any chance Andrew still had it, Calvin was going to try to get it back. He'd had to play it far safer than he would've liked so he wouldn't risk losing his parole, but Kessler didn't have that handicap.

And if Kessler didn't find what he was looking for tonight, maybe Calvin could convince him they should search Andrew's house the next time rather than watch it. If he'd been willing to skirt the law when it came to Calvin's warrant, maybe he'd do the same in that scenario.

The wind shifted, bringing the can back to taunt him again. It felt unreasonably cliché, but Calvin was bored out of his mind and desperate times called for desperate measures. He turned to the driver's seat. "So, you got any hobbies?"

For the first time since they'd parked, Kessler took his eyes off the house Andrew currently lived in. "Really? We're making small talk?"

He shrugged. "There's not exactly much else to do."

Kessler sighed and looked back out the windshield. "No."

"You mean 'no' as in there's not much else to do or 'no' as in no hobbies?"

"No, I don't have any hobbies."

Calvin could tell by the hint of irritation in his voice that he wasn't interested in small talk. Maybe he'd go for something a little more substantial. "Alright then, how 'bout this. What got you into law enforcement?"

Kessler tapped his fingers on the center console as if deciding whether or not he was going to reply. An uncomfortable silence lingered between them as a dog barked in the distance.

Damn. This was gonna be one long-ass, boring night. Well, he couldn't do more than try to break the ice. Maybe next time he'd bring a book or something to—

"My family," Kessler said. "A bunch of selfish, irresponsible assholes whose only measurable contribution to society is being a bad example."

Calvin found himself at a loss for words at Kessler's answer, but even more so at the calm, collected way he'd said it. His tone was so impassive that Calvin thought he might be joking.

The hard look in Kessler's eyes demonstrated he wasn't. "Sorry if that sounded harsh, but it's the truth."

"No, it's...not what I expected," Calvin said. "Figured you came from a long line of blue bloods or something."

Kessler looked down and ran his thumb across the car's shifter. "I grew up in a diminutive little shithole of a town, the kind of place you don't have to blink to miss. We had a few acres on the south end so none of our neighbors were particularly close. No local police, and a county deputy drove through every few weeks at best." He moved his gaze out the side window as he continued. "My father was an alcoholic with a nasty temper, and everyone in town knew better than to get in his way."

"He sounds like a real piece of work."

"Yeah, you could say that. I did what I could to keep his attention off my brother, but neither of us had it good."

"He was abusive?"

Kessler studied him for a moment, leveling his expression as he dodged the question. "At one point a new family moved to town, and a man came knocking late one night when he mistook our address for someone else's. Our father went out rifle in hand, telling the guy in no uncertain terms that if he didn't leave, he'd drag his 'sorry ass' into the house so he could shoot him free and clear. Of course, the guy called the police the minute he left the property."

"How'd that go?"

"It didn't. When the cops came, he denied everything. My mother covered for him as always, and with no other witnesses, there wasn't much they could do. Miles and I knew better than to say anything."

Miles, he must be Kessler's brother. "I take it your dad was drunk that night?"

"He was always drunk. For most of my childhood, I used to wonder what he'd act like if he wasn't," Kessler said. "The only time I ever felt safe was when the police were around, so when it came time to start considering occupations, I didn't have to give it a second thought. If I could give that sense of security to others, even just one person...I had every intention of doing so."

"What do your folks think of your career choice?" he asked. Even though they weren't assholes by any means, the scenario reminded Calvin a bit of his parents. They'd never approved of his preference for blue-collar work.

"No idea. I haven't talked to them since I left, which was the day I turned eighteen." He looked out the window. "My father died a year later at forty-seven. Heart attack."

"I'm sorry."

Kessler's expression hardened. "You'd be the only one."

Calvin shifted his legs again to buy himself some time. He couldn't think of a suitable reply, so he took the conversation in a different direction. "What about your brother?"

"He's the only other decent apple that rolled away from that rotten tree. He keeps our mother at arm's length, but visits her now and then for the holidays." Kessler paused a moment, shifting his gaze back to the floor. "I guess he's a more forgiving person than I am."

At the house, a light flicked on and illuminated the patterned glass of Andrew's front door. Kessler opened his door and got out. "Stay here."

"What? Why can't we both—"

"Two people makes it twice as likely we'll be seen. Stay put."

Rather than fully closing the door, Kessler set it quietly against the car's body. In one fluid motion he stepped into the darkness and over to—

Wait, what? Calvin looked around, trying to figure out where the hell Kessler went. Crouched down between the car and the curb? He rolled down the window and stuck his head out. Nope, just gone. Like a freaking ghost.

Calvin sighed and leaned back, stretching out his legs to make himself more comfortable. Andrew had walked around to the side of his house as usual, leaving nothing for Calvin to see thanks to the neighbor's disorderly shrubs. But even if there wasn't much to see, Calvin certainly had plenty to think about. For starters, what exactly had happened behind the public works before he'd made it there.

From the looks of it, Andrew had gone after Kessler with a piece of lumber, or at least that was Calvin's best guess. That, or he'd gotten his head slammed into the side of the other pickup. Either one would explain why his balance was shit right after the fight, and why his headache was so bad this morning that he'd made a point of carrying a bottle of Tylenol with him. Kessler didn't look like he'd gotten any sleep prior to their rendezvous tonight, but at least he seemed to be less sensitive to noise.

Still, it shouldn't have gone down like that. Not waiting for backup was reckless to begin with, but Calvin hadn't expected Kessler to run into anyone, especially not Andrew. He must not have seen the A8 parked on the far side of the shed. Calvin had assumed that, as a cop, Kessler would've swept the area for threats before getting too far from his car. And while his mistake had cost him, Kessler was damn lucky that for whatever reason, Andrew hadn't had a gun on him. If he had—

A dark figure stood motionless next to his door and Calvin nearly jumped out of his skin. "Holy shit! Why didn't you say something?"

"Sorry," Kessler said. "Didn't want to scare you."

"Well you did a bang-up job. Where the hell did you come from, anyway?"

"Over there." He pointed.

The bushes. Of course. "And why are you on my side?"

"I need a flashlight. Think I stepped in something."

"Why don't you use your phone?"

"I would, but it's in the glove box."

"Isn't that a bit overkill?" Calvin asked, retrieving the phone and handing it out the window. "You could silence it."

Kessler put a hand on his car for balance and swept the light across the bottom of his shoes. "Yeah, and next thing you know half a dozen gangbangers are on your tail because the dumpster behind them started ringing. Not worth the risk, trust me."

Apparently satisfied, he walked around the front of his car and got back in.

"So who's he talking to?" Calvin prompted.

"I couldn't tell, the call was too short. But tomorrow at noon he's going to be meeting a woman named Jaime Baker at Ohuta Beach, and we're going to be there."

"Tomorrow?"

"Yeah, is that a problem? I take it you don't work Saturdays."

"No, but that's the Float-a-Palooza."

"The what?"

"It's a yearly get-together where everyone brings an inflatable ring or whatever and hangs out at the beach," Calvin said. "I've gone a couple of times with my niece. It's not exactly my thing, but if that's your plan then we're gonna need to blend in."

Kessler's jaw tightened ever so subtly. "Alright. What do we need?"

13

THE BEACH WAS INUNDATED with music and laughter as the midday sun inched higher in the sky, the subtle blues, greens, and tans of the natural landscape drowned out by colorful arrays of blankets and umbrellas.

Calvin watched from a shaded bench in the grassy area along the northern edge of the park as he waited for Kessler to show up, keeping himself as far from the event's police presence as possible. He feigned interest in the ladies splashing in and out of the water, wondering if one of them was Jaime Baker. Now and then he looked nonchalantly over his shoulder to scan the streets behind him.

When he looked next, he saw Kessler pulling his Charger into a freshly vacated spot on the corner of Walnut Street. Calvin got up and walked across the street to meet him. "Took you long enough."

"I didn't think it'd be that hard to find a place in town that sold t-shirts," Kessler said, a slight edge to his tone.

"You don't have a single t-shirt in your closet? Why am I not surprised," Calvin said, glancing at the light gray one Kessler had on now. It had to be a hell of a lot cooler than his usual attire, but he didn't seem particularly comfortable in it.

"Don't act like you know me, because you don't."

Calvin's jaw tensed. What the hell was Kessler's problem? If he didn't want Calvin's help, then all he had to do was say so. Working together was his idea, after all. "I know we haven't even made it to the beach and you're already tense. Which is it, all the noise or the fact that you can't take your gun out on the lake?"

Kessler shot him a look, but didn't answer. He grabbed a plastic shopping bag from the passenger seat of his car, then they walked across the street and into the shade. The picnic tables were all occupied, so Kessler sat down in the grass before he proceeded to unwrap the items he'd bought for the day. Calvin sat next to him, stopping short when he saw the scars.

The marks were pale but extensive, tracing down the entire length of Kessler's right arm like jagged streaks of lightning. They weren't recent based on the color, but they couldn't have been more than a year old. No wonder he always wore long sleeves.

"Car accident," Kessler said, not bothering to look up.

Calvin's cheeks warmed as he pulled his eyes away from the lightning-like marks. He should've known Kessler would see him staring. It'd probably happened to him a hundred times. All of a sudden, Calvin felt like an ass for his earlier comment. "Must've been a pretty damn bad one."

Kessler's voice was distant. "Yeah, it was."

He didn't elaborate further, and despite Calvin's curiosity, he didn't ask him to. It was none of his business, after all, and it had nothing to do with why they were here today.

Calvin nodded toward the beach. "Aren't you worried that Andrew will recognize you once we get out there?"

"No. He came at me from behind and it was too dark to see much of anything after that," Kessler said as he ripped open one of the boxes. "You should probably be asking yourself the same question, though."

"Nah, he was fighting blind. I had the high beams on."

Kessler shot him a cold glance. "I noticed."

Once the second box was open, Kessler gave him a small air pump and a transparent wad of purple plastic. Calvin unraveled the purple wad, revealing a rainbow spiral horn set between two oversized eyes. "A unicorn? What's the matter, they ran out of inflatable donuts?"

Kessler kept his tone even and his attention on what he was doing. "If I had to explain myself to you—which I don't—I'd probably say something along the lines of 'these were the only two pool floats I could find and I had to drive to three different stores to get them'."

Calvin tossed it onto the grass. "I'm not going out in public on Rainbow Dash."

"Suit yourself," Kessler said. He handed him the other chaotic mess of plastic before retrieving the purple one for himself.

Calvin had to unravel it all the way before he could tell what it was. "Absolutely not."

"What is it this time? The shape or the glitter?"

He lifted the floppy heart-shaped ring for Kessler to see. "It says 'Bride' on it."

"You're lucky it's not pink. Just put that side down."

"It's transparent."

Kessler sighed and rubbed his eyes. "Look, you're not an unattractive guy. The long hair, your build, the accent…trust me, they're not going to be looking at the float."

"I'm flattered."

"You wanted to trade," Kessler said, his tone inoffensive yet firm. "Live with your choices."

"Give me the damn unicorn."

"No."

"Give it to me…"

Kessler gestured in the direction of a squad car, barely visible thanks to the bouncy castles and food stands. "You know you're the one with the warrant, right?"

Calvin pointed a finger at him. "Next time you get in trouble, I'm just gonna let 'em shoot your ass."

Kessler unfolded the large equine's wings. "You say that like I'd actually need your help."

*   *   *

They socialized their way across the sand, working from one end of the beach to the other. Kessler put on a far better facade than Calvin had expected him to, coming across as someone who wanted to be here. If it wasn't for how he kept scanning the area for threats when no one was looking, Calvin might've thought he was having a good time.

Calvin was equally capable of pretending to enjoy himself, a skill he'd honed thanks to all the events his socialite family had forced him to attend. He'd put an end to that once he turned sixteen and figured out what a spine was, making this the first time in a long time that he'd found himself stuck somewhere he didn't want to be.

Actually, make it the second. The Fairbault Prison would be offended if it didn't make the list. But to be fair, he'd never had to float around on a giant heart-shaped bachelorette ring when he was locked up. Not that half of the floats out here were any more dignifying. The lily pads fit in with the landscape decently enough, but some of these really had Calvin shaking his head.

An inflatable pineapple bumped into him, and Calvin shoved it back to the two guys who seemed to be fighting over it. Going to an event like this with Ellie was one thing, but being paired up with a tense cop was certainly another. "This is ridiculous."

"Nothing's ridiculous if it works," Kessler said.

"Oh, like those letters you send out to fugitives telling them they won a flat screen or something? No one falls for that."

"You'd be surprised."

"Seriously, though. We've been here for at least an hour. Your guy isn't here, and no one knows a chick named Jaime. You sure you heard right?"

Kessler glared at him. "I'm positive."

"Alright," Calvin said, lifting a hand to shield his eyes from the sun's glare as he looked across the water. "Short of going out on a boat, those five are the only ones we haven't talked to yet."

Kessler followed his gaze to the group of young women in jewel-toned bikinis, each lounging on a color-coordinated slice of fruit. "Your turn," he said.

Calvin rubbed the back of his neck. The group's high-pitched, giggly voices were grating on his nerves even from this distance.

They looked to be roughly eighteen or so, too caught up in their gossip and drinks to notice when he and Kessler paddled toward them. The cooler sleeves didn't fully mask their grocery-store beers, but whatever. At least they'd had the decency to bring cans instead of glass bottles.

"Hey," Calvin said, flashing them a charming smile he hoped came across as genuine. "I was supposed to meet someone here, but lost my phone. Are any of you Jaime, by chance?"

Five sun-kissed hands hit the sky.

Behind him Kessler stifled a laugh, and Calvin had to avoid the temptation to turn his inflatable ring around and wipe that *I told you so* expression off Kessler's face. They hadn't gotten lucky so far, and Calvin didn't expect them to now, but he asked the five Jaimes for their last names anyway.

None of them said Baker.

Well, so much for that. Maybe he should double-check how sure Kessler was that—

"Mind if I ask how old you ladies are?" Kessler asked.

The girls laughed before the blonde in red waved a dismissive hand in his direction. "Not in your age bracket, dad."

Kessler reached into his pocket, seemingly unfazed by her insult. "That's not quite what I meant, so let me phrase it a little better." He held up his badge for them to see. "Since you're all clearly of legal drinking age, you wouldn't mind showing me your IDs, would you?"

God, the nonchalant way he said it combined with the sheer look of horror it brought to their faces. It took all Calvin had not to laugh.

Aquamarine spoke for the group this time. "We, um…left them in the car. We'll go get them. Right, girls?"

The rest of the rainbow nodded in agreement.

"Good," Kessler said. "You ladies go ahead and do that."

As they paddled out of earshot, Calvin elbowed the unicorn. "You're off-duty. Can we focus on the task at hand?"

"It only cost us a minute. And besides, they won't be back."

"And on another note, are you sure Jaime's a woman?" Calvin asked. "It's a unisex name, after all."

"So we had it narrowed down to half of the population and now we don't even have that?"

Calvin shrugged. "If you're not sure, it's an angle we should probably consider."

Kessler looked out across the water as he took in the people around them with additional scrutiny. His gaze hovered in place for a few seconds. "You know what, never mind. I found her."

Calvin shielded his eyes from the sun as he followed Kessler's gaze. There were at least half a dozen people splashing around in that direction. "Which one?"

Kessler gestured to the small yacht behind the group. "The one with the words *Jaime Baker* plastered on her ass."

14

IT TOOK ALMOST an hour for the *Jaime Baker* to pull into the marina, but only a few minutes more for everyone on board to vacate it. Calvin used that time to go back to his place and get his lock pick set, not that he'd told Kessler that's what he was doing. They'd likely need it if they wanted to do any kind of meaningful search, but on the off chance that the boat's owner was a complete idiot and left everything unlocked, he could spare himself the judgment.

Kessler was waiting for him by the entrance ramp of the 300 dock when he got back. The southern part of the marina housed sailboats, but this section was almost exclusively yachts, and with everyone busy socializing on the lake itself, it was quieter than Calvin had expected. The retired couple on the white and navy Sundancer near the middle of the walkway were busy packing up while their multicolored herd of Goldendoodles meandered back and forth between the boat and the pier. Besides them, there were no other tenants.

The dogs took a friendly interest as he and Kessler squeezed past them to get to the *Jaime Baker*'s slip at the end of the dock. Calvin took up the rear and gave the vessel a quick once-over as they approached, its pristine white hull adorned with chrome hardware, black accent lines, and a matching Bimini top. It was similar in size and appearance to his dad's Sea Ray, but despite its obvious value, they'd done a shitty job tying it up, leaving the crossed rope stern lines lying slack on the boat's swim platform. Calvin's father would've thrown a fit if he'd ever left any of their dock lines that loose.

"Should we get the registration number?" Calvin asked as he glanced at the decals on the hull.

"What for?"

"Can't you run it and find out who the owner is?"

"Right, because I pull over boats all the time."

Despite the sarcasm in Kessler's voice, his face was nothing but serious. He'd stopped on the finger pier to glance over his shoulder toward the four-o-clock position, the direction of the clubhouse's windows.

"Now'd be a good time to walk away if you're having second thoughts," Calvin said.

Kessler took one more look around before stepping onto the yacht's swim platform. "No. We've gone this far."

Calvin stepped onto the platform next to him. "Have you given any thought to how far you're willing to take this?"

His expression darkened. "As far as I have to."

Calvin followed him through the small stainless-steel gate that closed off the passageway between the boat's stern and cockpit. The white leather seating contrasted sharply with the glossy black finish of the dashboard, its controls lined with gray accents and chrome edging.

It didn't take Kessler long to spot the glove box tucked on the lower left of the helm beneath the radio. He tried the handle, but it didn't budge. "I hope you brought a screwdriver back with you."

"Somethin' like that," Calvin replied. He reached into his back pocket and pulled out a small black leather case, the gold SouthOrd logo on the front shining as he snapped it open. After selecting a stainless-steel tension wrench and a single hook pick, he put the case back in his pocket and swiftly began working the lock.

Kessler watched him intently. "Let me guess. Another hobby of yours?"

"Yeah, actually," he said, feeling for the click of the pins as he lifted them one by one over the shear line. "There are people out there who pick locks for fun."

"Of course. They're called thieves."

Calvin cast him a sideways glare. "Regular folks, too. And for a while, locksmith was high on my list of potential careers."

It hadn't been his top contender, but he'd had to axe it after his conviction anyway. That and every other profession that required passing a background check. Not that he owed Kessler an explanation, but it'd be nice if he could cut the judgmental crap once in a while.

The cylinder gave as the last pin fell into place. Calvin rotated the lock all the way and then pulled out his tools, slipping them back into the case with the others. "There. Have at it."

Kessler didn't spare any thanks before he opened the glove

box and started to rifle through its contents. The papers on top didn't catch his interest, but the black pocket notebook near the bottom of the compartment did. He pulled it out and began to flip through its pages.

Calvin couldn't tell what was in it from where he sat, but it obviously had Kessler's attention. "What'd you find?"

Kessler tilted his head as he studied one of the pages. "Looks like a dossier of some sort. All kinds of handwritten notes—"

Footsteps approached on the walkway and Kessler instantly quieted, his gaze dropping as he shifted his attention to the sound. "Don't turn around," he whispered. "It'll look suspicious if you do."

The footsteps came closer, now at their eight o'clock position from the sounds of it. Calvin kept his voice low. "What if that's one of Andrew's buddies?"

"Then he'll say something. Don't give yourself away until you know you've been made."

The footsteps slowed. From the corner of his eye Calvin saw a man stop on the walkway to pull out his phone before boarding the speedboat one slip over from them. "Looks like we're in the clear," he whispered.

Kessler turned his head enough to glance over Calvin's shoulder. Despite his seemingly calm exterior the false alarm must've spooked him, as he quit skimming the book in favor of taking out his phone to photograph some of its pages.

While he was busy, Calvin sifted through some of the other paperwork for the sake of occupying himself. Charts, manuals, a pile of weekly cleaning receipts, and…no, it couldn't be. Did he seriously just get that lucky?

The ring. Big, gaudy. Vintage but not valuable.

Not to most people.

Calvin pretended to flip through a few receipts, making sure Kessler was still preoccupied before he discreetly palmed it. While feigning an itch he slipped it into the side pocket of his shorts. He stole another careful look over to see if Kessler had noticed his sleight of hand.

Nope, still busy.

The ring felt heavy in Calvin's pocket. With all the time that had passed he didn't know if he'd even be able to track it down, but now—

Kessler jumped as the phone in his hand rang. A split-second look of embarrassment crossed his face before he switched the ringer off and looked at the caller ID. Calvin glanced at it as well. Based on the area code, it looked to be a Minneapolis number.

"Freaking FBI," Kessler muttered as he quickly declined the call. "Kind of busy right now…"

"Seriously? You just hung up on the FBI?"

"It's my brother calling from work. I'm sure he'll live."

"Prestigious. You didn't mention he was older."

"That's because he's four years younger," Kessler said. He put the phone in his pocket and the book back in the glove box. "Anyway, let's get out of here before someone sees us."

"What about the cabin?"

"Too risky. If anyone shows up, we'd be cornered."

Calvin didn't argue. He took the lead as they made their way to the back of the yacht, stopping briefly to see who was or wasn't around. The couple with the Goldendoodles had left, and Cell Phone Guy was still busy talking it up.

Good. No new faces.

The wake from a passing yacht caused the *Jaime Baker* to

lurch against the ropes as Calvin was stepping off the swim platform. He quickly adjusted his footing to bridge the gap, when Kessler slammed into him and they crashed onto the weathered gray surface of the pier. Calvin pulled himself out from under him and turned around. "Dammit, Kessler! Can't you watch what the hell you're doing?"

Kessler muttered quiet obscenities to himself as he untangled the stern line from his ankle and pulled himself up. This time he double-checked his footing before he stepped onto the pier, but Calvin moved back to give him extra space anyway. The guy on the speedboat had lowered his phone to see what the commotion was about, so Kessler gave him a reassuring wave to let him know he was alright. As he went back to his phone call, Kessler threw Calvin another glare, his signature look today. "Keep it down, will you?"

"Then try not to land on me next time," he retorted. Even so, his testiness was only for show. He'd gotten Rodney's ring back, and he'd been able to do it without Kessler noticing.

It was turning out to be a good day, after all.

15

BEN HAD NO IDEA what Haggerty could possibly want with that monstrosity of a ring. There was no way it was his size, and it most certainly wasn't his style. The only piece of jewelry Ben had ever seen on him was that silver pendant he always wore, and it was by no means gaudy.

The thing he'd swiped on the boat looked like some hideous family heirloom, something worthless in a monetary sense but kept around purely for the sake of posterity. But whatever his motivation, if Haggerty wanted to give himself the five-finger discount at Dixon's expense, then Ben was more than willing to turn a blind eye.

They took a detour to pick up Greta, then stopped at Hok-Si-La Park and took up residence at one of the picnic tables near the shore. The surrounding campground and abundance of trees gave Hok-Si-La a more secluded feel than Roschen had. Fitting, since they were about to go over their illicitly gained intelligence with a fine-toothed comb.

Haggerty had initially suggested they grab a bite to eat at Heidi's café, since it was only a one-block walk from the beach, but Ben had quickly shot that idea down. It was well past lunch, and even though he would've killed for a sandwich and a cup of soup right now, Ben had no intention of being seen around town with a convicted felon.

On the bright side, stopping at Haggerty's place meant Ben now had a way to charge his dead phone. Even if the external battery pack barely had a charge itself, it was better than nothing. Since he was still waiting for the phone to turn on, he watched Haggerty practice another round of obedience with Greta. He was using hand signs instead of verbal commands this time. Haggerty's back was to him, and since Greta was looking his way, Ben decided to have some fun. He put his arm out, then brought it to the opposite shoulder to cue "come".

Greta bumped into Haggerty's leg when she took off in Ben's direction. As soon as she was in front of him, he put a hand up and she sat.

"I thought you never had a dog," Haggerty said as he walked up to the picnic table.

Ben swept his hand down, and Greta plopped on the grass. "I didn't, but my father-in-law trained police and hunting dogs up in the Cities. I watched him work quite a bit over the years."

A soft buzz brought Ben's attention to the table. His phone's screen was lighting up.

"About time," Haggerty said, flinging a tennis ball across the grass. As Greta took chase he sat at the picnic table.

Ben tried to decipher the first row of words. He'd assumed

he'd have an easier time reading it now than he did on the boat, since he didn't have to be preoccupied with his surroundings, but he'd assumed incorrectly. Were those letters or numerals? When squinting didn't work, he tried zooming in and out to no avail.

God this guy's handwriting sucked.

"Well?" Haggerty pressed. "What's it say?"

Ben adjusted his viewing distance to see if that would help. "I'm still working on it."

"Gimme that," he said as he snatched the phone from Ben's hand. He extended a different item in its place. "Here."

Ben grabbed the ball without thinking. It was wet. He shot Haggerty an incredulous look. "Really?"

He reflected the exact same expression right back at him. "It's not gonna throw itself."

Greta flinched at the ball's every move as they conversed, her eyes glued to the soppy sphere of joy. Ben hurled it as far as he could before shaking the drool off his hand as she barreled off into the distance.

Haggerty looked at one of the images. "Seriously? You can't read this?"

"What's there to read? It's chicken scratch."

"It's a list of dates and places they're gonna hit. Or have hit, anyway. Some of these are addresses, the type of vehicle, times they're parked or when they're left warming up...I mean this alone is more than enough to give you grounds to arrest him."

"No, evidence obtained without a warrant is inadmissible in court. If I try to bring him in on this alone, he'll walk."

Haggerty swiped through a few other photos. "Most of these are dated from May, June, and July. Can't you match them up to any unsolved thefts and use that as probable cause?"

"Again, same problem. We can pin him to all of these, but we need to catch him in the act first. Then we can get a warrant to search his property."

"That might be fine and dandy for you, but how's that gonna help me clear my name? Hansen's isn't on here, and neither is the public works, so I'd say Andrew keeps his extracurricular activities to himself."

"Then what the hell was he doing back there? Trying to steal that plain-Jane pickup?"

"I'd say loading up those spools of copper grounding wire," Haggerty said. "The big ones are worth at least a couple hundred each, and you can fit quite a few of 'em into a trunk or backseat."

"Is that his usual MO? Taking whatever random crap he can find laying around?"

"From what I heard in prison that's how he got his start, but for the last year and a half or so he's been taking on jobs for some bigwig he met up in the Twin Cities. That's who got him into boosting cars on a more professional level."

"A more professional level?"

"Yeah. Before that he'd taken two or three total, and only because the owners had left the keys in 'em. Lately he's been trying to up his game."

Ben thought about that. It'd be nice to take down Dixon's boss as well, but if he wanted to increase his chances of success he'd have to resist the temptation to bite off more than he could chew. Even so, getting Haggerty's warrant taken care of was still on Ben's to-do list. He owed him that much. "If I can get Dixon in an interview room, I can make something work. Tell him I have evidence proving he was at Hansen's, but if he admits to it, I'll cut him a deal."

"But you can't cut him a deal. That's up to the prosecutor."

"You'd be surprised how many people don't know that." Ben leaned over to look at the screen. "Can you see if any of those say what the next place he plans on targeting is?"

Haggerty scrolled through a couple more. "That'd be...this coming Tuesday, but there's no vehicle or location listed. It just says 'jewel'."

"The Jewel, it's a golf club on the west end of town," Ben said, remembering it from the map. It wasn't hard to miss since it took up a fairly large chunk of it. "That's perfect."

"How so? Unless you plan on going golfing, there isn't a lot of cover for someone like you in a place like that."

"What I mean is, it's perfect for someone who steals cars," Ben said. "Most of the vehicles are high-end and they're parked there for hours, which means he'd have plenty of time to decide what he wants, take it, and get it out of the area before anyone even notices it's missing."

"That wouldn't be like him. He always does his thieving out of the city limits."

"Two nights ago he didn't, and you said he's been trying to up his game. I bet if we checked we'll see there's an event on Tuesday, which means plenty of possible targets who aren't from the area."

"Alright," Haggerty said, stroking his chin. "Assuming there is something going on...what's your plan?"

"I'm on duty that day. We get a bait car, you park it there and I'll watch the area. If he takes it, I'll light him up and he'll run because that's what he does."

Haggerty looked at him with veiled suspicion. "How would you know?"

Damn it. He really needed to be more mindful of his word choices. "I mean he'll likely run. Most do if they're in a stolen vehicle."

Haggerty hesitated before moving on. "Why get a bait car? Can't you pull him over if he takes any of them?"

"I can and I will, but having something with a tracker on it if possible is always better."

"Well, according to this his usual targets are luxury SUVs, so we'll need something nice. Infiniti, Volvo, Land Rover—"

"I'll get us a car," Ben said.

"I doubt you're gonna have anything he's looking for in the impound lot. Rochester's probably the closest place to get a rental unless we wanna drive all the way up to—"

"This isn't my first rodeo. Like I said, I'll take care of it." Ben took his phone back from Haggerty and got up. He knew what they needed.

And they weren't going to find it at Hertz.

16

CALVIN WAITED for Kessler's tail lights to disappear before he pulled his phone out of his pocket. Greta whimpered from the passenger seat, eager to go home and get fed. He reached over and rubbed her ears. "Settle down. We'll leave in a minute."

She sighed and laid her head on his lap. He patted her on the shoulder before dialing and putting the phone to his ear.

"Hello?"

"Hey, Rodney. How's it going?"

"Cal, hey! Life's good. Owen starts kindergarten this fall, and we're getting ready for the baby shower next month."

"Damn. He's starting school already?"

Rodney laughed. "Yeah, they grow up fast. We still can't agree on a girl name, though. You'll come to the shower, right?"

"I wouldn't miss it," Calvin said. "But I've got some other good news for you."

"What?"

"I got the ring back."

The line was quiet for so long, Calvin started to wonder if the call had dropped.

"Are you serious?" Rodney asked.

He smiled. "Yeah. I'm holding it in my hand right now."

"Oh my God…how did you find it?"

Greta rolled on her back and pawed the air, so Calvin rubbed her belly. "I had a little help from a cop in town. We ended up on Andrew's boat, and I found it in the glove box."

"Andrew?"

"Sorry, Rude Dog. Andrew's his real name."

"You didn't, uh…tell that cop what I did, right?"

"No, he has no idea. He's looking into Andrew for other reasons, and I've been helping him."

"That's great," Rodney said. "You should drive up and join us at the campground tomorrow. We'll be staying the week, and you can bring your dog along, too. My treat."

He rubbed Greta's ears again. "As much as I'd love to, I'll have to pass. We're right in the middle of trying to catch this guy."

"Leave it to your cop friend. That's his job."

"No, I don't want to ditch him like that," Calvin said. "And besides, you know this kind of thing's right up my alley. Sneaking around, making a difference…I miss that."

Rodney sighed. "Okay, just…be careful, you hear? Don't get yourself in trouble playing cops and robbers."

He smiled. "See you next month, Rodney."

"See you then, Cal."

Calvin hung up, and flipped the ring between his fingers. He'd waited five years for this moment. Gathering intel behind bars, putting that intel into action once he was out. Tackling a problem Rodney didn't have the confidence to tackle himself. It had occupied Calvin's time. He liked fixing cars, but it didn't give him a rush like tracking down the ring had. Didn't give him the same level of fulfillment. But as of today, the hunt was over. It felt so…sudden.

It felt like he didn't have anything meaningful to do now.

He slipped the ring back in his pocket. His personal business with Andrew might be finished, but Kessler's wasn't. Rodney had a point about there being risks involved, but risk only added to Calvin's level of satisfaction when he was doing something for someone else. Something they couldn't do for themselves. It gave him back that sense of purpose he'd lost when his military career was cut short. He started his truck and shifted into drive.

He'd keep offering his help. Kessler needed it, and in the end Calvin didn't have anything to lose.

17

BEN TUNED to the local '80s station and listened to some of his favorites as the vehicle glided effortlessly down the rain-slicked highway. Don Henley, U2, and—ironically—the Police. The drive back from the Cities wasn't his favorite, but he had to admit his ride was damn nice.

It was a luxuriously imposing Range Rover, gunmetal gray with black accents and a mirror-like finish. Not only was it the current year's model, but it also sported the premium package, which should make it more than enough to catch Dixon's eye. The large SUV was also about four times more expensive than Ben's car, something Miles had made a point of rubbing in when he'd taken delivery of it last month.

As the miles passed, Ben couldn't help but appreciate how perfect the timing was. His brother always took a company car when he traveled out of town for work, and he'd be gone for another two or three days at least. On top of that, whenever he arrested a high-profile target, he always called within the hour to gloat about it. That combined with processing time and writing up a hefty report meant Ben would have a solid day to day-and-a-half heads-up before Miles got back. Which was good, because Ben had to leave him completely in the dark for this to work.

Other than booking a rideshare to Minneapolis, getting the vehicle had been easy. His brother kept a spare key for his front door in a fake rock under the hydrangeas and a quick *sorry, just me* got the security system company to turn off the alarm. The property was secluded and didn't have any security cameras, so Ben wouldn't have to worry about being caught on tape. There'd be nothing to prove that Dixon didn't steal the vehicle right out of Miles's garage.

From there the plan was simple yet elegant. Get the Range Rover to Lake City and park it at the Jewel during Tuesday's event. Once Dixon was behind the wheel, Ben would follow him and call Miles to ask why he was in town, to which his brother would respond that he wasn't. That'd give him probable cause to pull over the vehicle and arrest the perpetrator. Simple, and other than Dixon deciding to steal a different car, there wasn't a lot that could go wrong.

As much as he hated doing it this way, it was the only viable option. If he used a car he rented solely for the purpose of bait, there was a chance the case would get thrown out for entrapment when Ben's involvement came to light, which it most certainly would. Dixon had already gotten off once due to a technicality, and Ben wasn't about to risk it happening again.

Still, as he ran his thumb along the sleek black steering wheel of a vehicle that was technically stolen, he found himself questioning whether or not the end justified the means. Would his former self have even considered doing something like this?

His former self. That was an interesting concept. At least he'd known the ins and outs of that person. His motivations, his goals, and his limits. Not only the specifics, but the fact that he actually *had* limits. Had lines he wouldn't cross. His current self was much more of a wild card, and what little he did know he didn't like. He'd adjusted too seamlessly to working the wrong side of the law, and while he knew that should bother him, it didn't. And *that* bothered him. When was the last time he'd done some actual good in the world? Made a difference in someone's life? Saved someone? It hadn't been this year. If anything, he'd done nothing but the opposite.

Maybe he was the problem.

Ben set his signal and exited the highway, knowing he needed a distraction and knowing just the place for it. The traffic, high-rises, and tangle of streets he used to frequent had reminded him of so many milestones from his past. Training the new recruits. Getting promoted. His best friend's wedding.

His own.

Now all Minneapolis had for him was bad memories. Funny how things change.

The farther the urban sprawl faded into the distance, the more his mindset improved. Endless farm fields bordered either side as he took familiar turns, moving between alternating paved and gravel roads before taking a right at the four-way stop past the brown *Whitetail Woods Regional Park* sign. The landscape became more forested as he continued to the end of Station Trail, stopping at the entrance of the Dakota County Gun Club.

Rain dotted his sleeve as Ben swiped his membership card at

the gate. It was a good day for shooting, by his standards. The inclement weather meant there'd be less people around, and more than likely he'd have the entire place to himself.

Ben followed the gravel drive slowly, not wanting to kick up rocks and damage the SUV's pristine finish. After parking near the pistol range, he pressed the start/stop button before throwing the keys in the center console and closing the lid. Aside from not seeing the need to lock it way out here, Ben also didn't feel like hauling around the five pounds of random clunk Miles kept on a single keychain. An actual thief wouldn't have taken the time to separate the vehicle's keys from the others, so he didn't, either.

He got out, then opened the rear door to grab his range bag from behind the driver's seat. He rarely got pulled over, but since he was wearing a black hoodie and driving a stolen car, it seemed like a wise precaution to keep it out of sight. He grabbed his phone and shut it off before sliding it into the side pocket of the bag. He wanted complete solitude while he was here.

While the last remaining patrons scurried back to their cars, Ben walked as if the rain didn't exist.

Once under the protection of the canopy, he shucked his bag and set it on the table. After unzipping it and taking out the gun case, he reached in to grab one of the black and gold fifty-round boxes of ammo. He only had two left, which meant he'd need to buy more soon. When he reached in for the other, he accidentally pulled out the brand-new box of 9mm blanks his father-in-law had given him when he'd retired.

Ben held the blue package in his hand for a moment, not even sure why he'd kept them. They didn't fire with enough force to cycle his gun's slide all the way back, which made them good for pretty much nothing except practice clearing a malfunction.

It was something he should probably work on again, but he put them back anyway. Today he just wanted to shoot.

Last time he'd practiced with the Glock 19 he carried under his jacket, so today he'd brought along his larger Glock 17. The 17's higher capacity meant less time reloading and more time shooting, something Ben appreciated when his thoughts were bothering him more than usual. The rain started to come down in sheets as he loaded his magazines.

Bullets whizzed through the downpour as he fired, each one's path to the center of the target highlighted by a trail of steam. Before long the sound of his gun was echoed by the rumble of approaching thunder, bringing a slight smile to his face. The rain may bring him inner peace, but storms energized him.

With the range empty, he palmed in his next magazine before switching to rapid fire.

18

BEN TURNED RIGHT a block up from the Sunset Motel to pull into the parking lot of the AmericInn. Maybe he was being overly paranoid, but Lake City wasn't a big town, and he didn't want the Range Rover to be seen near his car. The location was convenient, and the ever-changing array of vehicles at a hotel meant it would blend in. He drove past the building and to the small lot alongside it, the one facing Lincoln Street, then parked and pressed the start/stop button.

He ran his hand along the steering wheel, wondering how smooth it would feel if he didn't have gloves on. The door handle, the seat belt, the controls, the wheel. He hadn't touched a single thing with his bare hands. Leaving fingerprints was another risk he wasn't going to take, but the longer he looked at his gloves the more they seemed to transform from a precaution to an admission of guilt. They separated him from the acts he was committing by nothing more than the thickness of their fabric. Nothing more than a few rows of black thread.

A wolf in sheep's clothing.

No, he couldn't slip back into that line of thinking. He'd just managed to get out of it. He got out and slammed the door, yanking his gloves off as he shifted his gaze to the darkening clouds of the northwest. The smell of rain was heavy in the air, and he took in a few calming breaths of it. The forecast had said the storm would miss Lake City, but he hoped their prediction would be wrong. Rain meant a better night's sleep, something he could use before the future successes he needed to believe in.

He could do this.

As he walked the rest of the way back to the Sunset Motel, he put his hands in his pockets to combat the gusts that had started to move in. He ran through his mental list of things to do tomorrow, for the first time in a while looking forward to what the next few days would bring.

Since he was coming from that direction anyway, he decided to stop at the motel's office to grab his mail. If there was any, that is. Most of his bills came via an email reminder, but once in and while he did get something tangible. Never anything important enough to warrant checking more than once a week, though.

The wind lost its edge as he walked alongside the building, its second-story wrap-around deck shielding him from the light raindrops that were starting to make their appearance. The white trim on the windows complimented the structure's dark gray paint nicely, a fitting color scheme with the approaching storm in the background. The rainbow-striped beach chairs on the patio gave a contrasting splash of color, as did the planters standing guard near the glass entry door.

Ben pulled open the door and stepped in. Even he had to admit that the drop in temperature was a refreshing break from the humidity. A gray tabby cat darted out of sight while another lounged across one of the two teal office chairs to the right, stretching out her feet as if reinforcing her monopoly on the spot. Ben let her be as he walked up to the counter to ring the service bell. While he waited for someone to come, he turned around and leaned back against the counter. The lobby was more like a foyer in size, and fit in well with the nautical theme that seemed to dominate the town. Large windows looked out across Lakeshore Drive and the river it flanked.

Footsteps sounded, and Ben turned back to the counter. The woman walking up to the far side of it greeted him with a smile as usual, her sandy blonde hair and navy-and-white striped shirt a subtle compliment to the nautical theme. He gave her a kind wave. "Hi, Kris."

"Hey, Ben. Good to see you," she said. "Sorry Happy took off on you again. He takes a while to warm up to strangers."

"That's alright. At least Neko doesn't mind me," he said as he looked back at the chairs. The cat hadn't moved, but her green eyes were now boring into him from across the room like laser beams, prompting him to revise his statement. "I think."

"She does, don't worry. If you scratch her forehead, she'll be your friend for life."

"I'll have to take your word for it. I'm allergic to cats and dogs, unfortunately."

"Oh, I had no idea," she said. "We'll have to make a point of vacuuming the lobby even more often while you're here."

"No need, it's a mild allergy. As long as I don't pet her and then rub my eyes, I'll be fine."

"That's good, then," Kris said, straightening out the business card holder on the counter. "Have you been enjoying your stay so far?"

"I have, thanks. Just came to see if I had any mail."

"Nothing yet. We did have a gentleman call and ask if there was a Mr. Kessler registered here, though."

Ben sighed. Really? Maybe he should tell Miles to practice what he preached and get a hobby for himself. "Did he leave a message?"

"No, and he wouldn't give me his name either. He was very polite, though."

"Yeah, that'd be my brother."

"Oh. You didn't tell him where you were staying?"

"I don't need to, as you can see."

"I'm sorry. Should I not have told him that you had a room here?"

Ben forced a smile. "No, that's alright. He must've forgotten. Miles is harmless, but he tends to have his fingers in too many pies for my liking. If you hear from him again, remind him that he has my number."

"I'll do that. And if there's anything else we can do to make your stay more comfortable, be sure to let us know."

"Thanks. And say hi to Doug for me."

Kris smiled. "Will do."

19

THE MORNING SUN was soft as it filtered through the trees, dappling the landscape with gentle shadows.

Ben set his signal and took a right onto Lakeshore Drive, his mind elsewhere after seeing the U-Haul parked next to his car when he'd walked out of his room a minute ago. Each and every one of those trucks seemed to have a different graphic on it, but his mood took a somber turn when he laid eyes on that one.

Bats. She'd done her thesis on those.

He tried to keep his thoughts on the task at hand. The view of the lake disappeared after he passed the veterans' memorial, replaced by rows of houses and vacation rentals. It was only a three-mile drive to the Jewel, which he wanted to scope out in person before tomorrow's event. Some corporate fundraiser according to the website.

As he continued into the more business-oriented stretch of Lakeshore, he couldn't help but notice the unmarked Explorer running traffic from the Gillford Mutual lot. It was easy to spot from his direction, but the small corner building would make the vehicle invisible to northbound traffic. Ben hadn't considered that location before, but it looked lucrative. He'd have to try it on his next weekend shift.

At the end of the block, he set his signal and pulled into the turn lane, stopping at the red light as he waited to make a right onto Lyon Avenue. The squad exited the parking lot and pulled up behind him. Ben glanced in the mirror, surprised the officer had a front passenger who was on the phone but seemed to be in uniform. The department hadn't mentioned anyone was going to be on training, but they didn't usually double up their officers. Hell, on some day shifts they didn't have more than one on duty.

The light went green and Ben turned, the squad and line of the cars behind them following suit. Only three blocks passed before movement brought his attention to his driver's side mirror. Another squad, a marked one this time, took a quick left from one of the side streets to position itself behind the first. Ben's gaze hovered in the mirror longer than it normally would.

Something was going on. Shift change was only an hour ago, and most departments liked to keep their officers spread out a bit more. No lights, though, so it must not be emergent. Were they looking for someone? Could be, but if that was the case then they should be using the radio and not a phone. He'd have to ask about this one when he went in for his shift tomorrow. Which reminded him, he still needed to stop by Haggerty's place and drop off the keys for the—

Damn it, the keys. He'd left them in it. Thinking back, he

couldn't remember if he'd locked the Range Rover either, which was fucking fantastic since he'd left his backpack with his phone and other gun in it, too. He *never* forgot his gun.

Don't panic, Ben told himself. It'd be fine. He'd take Tenth Street to circle back, and in five minutes he'd be pulling into the AmericInn and would see that the Range Rover was untouched. This was Lake City, after all. The level of crime here certainly didn't compare to that of Minneapolis.

Regardless, he needed to get his shit together. There'd been so much going on in his head the past year that his usually cohesive thought processes had felt more like shattered glass, and he'd been making mistakes because of it. Look what it'd got him behind the public works. It was just dumb luck that he'd been able to cover for that.

He kept an eye on the street signs as he drove.

Another Kwik Trip came up on his right, and he started to wonder what became of the kitten-clad sandwich bandit he'd caught at the other location on his first day in town. He'd have to look that up. No matter how many of her type he ran across, he still never understood how so many people couldn't grasp the basic concept of right and wrong. Granted, it was nothing more than a three-dollar item, but still. It was the principle of it.

Ben didn't notice the sign until he was almost on top of it. He slammed on the brakes and flipped his turn signal on before making a hard right onto Tenth. The tires chirped in protest as his car swayed through the corner. He straightened the wheel, chastising himself for almost missing the turn. But the last street he'd passed was Eighth, so what the hell happened to Ninth?

The squads behind him both made a right as well. Of course. The station was on Tenth Street, so it made sense they'd be heading that way. Hopefully none of them recognized his car or he'd never hear the end of it. Crappy driving at its best.

Past the back exit of Kwik Trip, a large barn-style boutique stretched alongside the road, its khaki-brown facade bringing a slight frown to Ben's face. His parents' house had been exactly the same color. He always took Tenth Street from the other side on his way to work and made a mental note not to come up from the south again.

A siren pierced the air as red and blue flashed in his mirrors. So much for not being recognized, but as embarrassing as it was, he would own up to his mistake. The law required signaling for a distance of no less than one-hundred feet and he'd done so for a third of that, at best. He wondered which of his co-workers would be doing the honors.

There wasn't much of a shoulder, but at least the lane was wide. Ben set his signal to the right and pulled his car as far to the side as the street allowed for. After coming to a complete stop he glanced in the rearview mirror, the creases on his forehead deepening at what he saw.

The squads were too far back. The first one had moved to the right to give the second enough room to pull up alongside it and both had their lights on. Ben knew the procedure. They weren't pulling him over for his turn signal, this was a felony traffic stop. He cursed himself.

The Range Rover. They'd figured it out.

Ben's thoughts raced as quickly as the squads' lights flashed. This didn't make sense. He'd avoided the traffic cameras. Miles shouldn't have been back this early. Even if Ben had missed his brother's call, it should've taken him at least another day to tie up all of the loose ends the Leighton case entailed. Damn it. To say this put a wrench in things would be the understatement of the year.

Breathe, he told himself. Focus on the present.

Ben shifted into park and pressed his car's start/stop button before rolling the window down. Normally he'd put the keys on the dashboard as well, but this was a high-risk stop. Pockets were off limits.

With his hands on the wheel, he turned his gaze back to the rearview mirror. Standard formation, two squads side by side and four officers with guns drawn taking cover behind the doors.

A voice came over one of the squad's loudspeakers. *"Everyone in the vehicle, slowly raise your hands outside through the windows."*

Ben put his hands out.

"Driver, turn off the vehicle with your left hand and drop the keys on the ground outside."

He'd already shut off the engine, so he slowly reached his left hand over to his right jacket pocket to retrieve the keys. Having his right hand still out the window made it awkward as hell, something he appreciated a lot more when he was on the other end of the command. Once he managed to fish them out, he put his hand back out of the window and dropped them. A jingle sounded as they hit the pavement.

"With your left hand, unbuckle your seat belt."

He knew that one was next so he could've done it when he was getting his keys, but he had no intention of making a single move before he was explicitly told to. At least unbuckling was much easier than trying to get into his pocket. He clicked the release, and put his left hand back out the window.

"With your right hand, open the door from the outside."

Another purposefully awkward move. He reached down and

opened the door, slowly swinging it to the stop before putting his hand back up.

"Keep your hands up and slowly step out of the vehicle, facing away from us."

He stepped out and left the door open, keeping his hands visible and his back toward the officers. Quiet greenery lined both sides of the road, the peaceful view a sharp contrast to the scene playing out right behind him.

"Walk backwards toward the sound of my voice."

He began to walk back, taking each step with exceptional care as he distanced himself from his car. Roads always seemed more spacious on foot, but now the expanse of pavement curving off into the distance and the endless blue sky above it were nothing more than a painful illusion of freedom.

"Stop."

Ben halted. Next they would do a visual for weapons. He considered calling out to tell them his Glock was holstered, but he quickly decided against it. Right now wasn't the time for extracurricular activities.

"With your left hand, lift up your jacket by the collar and slowly turn in a circle."

This was the risky part from everyone's perspective. He lifted his jacket and began to turn, not able to bring himself to look the other officers in the eyes when he faced them. The soft chirping of birds in the evergreens was quickly drowned out by a shout over the loudspeaker.

"I see your gun! Do not reach for it or you'll be shot!"

He took a shaky breath. No wrong moves. Knowing they wouldn't shoot unless he gave them a reason to didn't seem to calm his nerves. He'd never had so many guns trained on him at once. After what seemed like an eternity, he finished his circle and stopped with his back toward the officers, once again taunted by the serenity in front of him.

"Place both hands on top of your head and lace your fingers."

So far so good. He let go of his jacket and laced his fingers.

"Walk backwards toward the sound of my voice."

He took several more steps back, now noticing there hadn't been any oncoming traffic. They must've blocked the road up by the station after the officers here had lit him up. A wise move. In their position Ben would've done the same thing.

"Stop."

The volume was louder now that he was closer. Next they'd have him move over so he was directly between the two squads. Knowing the exact procedure they were using made him feel the tiniest bit better about what was going on, even if he was on the wrong end of it.

"Take a few steps to your right until I tell you to stop."

Ben took three steps over.

"Stop."

He stopped.

"Walk straight back."

Four more steps.

"Stop."

Based on where the speaker's sound was coming from, he was close enough. Now they'd want him on the ground for cuffing. He stood patiently as he waited for the command, struggling to come to terms with the fact that he was about to be arrested.

"Get down on the ground and lay flat on your stomach. Arms out, palms up, cross your ankles."

Ben's right knee was more sensitive, so he went down on the

left first. He put his hands out and slowly lowered himself to the ground. Footsteps approached from behind before a knee on his right shoulder pressed him against the asphalt. He grimaced from the pain, but it seemed out of line to ask the officer to kneel on his good side. A firm hand grabbed his wrist and twisted his arm behind his back with equal vigor.

The only thing more painful was the sound of the handcuffs snapping over his wrists.

20

WHILE HE WAS NO STRANGER to an interview room, this was the first time Ben found himself alone in one.

He liked to think he was a capable officer, but apparently he made a shitty criminal. Rumor had it when someone got caught for a crime, they'd gotten away with it nine times prior, yet here he was, sitting in the hot seat over his first one. Well, not technically his first crime, but his first theft. Even if he was here over no one's actions but his own it was unnerving, just like it'd been when he'd stepped over the threshold of legality in the first place.

Except this time it was worse, because this time he'd gotten caught. And to think Haggerty would've gotten away with his theft, but he'd chosen to do the right thing and turn himself in. Maybe there was some honor among thieves.

There was a soft knock on the door before an officer stepped in, folder in hand. He was older than Ben but a bit more trim, with short gray hair and pale eyes.

"Hello, Ben," he said as he closed the door behind himself. "I'm Officer Banks with the Lake City Police Department."

"Good morning, Officer," Ben greeted. They'd met a handful of times already, and while he'd normally call the man Carl, he went with the more formal title for the sake of the recording.

Carl sat down on the other chair and handed him a sheet of paper, his usual smile absent. "Could you state your first and last name for the record, please?"

"Benjamin Kessler."

"As you know, before I ask you any questions I need to make sure you understand your rights." At Ben's nod he continued, reading his own copy of the document he'd handed him. "You have the right to remain silent. Anything you say can and will be used against you in a court of law. You have the right to an attorney. If you cannot afford an attorney, one will be provided for you. Do you understand the rights I have just read to you?"

Of course, he'd read them aloud hundreds of times. "Yes."

"With these rights in mind, do you want to speak to me?"

Not really, no, but as much as Ben wanted to say that he knew it wasn't an option. Miles wouldn't press charges once he found out it was him, but he wasn't about to make things worse for himself by pleading the Fifth when he could play this as a misunderstanding. He'd certainly get a reprimand either way, but he needed to do what he could to stay on duty here if he wanted to make sure Dixon was caught. "Yes."

"Do you know why you're here?"

"No," Ben said. It was as untruthful as his last statement, but he knew better than to answer that one honestly. Case in point, the driver in Minneapolis who'd admitted to five serious traffic violations when he'd only pulled her over to tell her she'd forgotten to turn on her headlights.

"Okay." Carl flipped through the paperwork in front of him. "Can you tell me where you were last night between one and two A.M.?"

Two in the morning? That was an odd time. "Asleep in my hotel room," Ben said, wondering why Miles hadn't been doing the same. Normally his brother squeezed every last minute out of his hotel stays, not bothering to pack his bags until the required checkout time around eleven.

"You're staying at the Sunset Motel and Resort, correct?"

"Yes."

Carl jotted down Ben's answers as he gave them. "What time did you get to the motel prior to turning in for the night?"

When did he finish running errands? It was dusk. "Around eight," he guessed.

"So after you got back around eight P.M., when's the next time you left the motel?"

"This morning before I was pulled over."

"You didn't drive anywhere else last night?"

"No."

"Is there anyone who could collaborate that story?"

"It's not a story," Ben said, trying not to get frustrated with Carl's wording. He was simply doing his job. "I got back around eight, had dinner, did some reading, and went to bed at eleven. And no, there wasn't anyone with me."

Carl slid over a photograph of Ben's car on Tenth Street, the driver's door open as he'd left it. "This is your vehicle, correct? Minnesota license plate seven eight six, X-V-E?"

Ben tilted his head. They would've run his plates before the traffic stop, so of course they knew it was his.

"Yes it is," he said, knowing that a photo of the Range Rover was going to be next. At least they'd be getting somewhere. Carl wasn't inexperienced, though, so Ben didn't understand why he hadn't led with the vehicle in question to save time.

"Does anyone else have access to the keys? Wife, girlfriend, a roommate maybe?"

Ben tensed. *Wife.* "No, just me."

"You didn't lend the vehicle to anyone?"

"No."

Carl leaned forward, lifting his palms as if looking for an answer Ben had yet to give. "Are you sure?"

Ben hesitated. He didn't like where this was going. The time frame didn't add up, and neither did Carl's questions. Why the hell was he so convinced that someone else had access to his car? He kept pressing the issue, but Ben wasn't sure what else he expected him to say.

"I'm positive. Listen, Carl—Officer Banks, we're both professionals here. I don't have family nearby and I don't have any friends in town. Can you please tell me why I was brought in?"

Carl pursed his lips and pulled some items from his folder. "There was a drive-by shooting last night at around two A.M.," he said as he gave Ben several photos that looked to be stills taken from security camera footage. "The shooter's car was described as a black sedan, the driver a white male with black hair and a dark outfit."

While he and his car technically matched that description, Ben's first thought was that it wasn't specific enough to warrant a felony traffic stop. He couldn't be the only white male driving around Lake City in black four-door, after all. Asking him to come in voluntarily for questioning would've been more than sufficient.

He decided not to point that out and turned his attention to the photos. Night shots of two different vehicles. One was a Charger based on the tail lights, the other a sedan that was dark in color but harder to identify. The first two images didn't show much of the second car, but the Charger was interesting. Black rims like his. Same spoiler, too. Damn, wasn't that a coincidence. No wonder they'd brought him in the way they had.

The last photo was a video still that showed the two cars from behind as they went down Lakeshore side by side. Charger on the right, second vehicle on the left, with the glaring white burst of a muzzle flash visible from the Charger's driver's side window.

Point blank at the other car.

Ben took a slow breath. "Was anyone injured?"

"No, thankfully. But the partial license plate given to us by the intended victim was a match to the vehicle's full plate that we were able to get from security camera footage taken at US Gas minutes prior to the incident."

Carl handed him a photo of the black Charger stopped at US Gas. The way it was situated at the edge of the parking lot alongside Lakeshore Drive made it obvious that the driver was waiting for someone to come by. The car's brake and tail lights were on, its rear license plate pixelated from digital zoom, but legible. Ben read it three times over.

786-XVE.

What the hell—

"Do you know a Thomas Hoffman?" Carl asked.

Thomas? Tommy, perhaps? That had to be the victim, the one driving the dark-colored sedan. Ben was good with names, but that one didn't ring any bells. "No, not that I'm aware of."

"Thomas Joseph Hoffman?"

"Again, not that I know of."

"Would it help if I showed you a photograph of him?"

Ben sighed. "I'm sure it couldn't hurt."

Carl handed him one final image, a still taken from one of the squad's dash cams. As soon as Ben laid eyes on it, he regretted his choice of words.

Under the glow of streetlights, one of Lake City's third-shift officers stood next to Dixon, who was leaning against the driver's door of his black Audi A8.

21

BEN WAS PACING. He'd do at least fifteen years if he was convicted. Actually, scratch that. *When* he was convicted. Short of a taped confession from the actual shooter, he didn't have a snowball's chance in hell of getting out of this mess. They had all the evidence they could've possibly needed to charge him with first-degree attempted murder, and he'd buried himself further by telling them he was the only one who could've been driving his car. Fuck, he knew better. The first rule when talking to the police was don't.

And then there were the photographs of the shooter's car. Night images of vehicles were often hit or miss, but in this case the distinctive full-width outline of the tail lights was a dead giveaway. Clearly those of a Charger.

His Charger.

They were probably searching it right about now, meaning

they'd find the map with his handwritten notes about Dixon's habits. That would really cinch it. At least his phone with the photos from the *Jaime Baker* was still in the Range Rover, assuming they didn't connect the dots and search that, too.

Meanwhile, Dixon had given them a fake name. Well, not technically a fake name, but someone else's, since truly "fake" names wouldn't give the police a valid return. Either way, if he told them that, then the next thing they would ask is how Ben knew him. That wasn't a question he wanted to answer right now, and it most certainly wouldn't help his case, the same way being honest about the entire scenario wouldn't.

Carl had asked for that. Honesty. The disappointment on his face had pained Ben so much he'd almost considered admitting to everything—his prior history with Dixon, their run-in on the outskirts of town, finding the book on the *Jaime Baker*—but all that would've done was make him look more guilty. So instead he said the best thing he could think of, what he should've said in the first place.

I'd like to speak with my lawyer, please.

Ben could feel the sweat forming on his hands. He shouldn't be here. Shouldn't need a lawyer. Dixon was the one who was supposed to end up in prison. He found himself turning on his heels every few seconds. This damn room wasn't big enough.

What would his wife think of him now?

He sat down on one of the chairs, drying his hands on the leg of his pants. The last time he'd been this much of a wreck, he was still living with his father. He needed to calm down.

Maybe there was a self-help book for that. *How to Calm Down When You're Being Framed.* It'd probably be written by a guy named U. R. Fucked.

A knock on the door brought his thoughts back to reality. Transport time, no doubt. Since there was no jail in Lake City, they'd have to take him to the one in Wabasha. Hopefully he wouldn't run into any inmates he knew down there. That'd be his luck, and most certainly wouldn't be a pleasant experience.

An officer with blonde hair and glasses stepped in, younger than Ben but a bit heavier. Out of everyone in the department, he was the one Ben had worked with the most.

Taylor.

His presence alone helped Ben relax. Taylor was quiet but kind, and not the type to talk for the sake of it. Even if it was no more than a twenty-minute drive Ben appreciated not being paired with a chatterbox.

"Alright, Ben," Taylor said. "Do you need to use the restroom or anything before we head out?"

Ben thought about the one phone call thing, something Hollywood had made up. In real life he could make as many as he wanted, within reason, but there was only one person he felt like he needed to contact right now. He wasn't sure how much Dixon knew, but if he'd identified Ben's car and where he was staying, then he may also know he was working with Haggerty. Ex-con or not, the thought of someone else paying the price for Ben's bad choices didn't sit well with him.

"Think I could call a friend of mine? Make sure my dog gets a bathroom break here and there?" Ben asked. Taylor was a dog-lover, so that seemed like a good cover story.

"No problem," Taylor said, smiling at the mention of a furry friend. He gestured to the door in his usual professional manner before escorting Ben down the hall and to the suspect processing room. Once there, Taylor stationed himself near the door as Ben flipped through the yellow pages to find the section for car repair shops. With Haggerty recently released he probably still had friends in prison, so Ben hoped he'd answer a collect call.

Halfway through the fifth ring, a gruff southern voice answered. "Haase Truck an' Equipment."

"Hey. Listen," Ben said, aiming for subtlety since he knew the call was being recorded. "I was arrested in Lake City, so I was wondering if you could take care of my dog for a while."

Ben winced as the sound of something metal hitting the floor came over the line. Yeah, Haggerty probably hadn't expected him to say that.

"What's going on?"

He let out a slow breath. In a nutshell, what was going on was that someone who matched his description stole his car, used it in a drive-by shooting, and then parked it back where he'd found it. God, that sounded so completely ridiculous he couldn't even bring himself to say it.

"There was a drive-by shooting last night and one of the cars involved matches mine," Ben said. "It wasn't me, but I don't think this is going to be sorted out any time soon."

Haggerty was quiet for a minute. "Yeah, I can watch your dog. Is there anything else you need me to do?"

"No, just remember she hates people. Stay out of town."

*　　*　　*

They were never spacious to begin with, but the squad's backseat seemed even more cramped with Ben's hands cuffed behind his back.

The seat beneath him was cold and unforgiving, the divider in front of him a transparent yet tangible reminder of his severance from the career he'd dedicated his life to. His gaze was out the window, but his mind was elsewhere. Most notably, on his failures. Past and present.

While he never would've visited him in prison, Ben had always dreamt of the day when he'd see his father led away in handcuffs. Sadly that day never came, due to one stroke of luck or another. Fortune, in his father's case. Misfortune for everyone else.

And now here he was, living the dream from the wrong end of it. His father would never face justice for what he'd done and now, because of Ben's actions, Dixon wouldn't either.

A nightmare if there ever was one.

But in the end, he deserved this. He'd crossed the line. He'd broken laws. He'd thought he could pull this off, but he should've known better. A police officer should've known better. Apparently he didn't, and he'd lost his badge because of it. Dixon may have staged the shooting, but what happened was Ben's fault as much as it was Dixon's.

Just like last time.

The Explorer slowed, prompting him to register his surroundings. The traffic light was changing from yellow to red. Drab, colorless buildings sat on three corners of the intersection while an empty parking lot graced the fourth. Definitely not one of the more scenic blocks in town, but it was a much nicer view than the one he'd have after booking.

"So, what kind?" Taylor asked.

Ben shifted his gaze to the rearview mirror. "Come again?"

"Dog," he elaborated. "What kind of dog do you have?"

Shit, right. "Yellow lab," Ben answered. That had to be a safe bet, since everyone and their brother had one of those at some point in their life.

"Ah, we've got two chocolates ourselves," Taylor said. "Dolly's sharp as a tack but Gunner hates getting his feet wet. Hopefully we can work through that before duck season opens up but—"

Tires squealed behind them before a loud *POW* lurched the squad forward.

22

MILLISECONDS FELT LIKE HOURS, the crunching of metal and plastic giving way to an abrupt silence as the squad came to rest mere feet from the space it had occupied a moment ago. Everything stilled. Why the hell did time always seem to stop, too? Ben shook his head to clear the fog blanketing his senses.

"—freaking got rear-ended," Taylor was muttering, to no one in particular. His eyes met Ben's in the mirror as he increased his volume. "Are you hurt?"

Ben took stock of himself. He was shaken and his heart was beating out of his chest, but other than that he seemed to be unscathed. "No, I, uh…I think I'm alright."

His wavering voice must've lent doubt to his response. Taylor turned around to get a better look at him through the divider. "Are you sure?"

Ben added as much composure to his statement as he could this time. "Just caught me off guard, that's all."

"You and me both," Taylor said. "Hang tight and I'll go check on the driver." With that he flipped a couple of switches on the squad's console before grabbing his handheld radio to call in the accident as he stepped out.

Yeah, hang tight. Like he was going anywhere. His legs were trembling so badly that he probably couldn't walk if he wanted to. Distantly he could hear Taylor conversing with a woman, so he turned as far as he could to sneak a glance out of the back window. Blonde and petite, she looked to be barely out of high school. Her apologetic face was more or less canceled out by the rhinestone-encrusted phone still glued to her hand. Almost certainly texting while driving.

His heart was still racing, so he straightened in his seat and tried to focus on calming down. It was a fender-bender, after all, and a low-speed one. God knows he'd been through worse.

He was fine. Completely fine.

Sweat collected in the palms of his hands as he started to feel uncomfortably warm. Did Taylor turn off the A/C? Ben was overdressed to begin with and still hadn't managed to get his breathing under control, and now it felt like he was getting even less oxygen than before. He closed his eyes and tried to take a few deep breaths, but couldn't focus.

The interior was quiet.

Something was wrong. He could feel it. He couldn't put his finger on it, but he could feel it. It was like the scene in a movie when the music changes before something bad happens. One by one, scenarios ran through his mind, none of them pleasant.

No, he needed to settle down. The doors were locked, the

squad's lights were on, and there'd be another officer on scene in minutes. He was being paranoid. Nothing was going to—

The car started to tilt.

He tried to put his hands out to catch himself, but the cuffs held firm, his breath quickening as he pulled against their cold metal surface. Shit, how could he forget? He switched gears and splayed his legs for stability as he looked out the window to see what was happening.

Nothing. Literally nothing. Cars were being directed around the intersection and a small group of pedestrians had assembled on the sidewalk to watch the action. Not a single damn thing was touching the squad, but his surroundings kept spinning anyway. He closed his eyes and leaned forward, sweat running down his forehead as his stomach started to twist.

The repetitive *click-click-click* of snapping fingers prompted him to look over. Taylor and another officer were trying to get his attention, both of their faces wrinkled with concern. When had they opened his door?

"—need you to calm down," Taylor said. "What's wrong?"

"I...I think I'm gonna be sick," Ben replied. It had to be against some kind of moral code to vomit in another officer's squad, but at least Taylor's had a plastic seat. Even so, he'd rather avoid that scenario if possible. If he wasn't so hot, if he could get enough air—

"Help me get him out."

"Fuck he's pale..."

And then a panicky female voice. "Oh my gosh, did I kill someone?"

Ugh, that was the last thing Ben needed to hear. He already felt like he was dying. A hand reached in and released the seat belt before he felt himself being guided out of the vehicle and into a sitting position against it. Lengthwise in front of him sat another squad he was only now noticing despite its flashing lights. The other officer—Jordan, was it?—said something about a bottle of water and strode toward it. Ben did his best to calm down, trying to focus on the reality around him.

The cool pavement eased his discomfort ever so slightly, but the reprieve ended almost as soon as it began, his breath hitching as a split-second shard of pain cut through his chest. Moments later it struck again, his seemingly unwarranted freight train of fear suddenly gaining a very tangible basis in the sensation. His whole body started to shake as he realized what was happening.

Heart attack.

He was being framed for attempted murder, got rear-ended while in custody, and now he was having a heart attack. Just shy of forty-seven to top it all off. How sadistically ironic.

A stern voice commanded his attention. "Talk to me, Ben."

"Che…chest pain," he answered.

Taylor was on his radio instantly. "229, I need an ambulance here, now…"

Ben tuned out. The gathering across the street had tripled in size, but at least the other squad gave him a much-needed sliver of privacy. He'd always accepted that he might lose his life in the line of duty, but never in his wildest dreams would he have thought he'd die in handcuffs.

*   *   *

It took all of five minutes for another set of flashing lights to join the party. Taylor had walked over to meet the ambulance as soon as it pulled up and was conversing with one of the paramedics, no doubt giving her a quick summary of what was going on. The second had a bright red bag of equipment in her hand, and after a brief gesture in Ben's direction, the three of them approached.

The one carrying the bag also sported a ponytail, her black hair long and intricately braided. She set her gear to the side and addressed Taylor. "We'll need his handcuffs and jacket off, too."

Taylor quickly obliged, kneeling behind him to unlock the cuffs before helping him slip his suit jacket off. Once Ben had a free hand he put pressure on his chest to try to ease the pain.

The other paramedic knelt directly in front of him. Her jaw-length hair was dark brown with a streak of blue dyed on the right side. She greeted him with a smile, her hazel-green eyes not showing the slightest hint of anxiety. Ben wasn't sure if that made him feel better or worse.

"Hey. I'm Kayla, and this is my partner Nicole," she said. "Can you tell me your name?"

"Ben," he replied. Nicole's gloved hand took his and clipped an oxygen monitor on his finger, her dark skin making his seem even more pale than it already was. He felt a blood pressure cuff being strapped around his arm.

"Alright, Ben," Kayla continued. "Do you know where you are right now?"

"Lake City," he answered. Hopefully she didn't mean which intersection, since he wasn't certain of that. Lakeshore and… damn it, why the hell couldn't he think straight? Marion, maybe?

"What month is it?"

He closed his eyes as the pain resurfaced. "August."

Kayla took his wrist in her hand and felt for his pulse as she shifted her gaze to her watch. "And do you know why we're here today?"

"Because I'm having chest pain."

The questions seemed kind of silly, but Ben appreciated the distraction. The shaking had eased a little now that he had something to occupy his mind.

She placed the back of her hand on his chest but kept her eyes on her watch. "Has anything like this ever happened to you before?"

He tried to take a calming breath. "No."

"Did it come on suddenly or gradually?"

"The pain itself was sudden but I...before that I started to feel sick, and that came on a bit more gradually."

While he and Kayla conversed, Nicole was busy with the equipment. She took his blood pressure and some notes, then untucked his shirt and pulled it up, wiping his chest with a damp cloth. One by one she placed adhesive pads on his skin before hooking them up to what looked like a portable heart monitor of some sort.

Meanwhile Kayla continued with her part of the assessment. "On a scale of one to ten, with one being no pain at all and ten being the worst pain you've ever experienced, how would you rate your pain?"

Ben hated that question. There were too many different kinds of pain to make comparing them that easy. At least it didn't have to be an exact science. "Six or seven, maybe."

"And can you show me exactly where the pain is?"

With an open hand he gestured to the center and left side of his chest. "Right in this area."

"Does it radiate anywhere? Like your arm, neck, or jaw?"

"No."

That had to be a good sign, or at least Ben hoped it was. The audience of civilians seemed just as interested in his answers as Kayla, but thankfully the officers kept them herded a respectful distance away. It probably didn't help that they were blocking a main thoroughfare.

"Any shortness of breath, lightheadedness, or dizziness?" she asked.

"Yeah, all three. Nausea, too," he added, immediately second guessing himself. Had he mentioned that already?

Nicole took more notes as Kayla continued. "Okay, Ben. I have a few more questions for you. Are you allergic to anything?"

"Penicillin."

"Are you currently taking any medications?"

"No."

"Do you have a history of heart problems?"

"No, but my father died of a heart attack when he was forty-seven. I don't know the details."

His attention had shifted to Nicole, who was opening a disposable bag with plastic tubing and a sheathed needle inside. She must've sensed his concern, her voice even more reassuring than Kayla's. "I'm going to start an IV to help treat you. Okay?"

Ben's jaw tensed. "Yeah, go ahead." He looked away and tried to focus on Kayla, who quickly moved on to her next question. How many more could she possibly have?

"When's the last time you had anything to eat or drink?"

He closed his eyes, trying to relax as he felt the sting of the needle. "I had oatmeal for breakfast a few hours ago. Nothing but water after that."

While Ben didn't know the exact circumstances of his father's demise, he'd always assumed that the man's diet of bacon grease and nightly ice cream was the main driver of it. Ben had always made a point of exercising and watching what he ate, but right now was the first time he was seriously starting to consider that it might be hereditary.

Kayla pulled a stethoscope from the bag next to her and put the earpieces in before pressing the cold metal disc to his chest in several places. "Any recent fevers, illnesses, or surgeries?"

Surgeries, last year though. "How recent?" he asked.

She moved the stethoscope to his back. "Within the last month."

"No."

Kayla grabbed a bottle of pills from the bag next, glancing at the label briefly before opening it and tapping four of them into the lid. "This is aspirin. I need you to put these in your mouth and chew them," she instructed, putting the pills in his hand. "Don't swallow. They need to be chewed."

As she put the bottle away, Ben chewed the small tablets, which tasted a bit like orange. Once he was done, Kayla addressed her partner. "Nicole, can you take his blood pressure again?"

There was a firm squeeze on his arm as she took the reading. "One-sixty over ninety-eight."

With a quick nod Kayla turned back to him. "I'm going to have to ask if you've taken any erectile-dysfunction medications such as Viagra, Cialis, or Levitra in the last forty-eight hours?"

Ben paused. That wasn't invasive at all. "No, I haven't."

At that Kayla grabbed a small item that looked like a bottle of red nail polish. Like last time, she checked the label before taking the cap off. "This is nitroglycerin, which we administer as a single spray under your tongue. It might give you a bit of a headache, but that means it's working."

Ben followed her instructions as she gave the medicine. He'd dealt with his share of headaches this week, so what was one more?

Kayla put the bottle away and looked over to Nicole, giving her a thumbs up as she started to pack up her gear. Nicole nodded and pulled a cell phone out of her pocket before dialing and putting the device to her ear.

"Hi. This is Nicole with Lake City Ambulance." She paused a moment before continuing. "Yeah. We'll be en route with a forty-six-year-old male complaining of chest pain. Patient is alert and oriented, vitals are stable. We have an eighteen-gauge IV in the right forearm, three-hundred twenty-four milligrams of aspirin given and nitro times one, no other treatment at this time. We should be there in four minutes."

23

MORNING BECAME AFTERNOON. They'd been running tests for hours. Blood work, EKGs, X-rays. So far they hadn't found anything, or if they had, they'd opted not to tell him yet. Ben's pulse was still high, but he didn't care as long as it was still there. Even so, he couldn't keep himself from worrying that soon it might not be.

He needed to think about something else.

They'd stationed an officer outside of his room, but he wasn't cuffed to the bed like he'd expected to be. That was a plus. Or was it? What if the hospital staff had requested that in case they had to use the defibrillator?

Ben sighed. Really? He'd tried to put a positive spin on his situation at least a dozen times, but no matter which way he took his thoughts they always managed to circle back around to bite him. At one point he'd considered getting some sleep instead, but he had a feeling that whatever went on in dreamland wouldn't be any more pleasant.

There was a knock on the door before a man in his late fifties stepped in. The black stethoscope hanging loosely around his neck was a stark contrast to the white of his lab coat, but a perfect match to the frames of his glasses. "Hello, Ben," he said as he closed the door behind himself. "Sorry to keep you waiting."

"Doctor Query, welcome back."

He rolled a small stool over to Ben's bed and sat down. "I'm sure by now you're ready for answers, so I'll cut to the chase. Your test results all came back normal, which is great news. We didn't find any indications of heart disease and your EKG and X-rays looked good. We also did a blood test to look for certain proteins that are released into the bloodstream if heart muscle is damaged and that came back negative as well, which is the result we were hoping to see."

While that was reassuring on the surface, it didn't give Ben any answers. "If the tests are all coming back normal, then what exactly is going on?"

"What you experienced was a panic attack and not a heart attack."

A panic attack? No, that couldn't be right. He hadn't been simply freaking out. He was sure of that. But the man in front of him was a professional, so Ben tried to voice himself as tactfully as he could. "Obviously you're the expert here, but is it possible something was missed? With the pain and everything…I mean it felt so real."

"Real" as in he was certain he was dying.

"We see this quite often, and I can assure you that everything you felt was indeed real," Doctor Query said, lacing his fingers as he continued. "Basically it's your body's fight or flight response being triggered in the absence of an actual threat, and that can manifest itself in physical symptoms that mirror those of a heart attack. Chest pain, dizziness, and nausea are common with both. It can be frightening, especially the first time you experience it."

"And all of that from a minor traffic accident?" Ben asked. Frightening barely described it, and over a goddamn text message no less. He refused to believe he was losing it to that level.

"The cause isn't necessarily on par with your body's reaction," Doctor Query explained. "Prolonged stress is a common trigger, but panic attacks can occur in seemingly non-stressful situations as well."

"So it could happen again?"

"Yes, it most certainly could. The good news is that learning a few simple coping strategies and implementing better stress management techniques can go a long way toward preventing panic attacks, or at least keeping them manageable. Therapy or medication are also options depending on how things go, but that'd be something you'd want to discuss with your regular care team if you feel other methods aren't working for you. How does that sound?"

It sounded like something Miles would say, if Ben wanted to be blunt with himself. Either way, it wasn't a topic that needed debating right now. "That explains a lot. Thank you, Doctor."

"My pleasure," he said, leaning forward to shake Ben's hand before he stood. "The nurses are running a bit behind today, but someone should be in with your discharge papers shortly."

"Thanks again."

With a courteous nod Dr. Query exited the room, leaving Ben with nothing but his thoughts.

A panic attack, really? While that was better than having a heart problem, it wasn't what Ben had expected, and he wasn't sure if he believed it or not. He had his demons like anyone else, but he'd never had anxiety issues, never had a panic attack before. He was under a lot of stress lately, but he didn't let it get to him. Not like that. Did he?

No. He was handling everything just fine.

He closed his eyes and tried to think it over from a logical standpoint. An entire team of medical professionals had checked out his heart ad nauseum and deemed it healthy, so he should do his best to believe them.

Why the hell was that so hard?

Commotion echoed from down the hall. Voices, shouting. Reassurances being quickly discarded. Ben recognized it from all of the times he'd been in uniform responding to the exact same scenario. Combative patient. Except the last time he'd received that call, a nurse had been stabbed.

He got up without thinking.

A woman's scream sounded as he went for the door, but the plethora of tethers from the monitoring equipment yanked him back. Damn it, too many wires. He was wasting precious time. He pulled off the EKG leads and threw them aside before using his left hand to rip out the IV, stifling a cry as he did so. Once free he bolted to the doorway, and his training kicked in as he assessed the scene.

Down the hall, two hospital security guards in black were trying to subdue a man. The officer who'd been watching Ben's room had his taser drawn and was shouting at them to move. Both ignored his commands and continued struggling to get the patient's thrashing arms and legs under control. A woman in tattered street clothes, who Ben assumed was the man's girlfriend, was screaming at them to let him go but thankfully for her sake she kept her involvement limited to that. Everyone else had moved to the fringes of the room, all eyes focused solely on the action. Even if Ben had nothing more than his bare hands to bring to the fight, he couldn't stand idle by and let fate decide how this was going to play out.

Just as he was about to move into the hallway, the guards got the upper hand and quickly wrestled the patient face-down onto the floor. The officer holstered his taser, switching it out for a set of handcuffs as he approached to make the arrest. Ben let out a sigh of relief.

No one got hurt.

Wetness prompted him to look down. Blood from where the IV had been streaked his arm with crimson lines and the sight took him back to a year ago, to a place where someone did get hurt. He felt his breath start to quicken.

Don't. Panic.

He forced himself to look away. As the flashbacks played out in front of him, he tried his best to remind himself he wasn't there. But he had been there, and he knew how it'd ended. With Dixon still out...how long until someone else got hurt?

He dug his nails into his palm. No, not gonna happen. He wouldn't let it. But right now was his only chance and he couldn't afford to waste it.

Ben quickly scanned the room, his gaze stopping on one of the visitor chairs. Even though he was sure Taylor would've told them about his arrest status, an unknowing hospital worker had left his clothes in the room anyway. Rookie mistake. Luck rarely played in his favor, but he'd take what he could get.

They'd only had him undress from the waist up, so he untied the hospital gown and threw it on the bed before grabbing his button-up shirt. He shuddered as he felt the wetness on his arm smear, but he forced himself not to look. He'd have to deal with that later.

Once his shirt was buttoned up enough to be presentable, he slipped his jacket over it, thankful it was black. That'd hide the blood he could already feel soaking its way through the sleeve of the garment under it. He grabbed a couple of paper towels from the dispenser on the wall and pocketed them for later use. Under his breath, Ben apologized to the officer who was assigned to watch him, hoping his stunt wouldn't cost the man his job.

He took one more look down the hall before slipping out of the room.

24

THE OUTSIDE WORLD was a welcome sight, but Ben couldn't stop to enjoy it. They'd notice his absence in minutes, if they hadn't already. He walked briskly, hoping to find something that wasn't residential. He needed a phone.

Whatever street he was on right now didn't have sidewalks, which made him feel even more exposed. The view to the south had looked like an endless expanse of houses stretching as far as the eye could see, so he'd opted to play his luck and go north instead. So far nothing but single-family homes of various colors, each one staring him down as if it had eyes of its own. He kept pressure on his arm as he walked, trying to be as inconspicuous as possible given the circumstances. At least the bleeding had mostly stopped.

A small cross street came into view in front of him. Houses continued past it on the right side, but through the trees on the left stood a few pole buildings and a gravel lot with boats strewn around it. It was a bit too close to the hospital for his taste, but it'd have to do. He grabbed the last paper towel from his pocket and cleaned off the rest of the blood visible on his hand. That would draw the wrong kind of attention.

Gravel crunched under his shoes as he read the sign on the windowless brown building. *Smitty's Marine.* The only vehicle parked in front was a late-model GMC pickup, its sapphire paint bright enough to give the lake a run for its money.

Good. That meant someone was here.

The front door was white and also windowless. Ben increased his pace, but it swung open before he made it to the cement entry stairs. The man who exited was bald, bearded, and burly, the sun glinting off the propeller in his hand as he walked down the steps.

"Hey. Are you a local by chance?" Ben asked. Initially he'd planned on going inside to see if an employee would let him use the phone, but that wasn't without risk. The police would be showing his mugshot to every business within walking distance to see if anyone recognized him, but by then this guy would be long gone.

"Sure am," the man answered. "Are you here for the fishing tourney this week?"

"No, but my car broke down a few streets over and I was wondering if I could borrow your phone. I forgot to bring the charger for mine."

"No problem." he said, switching the propeller to his other hand to fish the device out of his pocket. He handed it to Ben.

"Thanks."

Ben grabbed it and checked the time. 4:54. He did a quick

internet search for the phone number and pressed *call*, hoping to hell Haggerty hadn't left work yet.

It was on the third ring when he picked up. "Haase Truck an' Equipment."

"Hey. Glad I caught you," Ben greeted, speaking as if he was calling a friend. "I was hoping you could give me a ride."

*   *   *

Smitty's must've closed by now, since Ben hadn't heard any other traffic. As long as none of the employees did a walk-through of the property before going home, he should be alright, assuming Haggerty got here before the police did. No sirens yet, but no tow truck either.

Not that they'd use their sirens before they got a visual on him. No, they'd be canvasing the neighborhoods quietly and systematically. Even so, telling himself that he might hear them coming was reassuring even if he knew it was flawed logic.

The sound of tires on gravel gave him a sense of unease when the accompanying low rumble of a diesel engine was absent. He crouched down further, keeping himself in the shadows as he tried to get a glimpse of the vehicle from his narrow hiding spot between the two sheds. Within seconds its front bumper slowly moved into his line of sight, its black paint causing his heart rate to spike until the rest of the car came into view.

A black Camry.

Ben relaxed slightly as he adjusted his position. He couldn't tell for sure if it was the same one from Haase, but how many black Camrys in that style could there be in a town this small?

Hopefully just one.

The car swung around before coming to a stop in front of the main building. Ben decided to chance it and stepped out, hoping the vehicle's driver was either Haggerty or a complete stranger who had no idea he was a fugitive. As he walked up from behind he looked through the rear window, breathing a sigh of relief when he saw Haggerty's long hair. He glanced around one last time before getting in on the passenger side.

"I heard about that drive-by of yours through the grapevine," Haggerty said, his tone leisurely. "Surprised they let you out on a sig-bond."

Ben shut the door and buckled. "They didn't."

Haggerty's expression did a one-eighty. "Wait, did you—"

"Just drive," Ben said before promptly changing the subject. "Can I borrow your knife for a second?"

Haggerty furrowed his brows at the request, but he handed the item over without question. Ben flipped it open and pulled up his right sleeve, swiftly cutting off his hospital bracelets before snapping the knife closed and handing it back. "Thanks."

Haggerty's gaze shifted from the red and white bands to the blood stains on Ben's wrist that hadn't fully wiped off. "What the hell—"

"I'm *fine*."

Haggerty stared at him for a few seconds but didn't push the issue. Thank God. Ben was still grappling with what the cardiologist had told him, and that was one thing among many he didn't want to discuss right now. He had more pressing concerns. "You don't happen to know a place we can lay low for a while, do you?"

"It's a bit of a hike," Haggerty said. "But yeah, I do."

Of course. Why did he ask. "And stay off the main roads, if you could."

"I'll do what I can, but if we get pulled over that's the end of it. I'm not gonna run."

"I wouldn't ask you to."

Haggerty took the same road Ben had, and Mayo was coming up on their right. Ben knew he shouldn't look, but he couldn't keep himself from doing so. Rows of cars spanning the parking lot blocked most of the view, but thanks to the added height of their light bars he could see at least two squads parked near the entrance. Ben pretended to be shielding his eyes from the sun as he lifted a hand to cover the side of his face.

The road they were on was offset past the stop sign, so Haggerty took a left and then an immediate right to continue down it. Not long after it curved to the right before ending in another stop sign, and he took a left at that one.

"So do you know who's pointing the finger at you?" Haggerty asked.

"You don't?"

"No, they haven't released any names yet. Open investigation and all that crap."

Ben looked out the side window. "Dixon is."

"Are you serious?"

"I wish I wasn't."

The neighborhood was quiet, which only seemed to add to Ben's unease. He knew they were hunting him, and he knew how competent they were. He panicked for a second whenever a vehicle came into view, and his ever-increasing stress level didn't go down even though none of them turned out to be a squad car.

None of them yet, anyway.

The high school was coming up on their right when Ben saw it, the SUV a few blocks down. Black and headed their direction. This time he didn't have to wonder. Spotlight, push bumper. Lake City didn't use Suburbans, though, so it had to be a sheriff's deputy.

Haggerty slowed down. "That looks like a—"

"Squad car, I see it. Pull into that driveway on the left."

"What if someone's home?"

"We can either chance it or we're made for sure."

Haggerty set his signal and turned, pulling the Camry into the small parking area next to the covered entry of a two-story, light gray house. Lilacs bordered the drive on their left while a dense row of hedges lined the front and side of the property. It was as much cover as Ben could hope for on short notice, but it still didn't feel like enough, so he quickly unbuckled and climbed into the backseat. As he laid down, time once again seemed to come to a standstill.

Ben took in what little he could see, which was the door panel, the floor, and the back of the front seat. He couldn't bring himself to close his eyes, not that it would've helped. The black cloth interior reminded him of his first car, and studying it reminded him of all the time he'd spent in it when he was in high school. Cruising to nowhere, parking, sitting in it for hours as he read a book or took in the landscape around him. Anything to be out of the house as much as possible.

Haggerty spoke without turning around. "He's gone."

"Did you see who it was?"

"The Sheriff's Department. Goodhue County."

"Give it another minute," Ben said. "He might be watching his mirrors to see if you pull right back out."

"What if—"

"If someone comes out of the house tell them you parked because I was having a panic attack."

Which he very well might before the day was over. He started to wish he would've asked the doctor how frequently he could expect those episodes to be. Fucking hindsight.

"Wouldn't asking for directions be a better cover story?"

Ben sighed and closed his eyes. "Tell them whatever you want, Haggerty."

After what Ben guessed was another minute or so he sat up and looked out the windows. The street was empty. "I think we'll be alright now."

"You think or you hope?"

He chose a seat in the back and buckled. "I hope."

The rest of the drive took six nerve-wracking minutes, which felt more like twelve. As Haggerty drove, Ben kept an eye out for any other squad cars, thankful they were able to stay off of the highway until they were almost to the southern edge of town. There'd likely be units from Wabasha County heading their way from the south, but he tried not to think about that.

Before he knew it they were heading south on Highway 61, and he got a visual reminder of everything that'd happened in the last few days. The Pepin Heights Store, the public works, the towering pine trees, the grassy field.

The run-down trucks and the pole buildings.

Pulling into the gravel lot at Haase was a welcome relief for Ben. The lush fields and green bluffs surrounding the area gave him back a sliver of the sense of freedom he'd lost on Tenth Street, even if it didn't help squelch the guilt of knowing he shouldn't be free at all.

They got out, and Haggerty locked the car before going into the office to drop off the keys. He locked the office door on his way out but stopped prior to closing it, giving Ben's outfit a quick once-over. "I've got a spare work shirt inside if you want it. Might get kinda warm hiking in that jacket."

Ben thought about it. Tempting given the late-afternoon heat, but if Haggerty's spare shirt matched the one he was currently wearing, then it was short-sleeved. "I'll be fine."

"You sure?"

"Yeah," Ben said. "Lead the way."

Haggerty's idea of "the way" was far different than Ben's expectations. He'd assumed "hike" meant there would be some sort of path, but after entering the tree line behind Haase they'd spent the next half hour or so working their way through untamed forest like freaking Lewis and Clark.

Burbling creek and all.

At least Haggerty seemed confident of where he was going. Either that or he put on a really convincing act. He also seemed to be taking it slow, glancing back frequently to make sure Ben was keeping up. That was Ben's guess, anyway. Or maybe he was looking to see if he'd died of heat exhaustion yet.

"So I got a question for you," Haggerty said, stopping—and speaking—for the first time since they'd set out.

Ben tried to keep his voice from sounding too labored as he caught up. "Yeah?"

"Why didn't you report Andrew that night? Was your bruised pride really worth all this trouble?"

Yeah, that. Honestly he was a bit surprised Haggerty hadn't asked earlier.

"My gripe with him goes back a little further than that," Ben said. "It's not like I haven't gotten into a scuffle before. That's part of the job. This is personal."

"What happened?"

He stepped around Haggerty to continue along his so-called trail. "Like I said, it's personal."

Haggerty grabbed Ben's shoulder and yanked him back into the conversation. "He tried to kill you," he growled. "How the hell does it get more personal than that?"

Ben's anger flared at the unanticipated touch. He threw off Haggerty's hand and backed away, the words slipping out before he even realized it. "He killed my wife!"

25

THE LARGE ROCK Calvin sat on wasn't exactly comfortable, but he had a feeling it was going to be a lot more pleasant than the story he was about to hear.

Kessler had positioned himself on the mossy surface of a fallen tree, hands clasped and elbows resting on his knees. He kept his gaze on the leaf litter as he spoke, his face harboring an uneasiness that his voice didn't convey.

"We were about two and a half hours through a three-hour trip, heading back from a seminar at UW. It was late, she was driving, and we were talking about the keynote speaker. There was a car and a semi heading south in the oncoming lane, both probably doing fifty-five or sixty like we were. Nothing unusual for that time of night."

Calvin stayed quiet, shifting his weight as he contemplated the words *oncoming* and *sixty*.

"The car went past us, but before the semi would've, I heard what sounded like a gunshot and the truck swerved into our lane. I remember blinding lights and the next thing I know we're facing south, there's flashing red lights everywhere and I'm wondering why the hell there's blood running down my hand."

Kessler rubbed his left ring finger absentmindedly, as if fiddling with the wedding band that used to be there. He didn't even seem to realize he was doing it.

"I don't know how long I was out after the hit, but I had a pretty bad head injury, among other things, and I wasn't really processing what was going on at that point. Apparently I asked for a napkin and told one of the paramedics they needed to get that chopper off the highway before I cited them for impeding traffic."

If the story wasn't so grave, Calvin might've laughed at the last bit. Ticketing a chopper sounded like something Kessler might do, even if only for posterity's sake.

"Everything else I know about the accident is from the police report," Kessler continued. "I don't remember the flight or the first few days at the hospital, but once I was coherent enough, they had Miles break it to me that she..." He stopped and cleared his throat. "Had him tell me that I was the only one in the car who survived. If she hadn't jerked the wheel and made it an offset hit, I wouldn't have."

Calvin hadn't planned on saying anything until Kessler had finished, but based on his faltering tone, he needed a redirect. "So Andrew was, what? Shooting at the semi?"

"No. He and his buddy had lost the cops a few miles back after a failed theft, and when they got on the highway Dixon thought it'd be a good idea to ditch his slim jim by throwing it out the window. Blew the truck's left front tire and the driver lost control."

In his line of work, Calvin was all too familiar with blowouts. Dangerous as hell in any circumstance, but on a steering tire, at that speed…fuck. "You're lucky to be alive."

At that Kessler met his gaze, his expression hard and his tone resentful. "She should be the one standing here today, not me. He might've caused the accident, but I'm as much to blame for what happened as he is."

"How do you figure? You weren't even driving," Calvin said. Survivor's guilt, no doubt. He'd seen it in some of his comrades after operations gone bad, and it wasn't pretty. And if Kessler was suffering from that, he may very well be suffering from PTSD too. Looking back, some of his behaviors certainly suggested it. Being distant, refusing to walk in front of the flatbed, literally shaking when he was caught in the headlights—

"I should've been," Kessler explained, standing to pace in a short arc. "Trisha loves—loved taking photos of the river, so I always drove if we took that route. Always. I don't know why I asked her to drive, I…" He sat back down and ran a hand over his face. "For some reason I just felt like being the passenger that night."

Calvin kept his expression calm, hoping that'd help Kessler balance himself. He knew there wasn't a phrase in the world he could utter right now that would give even the slightest bit of consolation, but Calvin could at least try to redirect his thoughts before the guilt finished tearing him apart. "So what happened with Andrew after the accident?"

Kessler rubbed his hands on his knees. "As you can imagine, they fled the scene immediately, but since the police already had a BOLO out on the vehicle, they picked him up the next day. The trucker told the cops that it was the car's driver who threw something out the window, but because he was behind them he couldn't identify who that was. In the interview room, Dixon and his buddy both wouldn't say who was driving, probably hoping to get the case thrown out under reasonable doubt."

"Is that what happened?"

"It probably would've if his buddy hadn't taken a little victory video out the rear window as they laughed about getting away. When he panned over, it showed Dixon behind the wheel. He'd tried to delete the footage, but forensics was able to recover it."

"So what'd they charge him with? Reckless endangerment?"

Kessler rubbed his imaginary wedding band again. "Criminal vehicular homicide. That was almost a year ago."

Calvin's brows furrowed. "Then why the hell is he already out of prison?"

Kessler shot him a cynical look. "Local police jumped the gun and searched his phone without a warrant, so the defense attorney's motion to suppress the video was granted. The only person who actually saw Dixon driving was his buddy, and he fled to Iowa to avoid the subpoena. Without the footage or any other eyewitnesses the prosecution didn't have a case, so all the charges were dismissed."

"Shit, what a mess."

"Yeah, it was. When the DA called and told me he was going to walk I—" Kessler stopped short, shame flashing across his eyes before he closed them. He ran a hand through his hair and let out a slow breath, nothing but the rustle of leaves filling in the silence. Calvin sat quietly to let Ben gather his thoughts.

Had Ben tried to take a run at Andrew back then? He didn't come across as the murderous type, but it had to be damn hard for anyone to keep it together under those circumstances. Or maybe the stress from the accident was what led to the loss of his detective position. Whatever it was, it haunted him.

When Kessler looked up his expression harbored nothing but stone cold determination. "He already ruined my life. I'm going to make damn sure he doesn't ruin anyone else's."

"And you really didn't try to shoot him last night?" he asked, though he already knew the answer. Kessler had chosen a career in law enforcement for the same reason Calvin had joined the military—to protect people. *Save* people. And ever since his first tour of duty, he'd easily been able to recognize when others were driven by the same motivation.

"No, she wouldn't have wanted that. But I saw the evidence, their case is rock solid."

"But if it wasn't your car, they should be able to clear this up, shouldn't they?"

Kessler stood to pace again. "That's the thing, it *was* my car. I have no idea who was driving it or how the hell they even took it. Dixon played the victim and gave a fake name, but he can't be in two places at once."

Calvin leaned forward. "Wait, he's framing you?"

"Framed," Kessler corrected. "Past tense. Someone stole my car from the motel's parking lot, followed his Audi, shot at it, then drove back and parked it where they'd found it."

"That sounds—"

"Ridiculous, I know. And of course Dixon's description of the shooter matches me," Kessler said. He sighed and rubbed his forehead before continuing. "They have photos, videos, a full license plate…and my recorded statement during the interview saying that no one but me has access to my car."

"News travels quick around here, especially in his circles if there's a new cop on the roster," Calvin said. "You didn't think he'd be on to you in a heartbeat once he heard you were in Lake City? I mean you ran right into him and all."

Kessler shook his head. "No, Trisha kept her maiden name when we married. He doesn't know my name, my face…he has no idea who I am."

"Well he either figured it out or you seriously pissed him off back there behind the public works."

"Someone called the motel a few days ago and asked if a 'Mr. Kessler' was registered there. That must've been how they found me, but I have no idea how they got my name."

"You didn't think that was suspicious?"

"I figured it was my brother. Lately he's been taking more of an interest in my personal life than he should."

Calvin bit his tongue. He could understand the reasoning for that, even if Kessler didn't see it. Either way, something about the entire scenario bothered him. Andrew had no idea Kessler had a personal interest in him, and framing a cop for attempted murder simply because he'd gotten into a fight with him seemed drastic considering he got away with it.

He opted not to voice those concerns. Kessler had enough to think about as it was. "I'm sure we'll figure this out."

Kessler looked at him. "That makes one of us."

26

THE TERRAIN had gotten steep, and Ben was starting to fall behind. A cramp thorned his side as he struggled to catch his breath. How long had they been at it? An hour? Two? It seemed like more. He called ahead to Haggerty. "You know, it doesn't seem like anyone's hot on our trail at the moment. Think we could slow down a bit?"

Haggerty looked back, not seeming to be exerting himself any more than he would be if he was out grocery shopping on a Saturday afternoon. "You don't hike much, do you?"

"Not as much as you, apparently," Ben said. Even if he knew his way around a gym, his usual workout routine didn't include hiking up a bluff. At least now he knew for sure his heart was in good shape. He wouldn't have made it this far if it wasn't.

"There's an overlook past those trees," Haggerty said. "We can stop there for a minute."

"They look similar to all of the other trees we've gone past. Are you sure you know where we're going?"

"For someone who's got worse places to be, you sure do whine a lot," Haggerty said. "It's not a bad hike. Hell, most days I end up carrying Greta for at least half of it."

Even with his accusatory tone, Ben had to suppress a smile. The thought of Haggerty traipsing through the woods with a velvet hippo slung over his shoulder was amusing.

Soon the forest opened up, and as Haggerty had said, there was an overlook. Well, an overlook and then some. The grassy expanse was large and partially forested, the kind of place that could easily be a county park if they added restrooms and a shelter or two. To the left, a weathered, multi-colored stone barrier wall stretched along the edge of the bluff, the view of the river behind it unobscured despite the dense foliage they'd gone through to get here. To the right sat a poorly maintained and empty parking area. Between the two towered the area's only fixture, an ancient light pole Ben leaned against to rest. Its flaking black paint and rusted fasteners had him questioning whether or not it worked, especially since the bulb itself looked like something Edison had personally handcrafted.

Haggerty had already walked up to the stone wall and leaned over it to take in the view of the landscape. To his left stood a tarnished metal plaque that read *Larson's Point*, and below it a paragraph of smaller text Ben couldn't read from this distance. Probably the story of how it got its name.

"Not a lot of people come up here these days, but it's the best view in the area," Haggerty said, his volume telling Ben he hadn't noticed he'd stayed behind. "You can see along the river about forty miles in either direction."

"I'll take your word for it," Ben called over.

Haggerty turned around and took in the distance between them. "Not a fan of heights?"

Ben hesitated as he contemplated honesty. Heights didn't bother him, never had. Hell, he'd even been trained in crisis intervention and had talked someone down from the edge of a roof on more than one occasion. But after he was discharged from the hospital, when the full realization of what had happened finally hit him, it was different. Then the DA called. And just like that, he was the one standing on the edge. But unlike those he'd helped, no one had seen him there. He'd made sure of that.

He wasn't proud of his actions that night.

In the end he'd stepped back, but afterwards he didn't trust himself. Didn't know if he'd make the same decision next time. He'd been comfortable standing there. Too comfortable.

Ben sighed. He'd never told a single soul about that night, and even if he suddenly found himself wanting to say something, to get it off of his chest, none of that was Haggerty's problem. He'd already said too much as it was. "Not really, no."

Haggerty shrugged before turning his gaze back to the river. "You're missing out."

Ben looked the other way, now seeing the aged but functional road leading out the parking area and down the bluff. "Is there a reason we didn't drive up here?"

"It'd draw all the wrong kind of attention if someone found a car sitting here and no one around," Calvin explained. "They'd probably figure someone jumped. Besides, the route you gotta take to get here from Lake City won't get us to where we're going anyway."

"It would've gotten us this far," Ben muttered to himself.

"What?"

"Nothing."

Haggerty narrowed his eyes for a moment before shaking his head. "Let's keep going. We're only about thirty minutes out."

"Is that true or are you humoring me?"

"It's mostly level if that makes you feel better."

*　　　*　　　*

As they cleared the tree line forty-five minutes later, Ben expected to be standing face to face with some kind of shed or abandoned outbuilding. Something small and decrepit, half covered by tenacious plants. The kind of place that didn't currently have electricity and may or may not have running water. From where he stood now, it was clear the cabin in front of them was...well, none of those things.

It was large but not excessively so, the sizable asphalt parking area flanked by a paved walkway running in front of and around the house. The windows on either side of the decorative glass entry door were adorned with matching wooden flower boxes overflowing with summer blooms. A few trees and more than a few sumacs clamored past the split-rail fence that edged one side of the property, a panoramic view of the river visible past them. Haggerty's pickup was parked on the other side of the house, in a small nook flanked by white fencing that closed off a large clearing next to a detached but matching two-car garage.

"Where are we?" Ben asked.

"My cousin's place. She and her husband go on a family

vacation with their daughter every summer for a week or two before school starts up, so no one's home."

"It's nice," he said, taking in the bluff-top location. Drilling the well alone must've cost more than his first house. "What do they do for a living, if you don't mind me asking?"

"He's a large animal vet and she's a triage nurse at Mayo."

The hospital and department he'd been seen at not once, but twice this week. Damn.

Good thing she was on vacation.

Greta crowded the door as they entered, the entire back half of her body swinging with the momentum of her over-energetic tail as her nails danced on the tile floor. Haggerty threw his keys on the counter before kneeling down to pet her, and between his smile and her joyful whimpers Ben couldn't tell which of the two was happier to see the other.

While they bonded, Ben took a minute to look around, unable to find a single thing any less tidy than the exterior of the house. The kitchen stood in front of them while the living room was off to the right in an open-concept layout, behind that a corridor leading further into the house. Everything clean, updated, and coordinated.

Once Greta settled, Haggerty refilled her dish in the sink before offering Ben a glass of water. No longer hot and dying of thirst, the dried blood tugging on his skin became his next most pressing annoyance. He set his empty glass on the counter before turning to Haggerty. "Think it'd be alright if I took a shower?"

"Knock yourself out," he said, gesturing to the back of the cabin. "Bathroom's down the hall."

Ben walked down the corridor, the presence of a dog in the house leading him to infer that the only fully closed door must be the one to the bathroom. When he opened it the sight of blue and teal glass mosaic tiles lining the wall confirmed his hunch.

"Hey, Kessler."

He looked back down the corridor. "Yeah?"

"There's a first-aid kit in the medicine cabinet if you need it."

Ben lowered his gaze. Haggerty didn't owe him that level of kindness. No one did.

"Thanks."

27

AFTER A SHOWER AND A SHAVE Ben felt ten times better. He put some Neosporin and a gauze pad on before wrapping his arm, which was already starting to turn a lovely shade of purple. Even so, it was the first time since his arrest he felt like he could breathe.

He took another minute to savor the bathroom's humidity as he toweled his hair, then threw his jacket and blood-stained shirt in the hamper. He'd take care of them later. The shirt probably wasn't savable, but the jacket should be alright after a wash. His pants had more or less survived the hike, so he slipped them back on and fastened his belt.

A fleeting cloud of steam leaked out of the bathroom door as he opened it. The cabin was quiet.

"Calvin?"

No answer. Must be outside.

He walked into the living room. Calvin and Greta were nowhere to be found, but a red and black plaid button-up shirt was waiting for him on the sofa. Long-sleeved, of course. Calvin's thoughtfulness never ceased to surprise him.

Ben had a couple inches of height on him, but Calvin was stockier, so between the two it fit decently enough. Once it was buttoned up he went to the kitchen and refilled his glass, letting the complete silence of the cabin envelop him after he turned the faucet off. Even when things were going well in life, he'd always needed occasional solitude, but after the chaos of the last few days he appreciated the quiet more than ever. He'd needed a reset.

Movement drew his gaze out the kitchen window. Greta was snapping at the air in a half-hearted attempt to catch fireflies. Calvin had changed out of his work clothes and was leaning on the fence off to the side, rubbing the face of a dark-colored horse that was loving the attention. Ben watched them for a minute before setting his glass down on the counter and walking out to join him.

The twilight air was refreshingly cool. Muted pinks and purples graced the skyline where the sun had dipped below it, the rising moon the only irregularity in an otherwise flawless view. It was still too bright for the stars to show themselves, but the chirping crickets were far less bashful.

Greta's panting face turned Ben's direction when she heard the gravel crunching beneath his shoes, but Calvin didn't turn around, busy offering the horse something from his hand.

The animal was near-black, with reddish-brown undertones on her muzzle and below her eyes. The only bit of white she had was a small star on her forehead, which seemed even brighter against the dark backdrop of her coat. Once Calvin pulled his hand away, she leaned in and nuzzled his face, her ears pricked forward hopefully.

"This is Ellie's horse, Ember," Calvin said as Ben came to stand next to him. "I take care of her if they're outta town."

"She's lovely," Ben said. And a she, good. He'd guessed it right this time. He reached out cautiously and patted the horse's neck, but her large, dark eyes had no interest in him. "I take it Ellie's your cousin?"

"No, that's Tracy. Ellie's their daughter."

Calvin reached into his pocket and handed Ben a greenish cube that looked like compressed grass. Ember tracked its every move and snorted as she took in its scent. Ben held it out to her on an open palm, imitating the way he'd seen Calvin do it. She lipped the treat from his hand before sniffing to see if there was another.

Calvin reached up to tousle her forelock. "She likes you."

"You mean she likes treats."

He laughed. "She likes people who give her treats, so just take the damn compliment."

Greta brushed up against Ben's leg, whimpering as she nosed his hand. He reached down and scratched behind her ears. "I think she's hungry, too."

Calvin waved him toward the cabin. "She's a dog. They're always hungry."

True enough, but Ben was glad they were heading inside. The mosquitoes were starting to get thick.

Back in the kitchen, Calvin grabbed some dog food and a bowl from the cabinet while Ben went to the sink and washed his hands. Greta's tail thumped expectantly against Ben's legs as

Calvin filled her dish. While she ate, Calvin moved into the living room, sitting down comfortably on the sofa.

Ben took up residence in the armchair across from him. "So did you get Greta from some sort of inmate-canine rehabilitation program?"

"No. A few weeks after I got out, Tracy's best friend Rebecca was having problems with her soon-to-be ex-boyfriend sneaking around. Staying out late, not telling her who he was texting, that kind of crap. She asked me to help her find out if he was cheating on her again or not so—"

"Wait, again?"

"Yeah. Rebecca's plenty smart, but for some reason she can't make good choices when it comes to men," he explained. "Anyway, long story short, we followed him and found out he was looking to get into dogfighting. The property he'd been sneaking out to already had kennels and a pit set up, and ten or eleven dogs chained up there."

Ben leaned forward and rested his elbows on his legs. "I take it you called the police?"

"No, not right then. Rebecca took photos and videos of everything, including him there with the dogs. He didn't even see us. After we left, I told her to go home and act like everything was fine. That we'd go to the police in the morning."

"And?"

"Later that night I drove back out there to check on the dogs. Somehow all of them had gotten loose and they wandered over to my truck."

"Just wandered on over, huh?"

Calvin offered a sly grin. "Yeah. Not really sure how that happened."

"Ten or fifteen dogs, even if he only paid a couple hundred each…that's well over a thousand dollars' worth of animals," Ben calculated. "From a theft standpoint that's—"

"Felony level. Been there done that, remember?"

"What I was going to say is that's about as respectable as a felony can get."

"Maybe so, but I didn't get credit for it. The next morning, Rebecca called to confront him about it. By the time the police got out there he was trying to get rid of all the evidence like an idiot." Calvin leaned back, putting his hands behind his head. "Such a shame no one believed him when he told them he had no idea what happened to the dogs."

"The look on his face must've been priceless," Ben said. "I would've loved to have been one of the responding officers on that call."

The cheerfulness left Calvin's expression. "Yeah, me too."

"You too?"

Calvin leaned forward, looking at the floor as he continued. "I would've done the police academy. I mean a few years back, I was about to have an opportunity for a career change and…well, you know. If things would've gone differently."

Ben was all too familiar with regret, but seeing it so heavy on Calvin's face was unexpectedly painful. "I know we haven't known each other very long, but from what I've seen, you're kind, observant, and willing to take risks on behalf of others," he said. "Maybe too observant for your own good at times, but—"

"For my own good or yours?"

Ben suppressed a smile. "You would've made a good cop."

Calvin didn't suppress his. "Thanks."

Greta finished her dinner and sauntered over, licking the last of the crumbs off her lips. As Calvin reached out to pet her, Ben got up and walked to the kitchen to grab the glass he'd left on the counter. "So what happened to the dogs?"

"After the dust settled, Rebecca dropped them off at a rescue that specializes in pit bulls. She wore her vet tech uniform and told them they were surrendered by their owner," Calvin said. "She gave Greta to me as a birthday present and a congrats for getting out. Figured I could use a friend."

The house was quiet for a minute, each of them lost in their own thoughts. Greta laid her face on the living room floor and pushed herself along with her hind legs to get the crumbs off her muzzle. Calvin shooed her away before he turned back to Ben. "So while we're busy sharing stories, are you gonna tell me how you managed to escape custody?"

Ben leaned back against the counter and took a sip of his water before answering. "No."

"Why the hell not? You dragged me into this, too."

"Plausible deniability. The less you know the better."

"Is that the only reason?"

Ben steeled his tone. "It's the only one that matters."

The way Calvin's jaw tensed made it clear he didn't agree, but he had the decency not to push it. "In that case, can you at least tell me where we go from here?"

Ben walked over and sat down, bringing his drink along for the ride. "First of all, 'we' aren't going anywhere. I need to see exactly what evidence they have against me so I can figure out a way to prove this was a setup."

"You're going to break into the evidence locker?"

"No, photos and videos are stored digitally. Any computer at the police station will do."

Calvin shot him an incredulous look. "Oh, good. Piece of cake, then. And how do you plan on getting past all the cops on your way in?"

Ben lowered his gaze. "I haven't figured that part out yet."

"We also don't have any wheels unless you wanna show up in the flatbed," Calvin reminded him.

"I picked up the bait car yesterday. Unless they put two and two together, it should still be parked at the AmericInn."

"Won't they be looking to see if you rented a car?"

"It's not a rental. I borrowed it."

Calvin raised an eyebrow. "From who?"

"My brother."

"Your FBI brother let you borrow his personal car for a sting?"

Ben stared into the crystal abyss of his glass. "He's…not exactly aware that I have it."

Calvin let out a low whistle as he stood. "Damn. And here I thought you were keeping me in the dark." At that he walked past him and disappeared wordlessly into the hallway.

Ben turned his attention back to his drink, trying to shove Calvin's disapproving expression into the furthest corner of his mind. For reasons he didn't understand Calvin kept trying to get him to open up, and while Ben felt comfortable enough around him to consider doing so, he knew it'd be to no one's benefit but his own. The last person he'd been that open with was Trisha, and look how that'd turned out.

No. Whether Calvin liked it or not, this was for his own good. Ben wasn't going to let him get caught in the crossfire of his personal problems, and if keeping him in the dark as much as possible was the only way to accomplish that, then so be it.

Light from outside blazed across the walls, prompting Ben to get up and set his glass on the counter. He walked over to the window by the front door and peered through the sheer white curtains.

Headlights.

Ben called toward the back of the house. "Hey, Calvin?"

There was a moment of silence before the bathroom door clicked open. "Yeah?"

"Are you expecting company?"

The way Calvin strode to the window made it clear he wasn't. He parted the curtains and looked outside.

Greta sprung up when the headlights went out, her empty food bowl clattering on the floor as she stepped on it in her haste to get to the door. Ben flinched at the sudden noise and backed away from the window, positioning himself unobtrusively at the entrance to the hallway.

"Looks like it's just Tracy," Calvin said. "Don't worry, you'll be fine."

Ben ran a hand through his hair. He was a wanted fugitive, about to meet someone who may or may not have seen his face on the news or any of the hundred other places they'd probably pasted it, but yeah, don't worry. He'd be fine.

28

CALVIN OPENED THE DOOR for Tracy as she approached and greeted her with a warm smile. "Hey. Welcome home."

"Hi!" She gripped him in an exuberant hug that was far stronger than her petite frame suggested. "Wasn't expecting to see you here this late."

Wasn't expecting to see you here this week, Calvin thought. "Yeah, sorry. I would've called, but Greta dropped my phone in her water bowl again and it's still drying out," he said. He hated lying to her so much that he didn't have to fake the apologetic look on his face.

Tracy knelt down, the smooth blonde hair of her ponytail spilling down her back as she rubbed Greta's face lovingly. "Aww, I'm sure she didn't mean it. Did you, sweetie pie…"

While Greta grunted in appreciation, Calvin spared a glance over his shoulder, half expecting Kessler to have vanished into thin air again. Lo and behold there he was, standing with one hand against the wall as if it might provide him with some kind of emotional support.

Tracy followed his gaze, tilting her head with a curious smile when she saw him. She gave one more pat to Greta and stood, her eyes flicking to the shirt Kessler was wearing before she turned back to Calvin. "Who's this?"

"Ah, my friend…"

Shit. What the hell was Kessler's first name?

Calvin faked a cough and gestured to his throat before going to get himself a glass of water from the kitchen sink. As soon as Tracy took her eyes off him, he shot Kessler a glance, hoping to hell he'd get the hint. He did, thank God.

"Ben," he said smoothly, stepping forward to shake her hand. "Nice to meet you."

Calvin took another sip before clearing his throat one last time for show. "And yeah, isn't that my luck. Finally got to invite an old buddy over for a few days and the plumbing folds." He looked over at Kess—Ben, willing him to play along.

Tracy scrunched her face. "That sucks. Did the landlord say how long until it's fixed?"

"He said a couple of days, but you know how he is. Probably be more like a week."

"Well you know you're always welcome here," she said. She set her purse on the counter and went over to the fridge. "You fellas need a drink?"

"I'll take a Bud Light if there's any left," Calvin said.

Ben lifted the glass in his hand. "Water's fine for me."

"If you don't like Budweiser I can see if we have any Coors in the mini fridge," she offered.

"I don't drink," Ben said, a bit too forcefully. At Calvin's glare he softened his tone. "But thanks anyway."

Damn, he hadn't realized the mere mention of alcohol was enough to put Ben on edge. He turned to Tracy with a quick subject change. "They cut your vacation short again?"

"Yep, got called in. The new hire didn't show up for work, April went home sick, a guy got tased, and we had an elopement. Can you believe that?"

"Wow. That sounds like an exciting day," Calvin said. As she dug in the fridge he raised an eyebrow at Ben, mouthing *you got tased?*

He shook his head. *Not me*, he mouthed back.

"And I missed it as usual," she went on, completely oblivious to the silent exchange behind her. "They stuck me on thirds for the rest of the week, too."

"How'd Ellie take it?" he asked as Tracy gave him his beer.

"She was disappointed at first, but since they're going to let Scott fill in for the canoe race, she's still in good spirits."

She plopped down on the couch next to him and cracked open the lemonade she'd selected for herself. If Ben's earlier tone hadn't been enough to make him regret asking for a beer in the first place, the way his expression went almost imperceptibly hard when Calvin opened it certainly was.

Note to self, touchy subject.

Thankfully the conversation quickly went to the summers Tracy and Calvin spent together as kids, and all the mischief that went along with him spending three months with her family up here instead of his family down south. He let her do most of the talking, and by the time she finished the last of her stories Ben had visibly relaxed.

While Tracy and Ben moved on to discussing which parts of Minnesota were the best for sightseeing, Calvin quietly nursed his beer, preoccupied with other thoughts. Ben might not have gotten tased, but whatever he'd done to shake the cops had landed him in the ER for what must've been a sizable cut on his arm. Scaled a fence, maybe? The extent of the staining on the shirt he'd left in the hamper told Calvin it'd bled a decent amount before he'd been seen.

He wondered if Ben would ever share details of his escape or the resulting injury, since he was super eager to discuss both. At least he'd received medical treatment, or Calvin would've insisted he let Tracy take a look at him. And while he didn't look to be in any physical pain, Calvin was more concerned about his mental state than anything else.

It was hard to tell where Ben's head was at. His first instinct when faced with personal questions was to shut down, but if Calvin could get him started he more or less spoke freely, willing to go into detail and give explanations as asked. He seemed to be dealing with a lot of shit right now, and keeping things bottled up was never a good way of handling that. While he had opened up some, Calvin still wondered how many other scars—physical and emotional—Ben was still hiding.

Calvin looked at the two people conversing in front of him, his demeanor lightening as he saw a faint but genuine glimmer in Ben's face. Happiness. Calvin hadn't seen that in him since they'd become reacquainted, making him wonder how long Ben had been hiding behind that expressionless mask. It certainly wasn't something he'd worn five years ago.

"Did you hear about the drive-by shooting last night?" Tracy asked, bringing Calvin's attention to the conversation at hand.

While she'd likely heard about it through the grapevine as he had, Calvin was beyond thankful that she didn't actually watch the news herself. He did his best to feign surprise. "There was a drive-by?"

"Yeah, right out on Lakeshore. Nobody got hurt but they're still looking for the shooter."

He and Ben exchanged a glance.

"Don't worry," she said, misreading the source of concern on Ben's face. "The police department here is excellent. They'll catch the guy for sure."

29

LIKE THE HIKE up here, the reality of meeting Calvin's cousin was far different than Ben's expectations.

For starters, she didn't share his southern accent. He also hadn't expected someone named Tracy to be noticeably younger than himself, but despite her "older" name, the spring in her step made it clear she had the energy of someone half her age. If Calvin hadn't already told him she was a nurse Ben would've bet money she was a fitness instructor of some sort.

Tracy was also open and genuinely kind, something Ben hadn't expected from someone who'd found an unannounced guest in the home she shared with her husband and daughter. She treated him like someone she'd known for years instead of the complete stranger he was.

"So tell me, Ben," Tracy started as she cleared the dishes from the table. "What do you do for a living?"

"I work security at the tech college in Rochester," he said, setting the rest of the empty glasses in the sink. He didn't know how much of his story would end up making the rounds in town, so he opted to leave out his police career. Former career. Years ago he had worked nights as a security guard at RTC to put himself through college, so it wasn't a total lie. Lies were easier to keep straight if they were as close to the truth as possible.

"Oh, that must be interesting."

"It's uneventful most of the time. Other than a few drunk college kids and the occasional instructor who forgets their keys I don't see a lot of action."

Tracy laughed. "You sound just like Calvin when I asked him how his last deployment went."

Deployment, interesting. Calvin hadn't mentioned he'd been in the military. But then again, unlike Calvin, Ben hadn't bothered asking about his past. He'd have to change that.

"It was nothin', really," Calvin said.

She threw a dish towel at him. "Oh, come on. They don't give out silver stars for nothing."

Ben shot Calvin an inquiring look that he quickly dismissed. "No need to bore our guest with a story he's already heard."

"Eh, I'm sure he wouldn't mind hearing it again," Tracy said, plopping herself down comfortably on the sofa in anticipation. "I never do, anyway."

"Doesn't your shift start in half an hour?"

She glanced at the clock on the kitchen wall. "Shoot, you're right. Where are you guys bedding down for the night?"

"He can have the guest room," Calvin said. "I'm fine on the couch."

"Did you give him the grand tour yet?"

Calvin's gaze faltered. "I, uh, hadn't gotten to that quite yet. I mean, I told him where the bathroom was, but—"

"Seriously? You led with that and forgot the rest? What an atrocious host," Tracy chided. "Come on, Ben. I'll show you the room."

Ben smiled at the way she put him in his place. Playful yet firm. And here he'd thought Calvin was the one without a filter.

Tracy led him down the hall to the first door on the right and gestured for him to go in ahead of her. "He calls it a guest room, but he's pretty much the only one who uses it," she said, standing in the doorway as he took in the space.

The knotty pine walls were rustic and tastefully adorned with wildlife décor. Bed with a side table and lamp on the right, gray stone fireplace on the left, and a large window on the far wall that looked out across the river. Mounted above the fireplace was an assortment of shotguns and hunting rifles laid out in an eye-pleasing fashion. Ben walked over to the fireplace, glancing at the guns only briefly before turning his attention to the display underneath them.

There were at least a dozen family photos on the mantle. Tracy and her husband, who was a bit heavier set and looked to be at least fifteen years her senior. His hair and mustache were as gray as the plaid button-up shirt he wore, but his smile radiated energy, as did the photos of him kayaking with friends or bottle-feeding lambs with a group of high school students. Next to that was a photo of two girls in riding helmets. About fourteen, Ben guessed. A dark-haired girl—Ellie, he presumed—with Ember on the right, and a blonde with a palomino on the left. Most likely her best friend.

"You have a beautiful family," he said.

"Thanks. They keep me busy, alright." She repositioned the photo of her and Ellie on a bright yellow go-kart. "How about you? Married, got kids?"

"No, it's just me."

"Any relatives nearby?"

"Only my brother who lives in Minneapolis," he replied. His gaze backtracked to the photo of Scott with the lambs, the dark one in the background striking a chord that prompted him to elaborate. "Growing up I was the black sheep of the family, so I didn't stay in touch with anyone else."

It was the rated-G version, but still far more than he shared with most people.

Tracy lowered her head. "I'm sorry to hear that."

She meant well, but her sympathy reminded Ben why he kept to himself so much in the first place. His problems were his alone, and the worse they got the more strongly he felt that he didn't need to burden anyone else with them.

He skimmed a few more photos before his gaze stopped on the one on the end, a photo of Calvin in orange camo, holding a rifle while kneeling next to a whitetail buck. Ben wasn't a hunter, but he had to admit that the animal had an impressive rack. Calvin had short hair in that photo, unlike the one where he was teaching Ellie archery. "Your cousin's definitely an outdoors kind of guy, isn't he?"

"Cal lives for the outdoors. Hunting, fishing, snowshoeing, you name it."

Ben nodded in agreement as he looked back at the fireplace, making a mental note to use "Cal" when he was around her. He turned his attention to the assortment of firearms mounted on the wall. "Nice collection. Are they yours?"

"My husband's," Tracy said. "And don't worry, they're all unloaded. We keep the ammo in a safe in here."

She walked over to the small closet situated by the door and opened it to show him the contents. A tall cabinet-style gun safe stood on the left while organized groups of bedding, life vests, and outerwear were stacked neatly on the shelves occupying the rest of the space.

"Feel free to help yourself to any of the extra blankets in here if you'd like," Tracy said, grabbing a lightweight one for Calvin before bidding him farewell. "Have a good night, Ben."

"Thanks. Have fun at work."

Halfway out the door, she stopped and turned around. "You know, Cal lost a lot of friends when he went to prison. It's nice to see he still has one."

"He's a good person," Ben said, surprising himself with the certainty of his own words. It was something he wouldn't have said a week ago, but now it wasn't even a question. Guilt panged him at how he'd treated Calvin in the not-so-distant past. He certainly hadn't deserved any of the kindness he'd been offered.

Tracy's mouth tilted up in a sad smile. "I wish the rest of his family saw it that way."

With that she was gone.

He sat on the edge of the bed. It said a lot that Calvin had chosen to live in this area rather than down south where he grew up, where most of his family likely was. How many of them still gave him the time of day? His parents? Siblings, if he had any? Ben looked back at the photos.

At least Tracy and her family did.

30

IT WAS A LARGE RANCH-STYLE HOUSE with a walk-out basement, its khaki exterior every bit as neglected as the aging brown shingles adorning its roof. The trees flanking it were dark and deathly silent, their leafless branches reaching up into the starless night like the gnarled fingers of a witch.

Ben found himself outside, his back toward the dilapidated front door. Every window in the house was pitch black, but the dim yellow glow of a security light on the other side of the yard illuminated the gravel parking area in front of him. That, and the only object within the otherwise desolate space—his first car. It was an old '67 Toronado, its rust-stained white paint a mirror of the hues around it. The driver's door was open and waiting, the dash lights glowing softly while the engine idled. It couldn't have been more than twelve feet away.

If only he could get to it.

Miles wasn't there, and even though he couldn't see his parents he could feel their relentless pull trying to hold him back, keep him from leaving. He needed to get out now while he was still able to. But he'd been here before, and that was easier said than done.

No matter how hard he tried to escape, his movements seemed to be hindered by molasses. His father was like a wraith, barely visible but always a hair's breadth behind and on the verge of grabbing him. If he managed to get into the car, then a hand would clench the door, another reaching in to fight for the keys. Ben felt his anxiety rise as time ran out.

He woke with a start, his heart pounding as he tried to reorient himself in unfamiliar surroundings. Where the hell was he? He sat up and quickly threw off a blanket, wiping the sweat from his forehead as he tried to slow his jagged breathing. A few seconds later he'd calmed down enough to take an objective look around. Rustic décor, fireplace, family photos—

The cabin. Tracy's guest room. That's right.

Ben reached over for the small table lamp and clicked it on, bathing the room in a cozy, subdued glow. Being able to see what was around him gave his imagination less to run away with, helped him ground himself. He ran a hand through his hair, now noticing that said hand was shaking. Fucking nightmares.

He got up and walked over to the window before running a hand along the smooth, cool surface of its knotty pine frame in an attempt to remind his subconscious where he was. Or, more importantly, where he wasn't. He closed his eyes and took a few deep breaths to center himself.

It wasn't the first time he'd had that dream, in one form or another. What frustrated him was even though he hadn't set foot in that place in over two decades, he couldn't shake it. It'd been haunting him a lot more lately, something that always happened when he was under too much stress. His only other recurring dream played out at night, too, but from the inside of the car. Not his, but hers. The double yellow line, the infinite blackness surrounding the highway. The headlights he knew were coming, but couldn't see until the last second. Couldn't stop—

No, he couldn't go there. His father haunting him from the grave was nothing compared to that.

He pushed those thoughts out of his mind and shifted his focus to the glass. The last time he'd looked at his reflection— really *looked* at it—he still had his badge. Still did the right thing. At this point he wasn't sure if the person looking back at him now even knew what the right thing was. Where the line was.

And that person looked far too much like his father.

For as long as Ben could remember, he'd vowed to be nothing like the man. And he wasn't, personality-wise, but right now the windowpane taunted him with the fact that he'd never be able to shake the familial resemblance. Same blue eyes, same near-black hair. His father had always had a mustache and a short military-style haircut, so Ben always made sure he was clean-shaven and kept his hair long enough for the natural curls to show. Miles, on the other hand, had inherited the brown eyes and straight brown hair of their mother. Lucky bastard.

Ben sighed as he thought back to the conversation he'd had with Calvin during the stakeout. If he hadn't talked about his past he probably wouldn't have been thinking about it so much, and could've spared himself the joy of dreaming about it. Idiot move. He should've just lied from the start and said he liked to knit or some shit.

A gentle knock on the door brought Ben's attention to the other side of the room. He cursed himself as he turned, hoping he hadn't yelled in his sleep. "Yeah," he called.

The door cracked open and Calvin leaned in. "You alright?"

"I'm fine," Ben said, to Calvin as much as himself. Over the past year he'd grown tired of that question, but at least the answer came effortlessly.

"Greta seems to think otherwise," Calvin replied as he took a step past the threshold. "She's been staring at your door for the past fifteen minutes."

Of course. Blame the dog. From what Ben could see of Greta through the doorway, her flabby self had become one with the floor, her tongue stuck to the tile like she didn't have a care in the world. The concern on Calvin's face was well masked, but clearly he was the one who thought otherwise.

Ben turned back to the window, focusing past his reflection to the moonlit landscape. Trees past the split-rail fence swayed gently in the wind, the star-studded sky a few shades lighter than the distant bluffs beneath it. It was a beautiful view, really.

A floorboard creaked as Calvin came further into the room, most likely hoping to continue the conversation. The move didn't surprise Ben, but he chose not to acknowledge it. He never did understand why people found silence uncomfortable.

"Bad dream, or see a bear or something out there?" Calvin asked.

Bears, great. Like he needed that thought in his head. "Just a dream," Ben assured. "Like I said, I'm fine. Been dealing with it for a while now."

At that Calvin was quiet, probably assuming he'd dreamt about the accident. Which he did, plenty. Just not tonight.

When Calvin spoke again his voice was soft, mindful. "Have you thought about getting professional help?"

"I can handle it. I don't need help," Ben replied, his voice confident but his thoughts less so. He tried to shake off the self-doubt and changed the subject before Calvin asked any harder questions. "What are you getting out of all this, anyway?"

"Like I said, he screwed over a friend of mine. I want to see him behind bars as much as you do."

Ben laughed quietly. "I doubt that."

"And besides," Calvin went on as he sat down on the bed. "It isn't smart to say 'no' when someone has you at gunpoint."

"I wasn't going to shoot you."

This time it was Calvin who laughed. "And I wasn't about to take that chance. You weren't exactly Mr. Sunshine when you pulled me over."

Yeah, that. Not one of Ben's most stellar moments. He hoped his voice conveyed at least a fraction of the remorse he felt. "I'm sorry, but with you and Dixon both here I thought there might be a connection."

"To be fair, you weren't wrong."

A comfortable silence settled between them. Ben's intuition had served him well, if he could exclude his blatant distrust of Calvin when they'd first run into each other here in Lake City. It was astonishing how quickly Calvin had gone from someone he didn't trust to the only person he could. Ben walked over and sat on the bed next to him. "You realize if they catch us before we catch him, we're both going to prison, right?"

Calvin leaned forward, turning up his palms. "Kinda figured that. But sometimes you gotta do the right thing 'cause it's the right thing to do, consequences be damned."

Consequences be damned. Ben's exact thought when Chief had been reprimanding him for insubordination. Maybe that was why he felt so comfortable around Calvin. Ben had less trust in himself and those around him than Calvin did, but other than that they seemed to be on the same wavelength.

Even so, the more he thought about what Calvin had done to help him, the more it gnawed at Ben's conscience. Forcing his cooperation at gunpoint had been wrong. Asking him for a ride after he'd escaped custody had certainly been questionable. But letting him risk prison over Ben's actions? That was far beyond the definition of unethical. And while he knew he hadn't been making the most ethical of choices lately, at this moment he could see exactly where the line was.

"So far no one knows about your involvement in this," Ben said. "You should walk away while you still can."

Calvin shook his head. "My folks taught me to finish what I start. The military taught me to put others' needs before my own. If someone needs help, I give it. And right now you fit the bill, whether you care to admit it or not."

31

TRACY WAVED as she pulled out of the parking lot of Kelly's Lake House Bar & Grill, taking a left to head down Lakeshore Drive. Ben and Calvin stood next to one of the river-rock pillars at the entrance, and both waved in return as she drove past.

"She actually believed you when you told her your truck wouldn't start?" Ben asked.

"Yeah, why wouldn't she?"

"You're a mechanic. How likely is that?"

"It can happen to anyone," Calvin said. "The only difference is I don't have to pay someone else to fix it."

They cut across the parking lot and over the grass, taking a left on the walking trail to head toward the lighted crosswalk south of Kelly's. Ben glanced up at the building's sign as they went past it. The words *craft beer* printed in red at the top caught his attention. "Did you have to pick a bar?"

"It's the only place close enough," Calvin said. "If I told her we were meeting friends for lunch at Burger King, she would've known I was lying."

The back of Kelly's was situated right up against the lake, and as they walked past Ben did his best to keep his gaze off the riverboat he knew was usually docked there. With its gold-trimmed smokestacks, intricate white hull, and red sternwheel, the *Pearl of the Lake* bore a striking resemblance to the vessel he and his wife had gotten married on.

They crossed Lakeshore, then took the sidewalk and another left into the parking lot of the AmericInn. Ben looked to the southern end of it by the neighboring US Gas, relieved to see his brother's SUV still there.

"Which one is it?" Calvin asked.

"The Range Rover."

Calvin's eyes swept over it as they approached. "Damn. It looks brand new."

"That's because it is," Ben said as he opened the rear door. He lifted his backpack from the floor to the seat and unzipped it to take inventory of its contents, relieved to find everything exactly as he'd left it. He could feel Calvin watching him as he ejected the gun's magazine to check the number of rounds in it.

"Is that your brother's, too?"

Ben palmed the magazine back in before returning the gun to its case. "No, it's mine. He's more of a Sig kind of guy."

He closed the bag and put it back on the floor, then went to the front and opened the center console. He grabbed the keys from it and handed them to Calvin. "You drive. I don't know where this friend of yours lives."

"His name's Mason. And did you think hiding your gun and

keys in plain sight was a smart idea, or did you straight up forget both of 'em?"

"People forget things. It happens," Ben said. "And besides, we wouldn't even be doing this in person if Mason's phone wasn't disconnected."

"Forgetting to pay your phone bill isn't as dire as leaving your gun and keys in a vehicle worth well over a hundred grand, don't you think?"

"Yeah, well, they don't mail out reminders for that."

★   ★   ★

The tint on the rear windows made Ben feel better about being out during daylight hours, but being the passenger still made him anxious. At least the drive wasn't particularly long.

As they approached the outskirts of town, Calvin spoke to him from the front seat. "Just so you know, Mason's a good guy but he's couch-surfing at his stepbrother's right now. The people who hang out there can be…unsavory."

Ben met his eyes in the mirror. "How unsavory, exactly?"

The moment Calvin pulled along the curb to park, Ben got his answer. The drab white house across the street from them looked questionable enough as it was, but the cars around it were the real giveaway. Front and center was a mid-'90s Impala, dark cherry with blacked-out lights and oversized rims. That side of the street was lined with several other equally flamboyant vehicles, minus the beat-up LeSabre at the end of the block. Probably the stash car.

"You know these guys?"

"I know Mason and his stepbrother," Calvin said. "The rest are acquaintances at best."

Even with an ally, Ben hated going into situations like this blind. "Care to tell me what kind of business his stepbrother is into?"

"Officially? Lawn care."

"Lawn care, good one. And unofficially?"

"Dealing. Not sure what, so your guess is as good as mine."

"You didn't ask?"

Calvin laughed. "I didn't wanna know. But someone who forgot he had four grand in cash in the glove box probably didn't work too hard for it."

"Did you—"

"No, I didn't take it. He liked how his car ran after I did the intake, but he appreciated the honesty even more." Calvin shifted into park and turned off the engine. "I don't condone what these people do, but I'd rather be on their good side than their bad."

That wasn't what Ben was going to ask, and even if he was a bit offended at Calvin's assumption, he didn't correct him. He deserved as much.

Calvin nodded at the other vehicles. "Looks like a couple of his lieutenants are here, too."

Lieutenants, shit. That meant Mr. Four Grand was pretty high up the food chain, then. Ben kept his range bag on the floor as he retrieved the gun case from it. "You didn't think to tell me any of this before we left?"

"I bought you a pair of jeans and told you to leave the jacket behind."

"Right, because that's full disclosure."

"I don't need you pulling your judgmental crap on Mason.

Sure he's got a record, but he's been on the straight and narrow ever since he got out, and right now he's the only one who might be able to help us. Don't spook him."

"I'm not going to spook him," Ben said. He tucked the gun into his waistband and draped his shirt over it, hoping the plaid pattern would help keep the weapon as unobtrusive as possible. It didn't help that it was the larger of his two guns, but he wasn't about to go into this unarmed.

When Calvin saw what he was doing, he glanced out the windows. "Is that absolutely necessary?"

Ben slipped a spare magazine into his back pocket. "I won't pull it if it's not."

Calvin's jaw tensed and he unfastened his seat belt. "Oh, and one more thing. Don't mention you're a cop."

Ben glared at him. "I'm not a cop. And also not an idiot."

As soon as they got out, Calvin took off his button-up shirt and threw it onto the passenger seat. Ben had never seen him in only a tank top, and that combined with the necklace definitely gave off ex-con vibes. Not a look he'd seen Calvin sport, but a fitting choice given the circumstances.

They crossed the street and went up the wooden deck stairs. Calvin didn't seem the least bit nervous, but then again he knew these people, and with his record they wouldn't bat an eye at him. Ben knew he had the most to lose if things went south, and made a mental note of possible exits, not pleased with the relatively secluded location of the house.

As Calvin reached for the doorknob, Ben grabbed his hand. "We're just going to waltz in?"

Calvin leaned in, keeping his voice to a whisper. "The only people who'd knock around here are your kind."

Ben let go and followed him inside, knowing this was a bad idea but grudgingly admitting to himself that he didn't have a better one.

From floor to ceiling the rental screamed '70s, the wealth of material goods and electronics a stark contrast to the wood paneling and shag carpet. Talk was lively and overflowing with obscenities as the house's patrons conversed and traded playing cards, most of them sporting street wear and expressions that marked them as someone you wouldn't want to meet in a dark alley. On the sofa lounged a bald tattooed man wearing little more than a robe and gold chains, using the controller in his hand to commandeer some lowrider Cadillac on a towering flat screen flanked by two equally tall speakers. Obviously the boss.

Calvin didn't spare a glance as he walked past everyone and toward the back of the house. "Just here to see Mason."

The few thugs that did look up quickly went back to their activities. Ben took an unobtrusive look around as he followed Calvin, glad he didn't see any familiar faces.

Ben didn't like the inside of the house any more than the location. While the dated interior was certainly hard on the eyes, it was the floor plan that really bothered him. Short of walking backwards and putting his back up against Calvin's, there wasn't a single way he could position himself so there weren't any threats directly behind him. He put additional effort into making sure his discomfort wasn't visible on his face.

A narrow hallway opened up into a large rec room with people on either side playing cards or darts, most of them with a drink or a cigarette in their hands. The only innocuous person in the entire house looked to be the guy at the corner desk who had his back to everyone, his t-shirt and blue jeans setting him apart from the rest of the house's populace far more than his physical distance did. He stroked his chin as he contemplated whatever was on the screen of the laptop in front of him. Calvin patted the man's shoulder to get his attention. "Mason, how's it going?"

Mason glanced over and slid his chair out. "Calvin, hey! What are you—" His smile morphed into a wide-eyed stare when he turned around and locked eyes with Ben, who recognized him at the exact same moment. *Damn it.*

Mason Costello. Wednesday's busted tail light.

Calvin must've seen the recognition on Mason's face, too, and quickly addressed him before he could say anything. "Mason, I'd like you to meet Ben. He's a good friend of mine."

Despite the way Calvin emphasized "friend", Mason got up and stepped back. "*This* guy's a friend of yours?"

Ben tensed as Mason's tone got the attention of the group closest to them, who quieted their conversation to see what was going on. That in turn got the attention of the rest of them. Ben kept his face neutral as he took a careful look along the fringes of the room, the eyes upon him sizing him up like predators before a kill. Fuck, this wasn't good.

"Yeah, he is," Calvin said, his tone as hard as his expression. "From my stint in Fairbault."

As much as Ben didn't want to, he held his position. Pulling his gun right now would be suicide, and he wasn't ready to play that particular card just yet.

One of the larger thugs stood up, his arms so thick he probably couldn't straighten them at his sides if he wanted to. "What's the matter, Mason? You know this dude?"

Despite the looming threat behind him, Calvin kept his eyes on Mason, tilting his head ever so slightly in a warning gesture.

Mason's gaze went from Thug to Ben and back to Calvin. "Um, no, I was mistaken. I mean he looks like someone I met recently, but this guy's way too old."

Thug kept his eyes on Ben and gave him a slow, menacing once-over before he turned to rejoin his card game. The rest of the groups slowly went back to their activities as well. That made Mason's comment the most appreciated insult Ben had ever gotten.

Calvin lowered his voice. "That could've ended bad, so I'll keep this short. I'm here to call in that favor."

"Um, yeah. Whatever you need." Mason's eyes kept shifting between Ben and Calvin. "But first could you, um, you know, take a look at something on my car real quick? Alone?"

Ben had to keep himself from shaking his head. The epitome of subtle, alright.

"We'll be right back," Calvin said, shooting Ben a stern *don't do anything stupid* look. It probably rivaled the expression Miles had made when he'd told Ben not to do anything rash. Did literally no one have faith in his ability to make sane choices?

Calvin followed Mason out of the sliding glass doors leading to the back porch. Ben found a wall to lean against so he could keep an eye on the exits, doing his best to look casual and not attract any attention.

One minute became two before he couldn't take it anymore and went outside. Voices drifted over from in front of the garage so he walked quietly, keeping himself between the side of the building and the project cars parked next to it as he listened.

"No, he's not, and I wouldn't ask if that was the case," Calvin said, obviously trying to calm Mason down. "You're not going to get in trouble—"

"Yes, I will! Look, I don't know where the heck you picked this guy up, but I'm telling you he's a freaking cop!"

Ben stepped out from behind the cars. "Calvin's right, I'm not a cop. Not anymore."

Mason looked around as if he might run, but Calvin put a hand in front of him before he had a chance to. Ben debated mentioning the drive-by to prove his case, but he couldn't decide if that'd make the situation better or worse.

After giving Mason a reassuring glance, Calvin turned his attention back to Ben. "Didn't I tell you to wait inside?"

"What you actually said was you'd be right back."

"And what do you think I meant by that?"

"Two words," Ben said as he lifted the corresponding number of fingers. "Full disclosure."

"I disclose a hell of a lot more than you do, if you wanna start splitting hairs."

"Oh? Did you tell Mason here about your warrant?"

Calvin crossed his arms. "How 'bout I tell him about yours?"

"Go right ahead. It puts yours to shame."

"Maybe if I'd known it was a contest, I would've tried harder."

As they sparred, Mason looked back and forth between them like he was watching a tennis match. "Man. You and Judge Dredd really do know each other, don't you?"

"Shut it," Ben snapped as he redirected his glare.

Mason lifted his hands submissively. "Hey, settle down," he said. As he looked back at Calvin, he lowered his hands. "Purely for the sake of curiosity, what do you two lovebirds want from me?"

"We're not—"

"Do you still work for that cleaning company?" Calvin asked, cutting off Ben as he stepped between him and Mason.

"What do you mean do I still work there? It's only been three weeks."

"You made it three days at the last place."

Mason paused, bobbing his head as he considered Calvin's words. "Well, since you're putting it that way...yes, I still work there."

"Do you work today?"

"Yeah, at four. Why?"

Calvin smiled. "Good. We need you to trade buildings."

32

BEN KEPT HIS HEAD DOWN as he followed Mason through the least-used entrance at the back of the police station, hoping his gray uniform and matching gray baseball cap would be enough to disguise him as a custodian. It wasn't a carbon copy of what Mason had on, but at least the missing three-bubbles logo on Ben's shirt was too small of a detail to be seen on the security cameras. He didn't have to concern himself with how passable the outfit was face to face, since if that scenario came up he'd be kissing his freedom goodbye no matter what he was wearing.

Mason took a cautious peek around the corner before they rounded it, the series of closed doors on either side of the hallway a clear indication that the command staff had left for the day. He parked his bright-yellow cleaning cart in the middle of the hall and angled it to take up as much space as possible. Ben wasn't sure if the cameras here were actively monitored, but at least they were focused on the entrances, lobby, and the suspect processing area. None in the hallway. Which was good, because footage of Mason unlocking one of the offices to let him in would've looked suspicious, since Ben kept the lights off in the room. Almost as suspicious as Mason's next move, which was dumping an entire bottle of cherry soda on the floor between said office and the front of the building.

Quiet sopping commenced in the hallway as Mason started to clean his mess. Or maybe he was spreading it around for fun. Hopefully he'd learned something in the three weeks he'd worked for Scrub-a-Dub, or there'd be a lot of shoes sticking to floors tonight.

Ben turned his attention away from the hallway and to the computer tower below the desk in front of him. He plugged a small flash drive into it, then pressed enter on the keyboard to wake the machine. He leaned over it rather than pulling out the chair to sit, preferring to be on his feet in case he needed to move in a hurry.

As soon as the desktop loaded, he navigated to the Records Management System. There was no way his credentials for RMS would still be good, but thanks to a humble blue sticky note he knew someone's whose were.

His chief's.

The first-initial-last-name format of the username made it easy to get that right, but Ben had to guess on the last character of the password. It'd been either a two or a seven, or a really bad Z. He picked one at random and clicked *Sign In*, red letters popping up as soon as he did.

Your login attempt failed. Please make sure your username and password are correct.

He tried again, going with a seven this time. The circle of dots finished their happy dance, and the homepage came up.

Bingo.

Other than the sopping of Mason's mop, the hallway was still quiet. Good. Ben clicked *All Cases* to bring up the search box, familiar with the menus as his department used the same system. And luckily for him, using the same system also meant he'd be able to see Lake City's cases.

Ben didn't know the court or officer numbers assigned to the case, so he went with the only other option available, not pleased to be searching his name via the *Accused* parameter. At least spotting his case in the list of results was easy since there was only one. #79-CR-21-7731.

Looks like there weren't many criminally inclined Benjamin Kesslers in Minnesota. Wasn't he the odd man out as always. He clicked on the case and selected *More Actions*, followed by *Print Incident*. A PDF file opened in a new tab and he saved it to the flash drive before navigating to the case's evidence tab, clicking each photo and video file individually before selecting *Download*.

The progress bar moved far slower than Ben would've liked, so he double-checked the file sizes of the videos. Four of the five weren't particularly large, but the last one sure was. Great. Either the Sunset Motel used high-definition cameras or the recorder stored videos in unreasonably long chunks. In his experience, it was usually the latter.

From the front of the hallway a male voice carried over, one Ben recognized. "Whoa. What happened here?"

He turned off the monitor, not willing to risk its glow being visible if David came any further down the hall. What the hell was he still doing here?

"Yeah, sorry. Totally my bad," Mason said. "I, um, fumbled it putting the cap back on."

"I see. No Logan today?"

"No, he called in sick. Can I help you with something?"

"I need to sneak by. Think I left my keys in the office."

Damn it, *this* office.

With all the confidence of a wet noodle, Mason tried stalling. "No no, I mean, I'd hate for you to slip. I can let you know when I'm done if you'd—"

"That's alright, I can manage."

Footsteps.

In one seamless move, Ben positioned himself behind the door, his steps silent from years of experience. If there was one skill he'd mastered while living with his father, it was the ability to make himself scarce at a moment's notice.

He stayed motionless as the lights flicked on, keeping his breathing slow and even. Papers shifted on the desk before a frustrated sigh moved across the room. Checking the pockets of his uniforms next, most likely. Items shifted slightly closer to him before the room went silent.

Ben held his breath and listened for movement. Was David looking at the computer? The flash drive was small, but not unnoticeable if he were to glance in that direction. But if he bent down to look for his keys under the desk—

"Hey."

Ben's heart skipped a beat. Was he talking to Mason? No, if he was then Mason would've said something by now. But the door was plenty wide and Ben hadn't made a sound…how could David possibly have noticed him?

It didn't matter now. As long as he stepped out slowly and—

No, he'd made that mistake before. He couldn't move until he was absolutely certain he'd been made.

"Oh, perfect," David said. "I've been looking everywhere for them. I'll be over in a minute."

Footsteps quickly moved past before the lights went out and the door was pulled from in front of him, darkening the room as it closed in its frame. Out in the hallway, David kindly informed Mason that the office doors were to be closed and locked as soon as he was done. Mason spewed out a waterfall of apologies before David's steps faded away toward the front of the building.

Ben leaned his head back against the wall, closing his eyes as he let out a slow breath.

33

THE SOFA FELT A LOT SMALLER with Ben and Calvin squished together on one end of it. Greta had sprawled herself out across the rest, inching closer every time Ben moved to make sure her toes stayed pressed up against his leg. He would've long since relocated to the armchair, but two people certainly couldn't fit on that and Calvin was just as eager to see the evidence as he was. It didn't help that the only computer in the house without a password was the blush-pink netbook from Ellie's room, which also happened to have the world's smallest screen.

Not that Ben was looking at that particular screen right now.

"What are you doing?"

Ben didn't look up. Phone in one hand and a print-out of the police report in the other, he spoke quietly to avoid waking Tracy. "Putting Dixon's number in my phone."

"Dare I ask why?"

Unwilling to use a first name, Ben typed the entry in under the last only. "Because it's one more piece of information I now have on him. You never know when something like that might come in handy."

"You don't even have my number."

Ben slipped the phone into his pocket. "Keep your enemies closer."

Calvin gave him a look but decided to let it go. "Alright, then. What else does the report say?"

"Nothing useful," Ben replied as he skimmed it. "They didn't find any shells in my car, so Dixon's buddy must've cleaned up after himself. Prudent, since they wouldn't have been a match to my gun."

Calvin smiled. "Well, there goes your first shot at a defense."

"Really? I could go to prison for fifteen years or better and you're making puns?"

"I thought…it was…I mean, no."

Ben gave him a stern look before turning his attention back to the paperwork. Dixon's description of him, where the incident occurred, the locations of the vehicles in relation to each other, their speed. Five under according to the report, and Lakeshore Drive only had a limit of thirty to begin with. He glanced back at the video frame paused on the laptop's screen, his car mirror to mirror with Dixon's and the muzzle flash in between them. He shook his head. "Any officer of sound mind would never discharge their weapon from a moving vehicle."

"And the first thing the prosecution is gonna do if you say that is convince the jury you're not of sound mind right now," Calvin said.

"There's nothing wrong with my mental state."

"You might believe that, but twelve of your peers?"

Ben hesitated, unable to miss Calvin's choice of the words. "What do you believe?"

This time Calvin paused, dropping his gaze for a moment before he brushed the hair out of his face. "I see things in you I didn't see five years ago, things that remind me of every single army buddy I've known who was diagnosed with PTSD. You're distant, you startle easy, you don't sleep worth a shit—"

"I don't have PTSD."

"It's an observation, not a judgment."

"Since you're playing devil's advocate, does your 'observation' have a point?"

"If they get someone on the stand, someone who knew you before...what do you think they would say about your mental state since the accident?"

Ben looked away as the full realization of what he'd be up against in court started to set in. The evidence they had, the testimony he'd already given them. He hadn't even considered the angles that seemed to come so easily to Calvin, and the more Ben thought about it, the more he knew he was right. He was fighting a losing battle.

And he was fighting it alone.

Ben tapped his fingers on the sofa. He had better questions to ask, but there was only one he wanted the answer to right now. "You think I tried shooting him, don't you?"

Calvin laced his fingers. "I know you didn't," he said, the expression on his face as soft as the accent tinting his voice. "But the belief of a convicted felon you hardly know isn't enough to get you off the hook."

Ben took a slow breath. "As of right now, that's all I've got."

The room was quiet as Greta sighed and repositioned her feet across his lap again, except this time Ben didn't push her away. Normally he hated being boxed in like this, but for some reason he found her and Calvin's presence comforting right now. He put a hand on the dog's side, focusing on the warmth of her fur as her chest slowly rose and fell.

He turned his attention back to the screen. For a moment it looked like Calvin was about to reach out to him as well, but he redirected his hand to the keyboard and cleared his throat.

"We've seen this clip five times already," Calvin said, his tone more matter-of-fact. "How about we move onto the next and see if we can find something that actually resembles a defense?"

"Alright. You choose."

Calvin started the next video in the folder, which showed the empty but well-lit pumping area at US Gas from a camera mounted near the store's entrance. About thirty seconds in, Ben's car went past on Lakeshore Drive, heading north before taking a left onto Bay View Street and another immediate left to pull into the gas station's lot. It went past the pumps before the brake lights came on and it stopped alongside the road, where it stayed for a little under fifteen minutes before Dixon's car went by. As soon as it did the Charger pulled back onto Lakeshore and out of view to the south like the Audi had. Ben tilted his head.

"What'd you see?" Calvin asked.

"The motel is south of the gas station, so why would you drive past it to use the north entrance unless you wanted to make sure the driver's side would be facing away from the camera?"

"You don't live here, so the prosecution could say you missed the turn."

"It's the next block. Local or not, that's hard to screw up."

"Still thin for a defense," Calvin said, a slight smirk forming. "Is that all you noticed?"

"Why? Did you see something else?"

Calvin moved the video slider back and paused on a frame showing Ben's car stopped at the gas station. He pointed to the Charger's illuminated brake lights. "If you're gonna be sitting somewhere for who-knows-how-long, would you keep your foot on the brake instead of shifting into park?"

"I wouldn't, but what difference does that make?"

Calvin's brows furrowed. "You don't know much about car theft, do you?"

"That wasn't exactly my specialty, no."

"Does your car have keyless entry? The kind of setup where you walk up to the door and it unlocks automatically?"

"Yeah, why?"

"Where do you keep your fob?"

"It stays in my jacket," Ben said. "They didn't get a hold of the keys, though. I'm sure of that."

"Don't need to. Two guys with repeaters can clone the signal if one of 'em stands by the house and the other by the driver's door. Tricks the car into thinking the fob is right next to it and it'll unlock. Once they start it and shift into drive, they don't need the signal anymore and can take off. It's called a relay attack."

Ben stared at him. "Won't the engine kill or something?"

"Only if they shift into park," he explained, pointing to the Charger's brake lights again. "There'd be a warning on the dash about the key no longer being detected, but if they keep it in gear they can drive it as long as they want."

Ben paused, not sure if he should ask, but his curiosity

getting the better of him. "Is that something you know about through…personal experience?"

"I never stole a vehicle if that's what you're asking. But I did accidentally take a customer's Prius for a test drive without the fob once. It works, alright."

"That sounds like a design flaw if there ever was one."

"Would you rather have the engine quit when you're on the interstate and the battery in your fob dies?" Calvin asked.

"Okay, valid point."

Calvin closed the media player to bring them back to the folder. "So is there any footage from the motel?"

"Yeah. Twelve whole hours of it," Ben said. He leaned over to see the files. It was hard to differentiate between the thumbnails, since they were all night shots. "Click on that one."

Calvin opened the video, which, based on the time stamp, started at midnight. It showed the back section of the motel as viewed from a camera near the office. Ben's car was parked in the stall in front of his room and the room's door and window were both visible. The driver's side of his car wasn't visible, but anyone standing next to it would be.

"Skip ahead to a quarter to two," Ben said.

Calvin moved the slider forward. The U-Haul Ben had long forgotten about magically appeared on the screen because of the time skip, bringing back all of the negative emotions he'd felt the morning he'd seen it in person. To add insult to injury, its sizable box completely blocked the camera's view of Ben's room and almost all of the Charger, leaving nothing more than the car's left rear corner visible.

Wasn't that his luck as always.

Before Ben had a chance to rant about it out loud, his car's tail and brake lights came on. A few seconds later it backed out, swinging behind the U-Haul before driving forward toward the left side of the screen and away from the camera. It took a left onto Pepin Street and disappeared behind the other wing of the motel.

"Same thing here." Ben gestured to the roads on the screen as he continued. "Why would you use the exit to the south if you were planning on going north? If they'd left using the main entrance we would've had a perfect shot of the driver. He had to be avoiding the camera."

Calvin snorted. "Too bad the U-Haul wasn't."

"Yeah, if they would've parked it in literally any other stall we would've been able to see everything. I mean isn't that just—"

Ben stared at the U-Haul on the screen as he considered it.

"Just what?" Calvin prompted.

Fucking coincidental. "Go back. I want to see when that thing showed up."

Calvin moved the slider to halfway between the start of the video and where they were now. No U-Haul there, so he inched forward until it came into view. Then he moved the slider back a touch and hit the play button.

There it was, his Charger parked by itself. The entire area was motionless aside from the occasional bug hawking the camera. A few minutes later the U-Haul pulled in, using the main entrance like most people did. Of course that meant the driver's side was out of view of the camera, but there did look to be an occupant on the passenger side.

"Pause it and zoom in on that guy," Ben said.

Calvin paused and adjusted the frame. "You think that might be Andrew?"

"Not sure. The angle isn't good enough and neither is the resolution. For all we know he could be our mystery driver."

"Assuming these people are even involved in the first place," Calvin said. He zoomed back out and pressed play.

The U-Haul went by the camera, its headlights turning off before it made it past the office. After that it pulled into the stall next to Ben's car, its brake lights going out as it was parked.

"Looks like they didn't want to shine my window and draw attention to themselves on the off-chance I was still up."

"Or maybe they didn't want to wake everyone," Calvin said.

Ben threw him a glance. "No one's that considerate."

"That attitude is the kind of thing I was telling you about. Or trying to, at least."

"What the hell does that mean?"

"The way you think. You're always lookin' over your shoulder, suspecting everyone of everything. Even for a cop you're pretty damn distrustful."

"I'm being framed for attempted murder. Wouldn't you be?"

Calvin shrugged. "Probably. But if I had to wager a guess I'd say that overly vigilant tendency of yours started about a year ago, didn't it?"

He looked back at the screen, knowing Calvin was right but not willing to admit it. Miles wasn't half as perceptive, that was for sure. "It's my job to be suspicious, in case you hadn't noticed," Ben said before bringing the conversation back to the task at hand. "And why hasn't anyone gotten out yet?"

They both watched the screen for several more minutes, but nothing changed aside from the bugs.

"They could've gone into the room next to yours," Calvin suggested. "The U-Haul blocks the entire view of that one."

"If that's the case, then they both got out from the driver's side. Do you have any good excuses for that?"

Calvin rubbed his forehead. "I think you're grasping at straws here. None of these things point to foul play."

"Any individual one, no. But collectively?"

"How about we fast forward and see if anything changes?"

Ben nodded, hoping Calvin was wrong and they'd be able to find something he could use for a defense. Twenty minutes of footage rolled by in less than five before they made it to the next part of the video where something happened, the part where Ben's car backed out and left.

Calvin slowed the playback to normal. "I hate to say it, but there's nothing to see."

"Keep it playing," Ben insisted, a new theory forming in his mind. "You said it'd take two people to start my car, but there's no way Dixon left in it. If he had then they would've had to stop and let him out before they got to the gas station, but the time frame was too tight for that."

"Assuming he was even there," Calvin countered. "What if he had two accomplices handle that part for him while he waited in his car somewhere else?"

"Now you sound like the overly suspicious one."

"Alright, then where'd he go? The camera would've seen him if he'd walked anywhere. You really think he's hiding out in front of the U-Haul twiddling his thumbs?"

"The shooting was at two, so that gives him about fifteen minutes to get back to his car and into position," Ben said. "If it were me and I wanted to stay off the radar, I'd wait five or ten minutes after the Charger left before I did, since anyone reviewing the footage would've stopped watching by then."

"That seems a bit far-fetched, don't you—"

"There," Ben said as he pointed to the screen. "Right there."

A man stepped out from in front of the U-Haul and walked briskly alongside the motel, heading north until he disappeared off the right side of the screen. Calvin went back a few frames before pausing it and zooming in. "Damn. I mean this image is hella grainy, but that might be him."

"And his outfit looks similar to what Dixon was wearing in the dash cam footage taken right after the shooting."

"Gray suit?"

"Yeah."

Calvin stroked the stubble on his chin. "We should take this to the police."

"No, not yet," Ben said. "'Might' won't be good enough for a jury. We need to be sure."

"How?"

He pointed to the U-Haul on the screen. "We find out who rented that."

34

THE U-HAUL IN RED WING was about as small as a U-Haul place could get. Rather than having an actual sign, they let their largest rig do the honors, parking it lengthwise in the grass out by the road to alert approaching motorists of the store's presence. There were a few Kubotas parked there as well, but Ben could count the number of moving trucks on one hand. He didn't see the bat-adorned one as they pulled in, but that didn't mean it wasn't parked somewhere out back. Even so, Ben couldn't deny they were here on a gamble.

There wasn't a U-Haul in Lake City, so Dixon would've likely gone to either this one or the one down in Kellogg. Both were about the same distance away, but with Dixon's former addresses being up north, Red Wing seemed like a better candidate. The next closest one was in Rochester, but that was twice as far as Red Wing or Kellogg. They were running out of daylight as it was, so if they struck out here they'd have to wait until tomorrow to check out any of the others.

Ben drove past the tan and green building and parked alongside one of the white panel vans so the Range Rover would be out of view of the building's windows. He killed the engine and checked his watch. "Ten minutes to spare."

"Would've been more if you hadn't been driving like my grandmother the entire way," Calvin said.

"Just because everyone else is doing ten over doesn't mean I'm going to. The last thing we need is to get pulled over." He unbuckled and glanced around before pulling his gun from his waistband and stashing it in the center console. "Stay out of sight and walk the lot, see if you can find the truck. While you do that, I'll go inside and see if Dixon rented anything here."

"What if he used a fake name or something?"

"He wouldn't have expected us to come here, so I doubt he was that careful."

"Would you have been?"

Ben reached into the glove box and grabbed a business card with his brother's name on it. He held it up for Calvin to see. "I will now."

The two of them got out. Ben closed his door and proceeded to walk toward the front entrance, smiling to himself when he saw Calvin setting the passenger door gently against the vehicle's body to avoid making any sound. He was a quick study.

The inside of the building smelled heavily of cardboard, chrome, and tape. Mainly tape. The kid leaning on the counter didn't look up from the pages of his magazine when the door chimed, but he did call over a brief greeting. Well, less of a greeting and more of a reminder.

"We're closing in ten minutes."

Ben walked up to the counter. "Special Agent Kessler, FBI. I won't take up too much of your time."

At that, the kid pulled his eyes away from his magazine, staring at the business card Ben offered as if it might bite him. His hand trembled when he reached out and took it. "Um, how can I help you?"

He was nervous, good. Nervous people made mistakes. Mistakes like not asking to see his badge.

"I'm trying to track down someone who might've rented a moving truck from this location," Ben said. "I need you to pull up your customer database and show me a list of everyone who came in on Saturday or Sunday."

"Uh, yeah, sure. I think I can do that." The kid turned to the computer next to him, wiping the sweat from his hands on his shirt before he reached for the keyboard. "I don't really do this very often so it might take me a minute to figure out how to search it by date."

He glanced at the kid's name tag. TJ didn't come across as particularly skilled behind the counter, but he must've had even less experience dealing with law enforcement. "That's fine, take your time."

Ben's phone vibrated. While TJ was busy with the computer, he discreetly pulled it from his pocket and looked at the screen.

It's here. Only one behind the building.

He sent a quick reply—*get the plate*—before slipping the phone back in his pocket. Several clicks later, TJ gestured him behind the counter. "Okay. I got it."

Ben walked around the stand-alone displays of tape and over to the monitor. The list of names wasn't long, but Andrew Dixon wasn't on it. He read it a second time, ignoring the names and focusing on the addresses instead. Dixon's wasn't there either, but the sole entry with a Wisconsin address stood out.

Ben couldn't help but think of the Lexus he'd seen at the storage units. It had Wisconsin plates. "Do you store a copy of your customers' driver's licenses?" he asked.

"Yes we do."

"Greg Lundsford," Ben said. "Show me his."

A Wisconsin driver's license popped up on the screen. Ben didn't recognize the man's face, but he studied it anyway. Photos on the current Wisconsin driver's license design were black and white, but it wasn't hard to see that Lundsford was Caucasian.

Ben moved on to reading the information next to the photo. Name, address, physical description. Black hair, six-four, a hundred ninety pounds. Ben didn't usually have to look up at people, but this guy had a solid four inches on him. According to the date of birth listed, he had about four years on Calvin.

"Can you print me out a copy of this along with his rental contract?" Ben asked. He hadn't been able to get a glimpse of the Lexus's driver, but if he'd met with Dixon before, maybe Calvin would recognize him.

"Yeah, sure," TJ said, drying his hands again. After he reloaded the paper, the printer did its job and he handed everything to Ben. "Is that all you need?"

Ben flipped to the page with the driver's license, Calvin's earlier question about fake names sticking in his mind. "When a customer presents their driver's license, do you check the security features on it?"

TJ stared at him like a deer stared at Halogen lights. "What security features?"

Well, that answered that. Ben folded the papers and tucked them into his jacket. "Never mind, I'm sure you're eager to lock up. Thanks for your time."

"You're welcome. Have a good night."

Two steps from the counter Ben turned around, pulling his final question last second to catch TJ off-guard. "Oh, one more thing. The truck parked behind the building. When did it come in?"

"Um, the one out back? I think it's been down for repairs."

"How long?" Ben asked.

"I dunno. A week? But, you know, I'm not really sure."

"Would your supervisor know?"

"Uh, maybe? I mean I could call and leave a message, but I don't know how long it'll take for her to get back to me."

Ben's gaze drifted to the business card TJ had set on the counter. He grabbed that and the bright-orange pen lying next to it. "Tell you what," he said, scratching out Miles's phone number and writing his own in the space above it. "I'll be in the area for the next couple of days. When she does get back to you, or if you happen to think of anything else, don't hesitate to call me on my cell."

He gave TJ the card back, which he slipped into his shirt pocket this time. "Yeah, sure. As soon as I hear from her."

"Thanks. Have a great night."

"You, too."

Ben walked out the front door and back to the Range Rover. In the little time he'd been gone, the sky had shifted away from dusk and more toward night. He opened the driver's door and got in, thankful they'd have the cover of darkness for the drive back.

Calvin was waiting for him in the passenger seat. "Well?"

"Are you sure it's the same truck?"

"I'm sure. It has the same picture on the box and the same dent on the rear bumper."

"The kid behind the counter said it's been down for repairs all week."

"A week my ass," Calvin said. "With all of the rain we've had the brake rotors would've been rusty if it'd been sitting that long. It's been there a day or two, max."

"You checked for that?"

"Yeah, who wouldn't?"

Ben bit his tongue, appreciating Calvin's initiative and his knowledge of cars far too much to answer that one honestly. He grabbed the paperwork from his jacket and handed it over to him instead. "See if the license plate it had matches the one on this rental contract."

As Calvin used his phone to cast some light, Ben started the Range Rover and backed out. He drove past the building's now-darkened windows and to the edge of the lot before taking a right to head south.

"Plate's the same," Calvin said. "So it looks like your friend at the counter was lying to you."

"It's hard to say, he was practically shaking in his boots. I don't think he'd ever dealt with law enforcement before."

"You didn't go all 'bad cop' on him or something, did you?"

"No, just introduced myself and gave him a card," Ben said. He gestured to the papers. "There's a photo of a driver's license in there, too. I'm hoping you recognize the guy, because I don't."

Calvin flipped through them until he found the one in question. "Yeah, I've seen him before. Dixon's boss, I think."

"What do you know about him?"

"Not much," Calvin said. "He comes down from Superior every month or so to meet Andrew, but the timing's not right. He was here last week. Until you showed me this, I didn't even know what his name was."

"Last week at the storage units? The guy in the Lexus?"

Calvin lowered the papers to glare at him. "Is that why you were sitting out there?"

"You thought you were the only one following Dixon?"

"At the time, yeah."

"Well congratulations," Ben said. "Someone beat you to it."

"I've been following him a lot longer than you have. Even in prison I made a point of finding out what I could find out."

"And you didn't hear anything about this guy?"

"What can I say? He keeps a tight circle."

Ben took a right onto Highway 58. "Tight or not, if Dixon's in it, that could be all we need to introduce reasonable doubt."

35

CALVIN HAD INSISTED on picking a country station, but Ben wouldn't concede, so they'd decided to compromise and listen to nothing.

The road itself was equally quiet. County 5 Boulevard wasn't the most direct route from Red Wing to Lake City, but it was far less traveled than the main highway. The less likely they were to run into law enforcement, the better. Ben kept a loose grip on the steering wheel, deciding to take advantage of the silence and see if he could scratch an itch about Calvin's past. "Can I ask you something?"

Calvin looked over at him. "If you have to ask me before you ask, it must be a serious question."

Man, he had to point out everything, didn't he? It was like playing chess with words at times. "I wouldn't call it serious," Ben said. "Maybe a bit personal."

"You can always ask. Can't guarantee you'll get an answer, though."

Fair enough, Ben thought. "Back in Minneapolis, you didn't seem interested in discussing your gambling habit."

He kept his eyes on the road while he gave Calvin time to respond. He figured it'd be a touchy subject, but the level of irritation in Calvin's voice was more than he'd expected.

"That ain't a question. And besides, you if anyone know that people don't like talking about their problems."

"You seem more open than most people. When it comes to my problems, at least."

"So you're trying to, what? Get back at me by asking about mine?"

"No, nothing like that. Just curious is all."

Calvin shrugged. "There's nothing to talk about. I got help, I'm over it, and I won't be going back," he said. He paused to look out the window before continuing. "Out of all the things you could ask me, why do you wanna know about that?"

"My father had a gambling problem too, except he spent far more on drinks at the casinos than he ever lost at the tables," Ben explained. "Being close to Treasure Island up there had me wondering if it was the playing itself or the atrocious price for alcohol that put you in the red."

"Little of both, I guess. It adds up quick."

Ben hid a knowing smile. "Yeah, you could say that again."

"So did your father get help?"

He shook his head. "For that you have to admit you have a problem."

As the next side road approached, Ben noticed the glint of a burgundy sedan parked perpendicular to County 5, set back but facing the road. It was exactly the kind of place he would sit late at night if he was looking to pull someone over. He kept the wheel steady and tried not to think of the worse-case scenario. As soon as they were past, he discreetly checked the rear view mirror.

The sedan's headlights came on before it pulled out behind them. His grip tightened on the wheel.

"You alright, Ben?"

He looked in the mirror again. "We might have company."

"That was a cop?"

"I don't know. None of the municipal police in this area use Tauruses, but red isn't exactly a county color. I can't imagine who else would be sitting like that, though. There's nothing out here."

Red and blue lights from behind danced across the Range Rover's interior and Calvin lowered himself in his seat. "Please tell me you weren't speeding."

"Of course not. My best guess is we've got a tail light out or something."

Calvin ran a hand through his hair. "So let me get this straight. Every cop in the state is probably looking for us right now and you didn't think to check the lights before we left?"

"It wasn't exactly my first thought, no."

"Maybe it should've been."

"Listen, he'll have no reason to assume I'm not the registered owner. I'll say I forgot my license and give him the name and date of birth he'll be expecting."

"In that case I sure hope you two look alike."

"Officers don't see a photo when they run someone unless they specifically request it, which they won't unless they have a valid reason to," Ben said. He set his turn signal and pulled onto the shoulder. "As long as we play this cool we'll be fine."

"What makes you think he's not gonna ask for my ID?"

"I don't know if it'll work, but there's something I can try," Ben said. He shifted into park before turning to Calvin. "If this doesn't work and we're both brought in, tell them I forced your help at gunpoint. That'll keep you from being charged with aiding and abetting."

"What? You'll be throwing your life away if they think you did that."

"I did do that, and I already threw my life away," he said, turning his attention to the side mirror. "I'm not letting you go down with me. You've still got a future."

"I like to think we both still have a future."

Ben didn't answer, focusing instead on preparing himself mentally for the idiotic stunt he was about to pull. Calling his idea sketchy would be giving it way too much credit, but it was the only thing he could think of that might be enough of a distraction to keep the officer from noticing he had a passenger. Of course, for it to work, said officer would have to be extremely inexperienced or really, really bad at their job. Maybe for once dumb luck would play in his favor.

When the door of the squad opened, Ben got out as well. He couldn't bring himself to walk directly in front of the Taurus, but he kept his hands visible and in a non-threatening position as he approached.

The officer was in plain clothes, no badge visible and his gun tucked into his waistband. While he'd expected to get a forceful reminder to stay in his vehicle, the man offered him a polite wave instead. Ben stopped in his tracks.

That'd make this guy the most laid-back cop to ever walk the planet.

"Good evening, Sir. I'm Officer Flynn talking to you tonight. Mind telling me where you're headed?"

"Just passing through, Officer. Is there a problem?"

"Do you know why you're being pulled over?"

"I don't, no," Ben said, turning his attention from the officer to the unmarked car behind him. The only equipment it had was an LED light bar suction-cupped to the inside the windshield, something Ben had never seen on a legitimate squad car. He made sure his tone was casual. "What department did you say you worked for, again?"

"The Cascade Police Department."

Of course. Cascade was the nearest town, so naturally that's what he'd say.

Ben pretended to check his pockets. "Great," he muttered. "Forgot my damn wallet again. Sorry about that, but let me grab the registration for you."

"Sure thing."

He gave a quick nod before heading back to the Range Rover, doing his best to walk the entire distance leisurely. As soon as he got in he slammed the driver's door shut and threw it into gear.

"What are you—"

Ben pushed the pedal to the floor and threw both of them back into their seats. After grabbing onto the armrests Calvin raised his voice. "Seriously! That's your idea of playing it cool?"

Ben kept his eyes on the road as they picked up speed. "He's not a real cop."

"Really? 'Cause I didn't hear you calling dispatch to check."

"For one, a real officer would've told me to stay in the car."

"He made a mistake, it happens," Calvin said. "Or maybe he's a bit more laid back than you are."

"For two, he said he works for the Cascade PD."

"So?"

"He doesn't."

"And how can you possibly know that?"

Ben checked the rearview mirror again as headlights gained on them. "Because that's my department."

Bullets ricocheted off of the Range Rover's liftgate before the rear window shattered. Calvin put his hands over his head to shield himself from the flying glass while Ben jerked the wheel, sending the next round of bullets flying past them instead of into them. Running had been his first choice, but fuck this wasn't going to work.

Change of plans.

Ben nudged the steering wheel right and eased off the gas. Calvin looked over his shoulder as the headlights closed in on them. "Why the hell are you slowing down?"

Ben ignored him and kept his focus out the driver's side window. The Taurus was pulling alongside, its passenger window rolled down. As the driver raised his gun, Ben slammed on the brakes. Bullets meant for them pummeled the front of the Range Rover instead, but he kept his eyes on the side of the car as it quickly overtook them. He needed to time this right.

The instant the Taurus's rear wheels cleared his front bumper Ben jerked the steering wheel left and hit the gas.

36

SPARKS FLEW AS THE IMPACT reverberated between the two vehicles. Ben fought the wheel and kept pushing, sending the Taurus sideways in front of them and into a tailspin toward the right shoulder. White smoke from the tires blackened from dirt as the car skidded off the road and down the embankment. Ben had never done a PIT maneuver with his target behind him, but there was a first time for everything.

The Taurus's lights vanished behind them as Ben pushed the Range Rover's speed to the triple digits. He didn't know if he'd completely disabled their assailant or merely slowed him down, but he had no intention of sticking around to find out. It wasn't the route they'd planned on, but Ben decided to take a left onto County 2 Boulevard to lose their tail if he did end up back on the road. The interior was loud thanks to the wind noise from the bullet holes.

Calvin let out a tense breath and relaxed in his seat. "For a second there I thought you were gonna get us killed, but shit, that was some good driving."

"Thanks. I've done it a few times."

The warning chime went off just as Ben saw the wisps of smoke starting to dance along the bottom of the windshield. A red icon and a warning message flashed on the dashboard.

Engine Temperature High.

Calvin looked over at the gauges. "Son of a bitch. Must've hit the radiator."

The wisps intensified until steam poured out from under the hood and obscured Ben's view of the road. He slowed down to compensate. He was no expert when it came to cars, but he knew enough to know they were in trouble. "How long can we drive it like this?"

"Until the engine locks up. Minutes, at most."

"You know the area. What's our best option?" Ben asked. He didn't exactly revel in the idea of hiking their way out, especially in the dark.

"The only thing close is Frontenac Airport."

Ben had never heard of that one, but an airport meant lights, people, and security. "Which way?" he asked.

"See that substation up ahead? Take the next right after it."

Ben followed his instructions and took a right at the first intersection that came into view. After the turn there were two more options, go straight or take a near-immediate left.

"Keep going," Calvin said before Ben had a chance to ask. Trees lined the left side of the road while a cluster of buildings was set back on the right. Past that another road branched off to the right, and Calvin gestured toward it. "Take that one."

Ben turned right. There wasn't a lot of light to begin with, but as the road took its first winding turn, Ben got a better view of the landscape. Crops on the right, solar farm on the left. The road curved right alongside the boundaries of the crop fields, but the solar panels gave way to trees and a scattering of darkened outbuildings past the turn. He didn't know how far this airport was supposed to be but there was no way in hell they were going to make it there.

At the next curve the Range Rover's engine started to knock, the needles on the gauges dropping before the vehicle began to shudder. Gravel ground beneath the wheels as they locked up, throwing Ben and Calvin forward as the vehicle lurched violently to a stop.

Ben wasn't sure if it mattered or not, but he shifted into park and pressed the start/stop button anyway. He turned off the headlights and got out, waving a hand to clear the smoke and smell from his face as he took a look around. A large field to the north, trees to the south and east, and a handful of outbuildings to the west. So, basically, the middle of nowhere.

Fucking perfect.

Calvin got out and came to stand next to him. "Damn. Can't believe we made it."

"What do you mean 'we made it'? There's no airport here."

"That's a plane, isn't it?"

Ben looked where Calvin was pointing. Sure enough, in the shadow of one of the outbuildings, stood a small plane. Long blue-tipped wings ran across the top of its white and blue fuselage, counterbalanced by the pair of large white floats it sat on. It looked like something that belonged on a postcard from Alaska. In another life his wife would have insisted they pose next to it for a photo, but right now the machine didn't do them one iota of good.

He looked around in hopes of finding something that might be able to get them out of there faster than walking, but there was nothing. No car, no worn-out pickup, not even a tractor. Hell, he would've settled for a mule if there'd been one around.

At least their assailant wasn't around, either. That and the relative quiet of the moonlit landscape tempted Ben to feel a hint of security, but he knew better than to fall for it. They'd ditched their tail, but that might not last. Of course the Range Rover had to be smoking up the place like a fucking signal flare.

"You're hesitant to shoot someone, aren't you?" Calvin asked.

"Where did that come from?"

"Back there you could've and it would've been clear-cut self defense, but you didn't."

"There were still other options," Ben said. "If it comes down to it I'll pull the trigger, but that's a last resort. It has to be."

"At the price of your life?"

"Not at the price of yours."

Movement prompted Ben to look over. Headlights were approaching from the same direction they'd come from, going slower than expected given the speed limit of County 2. He couldn't make out the type of vehicle, but the passenger side tail light was out and one headlight looked to be about half as bright as the other. That kind of damage would be consistent for a car that'd gone off the road, but Ben tried not to make assumptions. Not yet. It could easily be some old farm truck and in a few seconds it'd pass by. Calvin was watching it, too.

As the car came within eyeshot of the clearing, its brake lights came on as it slowed down.

Ben cursed under his breath and went back to the Range Rover. He opened the rear door and swiftly grabbed his bag off of the floor before tossing it to Calvin. "Put this on."

He caught it in midair. "Why do I have to carry your crap?"

Ben went to the front and grabbed his gun from the center console, making sure there was a round in the chamber. "There's a Kevlar panel sewn into the lining. If shit hits the fan and you need to run, at least you won't have to worry about getting shot in the back. Or keep it in front of you if you need to hunker down."

"What about you?"

"I'll hold him off," Ben said. "If I…if things go south and I have to use deadly force, you were never here. I'll call it in."

Calvin's jaw tensed. "Maybe I got a better idea."

Ben glanced over to check their assailant's position. Making a right turn off of County 2 like they had. By the time he looked back, Calvin had gone over to the plane and was trying to force open one of the doors. When it didn't budge, he grabbed onto the tip of one of the wings and started to rock the machine like crazy.

Ben watched as the headlights came closer. They didn't have time for this. "What the hell are you doing?"

With one more rigorous yank, the doors popped open and Calvin let go. "Giving us another option."

"We're not taking someone's plane," Ben said. Grand Theft Aero, that'd look great next to all the other charges he'd already accumulated.

Calvin lifted the floor mat before climbing in and turning his attention to the sun visor. As he pulled it down, a small key fell into his lap. "Says the guy who stole his brother's SUV."

"*Borrowed.*"

"Look, we're sitting ducks out here. You don't wanna come, then you got about thirty seconds to come up with something else." The headlights swung onto the stretch along the solar farm. "Make that fifteen."

As Calvin closed his door, Ben jogged to the other side of the plane and climbed in. "Can you even fly this thing?"

"Bet your ass," Calvin replied. The dash lit up as he made quick adjustments to a dizzying array of levers and switches. "My folks own one of the largest independent insurance companies in Tulsa. Made sure each of us kids got our pilot's license." He put one hand on the large red knob to his right while using the other to turn what must've been the ignition on the far left, smiling as the engine roared to life. He raised his voice over the noise. "We learned on a cheap plane like this, but it's all the same when their only goal was impressing the neighbors."

"Since when is there such a thing as a 'cheap' plane?"

Calvin laughed. "You don't know my family."

"Then why are you working some blue-color job in a town of five thousand?"

"'Cause I want to. That's their lifestyle, not mine."

A shot rang out behind them and hit the building to their left. Calvin put his hand on the black knob to his right and pushed it in, the noise from the engine intensifying as the plane lurched forward. He steered onto the grass strip facing north when three more shots came from behind, all misses. It was a bumpy ride, but the jostling ceased as soon as the plane's wheels left the ground.

Ben looked back as everything beneath them shrank into the distance. He couldn't hear anything over the roar of the engine, but he could see the muzzle flashes as their assailant tried and failed to hit his target. Not that Ben was complaining, but it'd been a while since he'd seen someone who was that bad of a shot. Even a small plane was a damn big target.

He straightened in his seat and let out a sigh of relief. For the first time since he'd seen the glint of the Taurus, he felt like he could relax. Of course fate couldn't possibly let that stand for more than two seconds, something Ben realized the moment he saw the look of concern on Calvin's face.

"Shit…"

He leaned over, not sure what Calvin was looking at among the gauges. "You know, pilot is a lot like surgeon as far as careers go. You don't want to hear 'shit' from either one of them."

"Very funny. In that case the good news is you'll live."

"And the bad?"

"Plane's on fumes."

"You didn't think to check the gas gauge before we left?" Ben asked.

Calvin glared at him. "We were a little short on time, in case you hadn't noticed. I had to skip the preflight checks."

"Where's the next airport?"

"Red Wing," Calvin said as he pushed some switches. "We won't make it that far. I'll have to put it down in the river."

Ben stared at him. "You're joking, right?"

37

THE WATER LAPPING at Calvin's ankles was as cold as his parents' criticism.

It'd always been there, to some degree or another. One of the more major rifts came right after high school, when their vision for Calvin's future didn't line up with his own. He knew what he wanted to do with his life, and it didn't involve a desk, a pencil, or a calculator.

His parents disagreed. The insults had come first. *What's the matter? Don't you think you're smart enough?* Then the guilt trips. *After all we've done for you? Why risk your hide for total strangers when the family business needs you right here at home?*

And of course, his parents' ever-sunny prediction of his future if he didn't follow every piece of unsolicited advice they'd ever offered him. *One day you're going to find yourself on the side of the road with nothing more than the shirt on your back.*

Alright, that last one was fitting about now. River instead of road, but close enough.

Calvin trudged out of the water and onto the sand, holding the end of the rope that wasn't tied to the Cessna. Its floats were resting securely on the edge of the beach, but he wanted to moor it anyway. The ebbs and flows of the river could be unpredictable and the plane would be a hazard if it floated into the shipping lane. He slung the rope around the first sufficiently large tree he came across and proceeded to tie it.

"You look like you've done that before," Ben called over from beside the cabin. He'd situated himself on one of the floats and held a hand on the fuselage for support.

"My parents had me slated to be an accountant," Calvin said as he double-checked the knot's tightness. "Even signed me up at one of the most prestigious colleges in the area. Without my input, as always." Satisfied with his work, he turned back to the Cessna. "And when I gave them a firm but gentle 'no', they had the audacity to act surprised."

The water was barely ankle-deep but Ben ducked under the wing strut to avoid it anyway. "Hard to imagine you in a tie."

Calvin laughed. "Yeah, glad I didn't listen. To this day I have yet to run into a scenario where pencil-pushing would've served me better than my military training."

"I don't know about that. Tying a decent knot is a skill you probably would've learned in the office, too."

"The thought of me opening up my closet to some color-coordinated assortment of ties is vomit-worthy."

"Surely you have at least one," Ben said.

"I'll get one when I get married. Until then, my folks can go take a long walk off a short pier."

"That's a bit harsh, don't you think?"

The question almost came across as sincere, but Calvin could tell by Ben's half-veiled smile that he was toying with him. Ben knew what it felt like to be an outsider in his own family, and Calvin appreciated the show of solidarity. They came from similar backgrounds in that respect. "You got a tie?" he asked.

"No. Well, actually, yes," Ben corrected. "I have one for court, but it's a clip-on."

"A clip-on?"

"Yeah. So they can't strangle me with it."

Calvin stared at him.

"What?"

"Nothing. Need help getting off?"

"No, I've got it."

Ben stepped off of the float onto the sand but stumbled on the loose footing. He caught himself, but winced before putting a hand to his side.

"You sure you're alright?"

"Yeah. Just…you know, touchdown was rough."

"You almost nose-dived us when you hit the yoke," Calvin reminded him. "How the hell could you forget to put your seat belt on?"

"I didn't want it on in case the plane went under."

"You didn't trust my flying skills?"

"I didn't trust the machine," Ben countered. "Who uses duct tape on an airplane, anyway?"

"It's speed tape, not duct tape. World of difference and completely safe."

"How was I supposed to know that?"

"Next time ask."

"Heat of the moment. I was thinking about other things."

Calvin was about to point out how that particular mentality had gotten Ben in trouble behind the public works, but thought better of it. He'd been too busy focusing on the landing to even think of making sure Ben was buckled. Dumb on both of their parts.

Ben pulled his phone from his pocket and pressed the home button a few times, but nothing happened. "Looks like my phone didn't survive the landing," he said, tossing it aside.

"Hopefully it at least buffered your impact a little."

Ben glared at him before sitting gingerly in the sand. "It didn't."

"Well, before we hike outta here, let me see if there's anything in the plane we can use."

"What could we possibly need from it? Your phone should be alright."

Calvin waded back over to the Cessna. "A real flashlight'd be nice so I don't have to drain the battery on it."

He pulled himself onto one of the floats and climbed into the cabin. While he did find an ancient flashlight in the luggage compartment behind the rear seat, the batteries were dead. The towel would be useful before he put his boots back on, so he grabbed it. There were also a couple pouches of freeze-dried food in there, but Calvin left them behind. They weren't that destitute yet.

As he turned back toward the cabin door, Calvin looked out the windshield. Ben had found himself a twig and was doodling in a patch of sand he'd smoothed with his hand. Calvin climbed out of the cabin and splashed back to the beach, tilting his head when he got a closer look at it.

Ben's "doodle" was a near-perfect rendition of the Cessna. The proportions, the angles...damn. Everything was spot-on. And he'd done it in minutes. His handwriting wasn't half bad, either, illustrated by the clean yet simple 'sorry' he'd written in the sand next to it. And here Calvin struggled to read his own chicken scratch half the time.

"You draw?" he asked.

Ben's face was expressionless as he looked over his work. "Used to."

He took a few steps closer, only half surprised that Ben didn't see his own talent. "They say artists are torn between the desire to communicate and the desire to hide," Calvin said, repeating what Marissa had told him when he'd caught her sketching at the register on a slow, rainy day at Wise Ace Hardware. He couldn't remember who the actual quote was from, but it certainly rang true for her. As for Ben, it seemed to apply to more than his artistic talent.

"Donald Winnicott," Ben said, studying him curiously. "You know, I never would've guessed you were an artist."

Calvin sat down in the sand next to him. He'd been thinking the same thing. "I'm not. Just know a couple."

Ben and Marissa, so literally two as of now. Well, two and half. Ellie tried but...well, Calvin certainly wasn't in a position to judge.

Water quietly lapped the shore. Calvin dried off his feet and rolled his pants down before putting his boots on, comfortable with the fact that Ben wasn't the type to reply purely for the sake of filling the silence. He'd talk if he had something to say. And as long as Calvin wasn't expressly concerned about Ben's mental state, he was happy to respect that.

Ben's gaze swept casually over the landscape before coming to an abrupt halt at Calvin's side. His previously neutral expression took on a look of concern. "When did that happen?"

"What?"

"That cut on your arm."

Calvin turned over his left arm and exposed a smear of red. "That? It's just a graze. I'll take care of it when we get back."

"That happened in the car?"

"Yeah. Like I said, no big deal. It's hardly even bleeding."

Ben was silent for a minute. "You didn't say anything."

It took all Calvin had not to laugh. "Ain't you one to talk."

A high-pitched jingle brought both of their attention to the sand where Ben's phone was lying. The ringtone sounded normal, but not a single pixel on the screen illuminated. Ben reached over and picked up the device. "What the hell…?"

"Try answering it. If the ringer works, the rest of it might."

"I guess we'll find out," Ben said. He pressed the pitch-black screen twice before holding the phone out in front of himself as he answered. "Kessler."

"Hello, Ben," the caller said, sounding a little confused.

Damn, pretty good for tapping blind. He must use the speakerphone a lot.

Ben's jaw tensed but he kept his voice casual. "Hey."

"Random question," the man went on. His voice was deeper than Ben's, his tone more distinguished. "Why does my phone show your location as smack dab in the middle of the river right now?"

It must be Ben's fed brother, or so Calvin hoped. Otherwise someone had serious boundary issues and no concept of what stalking was.

"I'm out fishing," Ben said, quite smoothly. "Why else?"

"Fishing?"

"Yeah, what's wrong with that? You're the one who said to get a hobby."

"It's almost ten at night for starters," the man said.

"And there's no better time than the present."

Yeah, the rapid-fire way they went back and forth. Definitely brothers.

"How's the manhunt going?" Ben asked.

A pause. "So far it's been less than fruitful. Looks like he might've gotten wind and skipped town."

"That's unfortunate," Ben said. The disappointment in his voice contrasted with the look of relief on his face.

"We'll get him, don't worry."

"You always do. But hey, I need to let you go. Mind if I call you back in the morning?"

"Sure. Take a photo for me. If you catch anything, that is."

"Same to you. Goodnight, Miles."

Miles returned the sentiment, then Ben held down the power button to turn off the device before he put it in his pocket.

"Don't you think it might be a good idea to ask your brother for some help on this one?" Calvin asked.

Ben shook his head. "Miles has his life in order. I have no intention of dragging him into my shit show any more than I already have."

"So you like to struggle?"

"More like I have faith in my abilities."

"In that case you better have some damn good tricks up your sleeve, because your friends are tenacious and we're running out of options."

"Dixon's going to prison if it's the last thing I do. I'll think of something."

Calvin nodded before looking inland. The brown haze of city lights glowed in the distance. "Based on where we took off from, that's Wacouta over there, which means someone might've seen or heard us fly in. We should get moving."

He got up and offered a hand, which Ben surprisingly took. Even with help hauling himself up, he winced noticeably as he stood.

"We'll have Tracy look at you when we get back," Calvin said.

"No need. I'm fine."

"Think it'd kill you to be honest with yourself for once?"

Ben paused. "I'd rather not find out."

Calvin shot him a look, but for the sake of time decided not to get into it further. He wasn't going to waiver on Ben getting checked out, but they didn't need to be arguing about it right now. He grabbed his phone and dialed Tracy.

She picked up on the second ring. "Hello?"

"Hey. Sorry to call you so late."

"Nah, I was just catching up on a few chapters before work. What's going on?"

Lying to her again, Calvin hated that. He tried to focus on what little truth there was in his story as he told it. "We're up here in Wacouta and Ben's rental decided to break down. I was wondering if you could pick us up."

SO FAR ONLY CALVIN had seen his scars, and Ben planned on keeping it that way. At least a minor chest injury combined with his preference for button-up shirts made it an achievable goal. Tracy sat next to him on the sofa, her hands under his open shirt as she pressed gently along his ribs.

"So what exactly happened?" she asked.

The story they'd agreed upon—or the one Calvin had shoehorned, anyway—was so ridiculous Ben didn't have to fake his embarrassment. "While he was taking a look under the hood I dropped the flashlight, and when I tried to reach for it my feet slipped out from under me. Pretty much put all of my weight right on my ribs on the edge of that fender."

"And that's when you felt the pain?"

"Yeah," he said, trying not to grimace at her touch. "Felt like an idiot, too."

Tracy smiled. "Don't beat yourself up about it. It's not the worst I've heard by a long shot." She turned to address Calvin over her shoulder. "You, on the other hand, should've known better than to be poking around next to those cooling fans. 'They can start up whenever they want', you always told me."

Calvin put his hands up, his wound already cleaned and bandaged. "I know, I know. Next time I'll be more careful."

"Or he could try to be more careful in the first place…" she mumbled to Ben.

"Hey, I heard that."

Their banter was playful, and while Ben did his best to sit there and act like everything was fine and dandy, his mind was running at ninety miles an hour. Tracy had agreed that Calvin's wound was minor, but Ben still couldn't get it out of his head. He thought he'd been careful, thought he'd done what he could to keep Calvin out of harm's way, thought he'd made the best possible choices given the circumstances. He'd thought wrong.

And Calvin almost paid the price for it.

During the chase, everything had been so fluid. His vehicle's position relative to the other, the exact aim of the shooter's gun, the precise moments when their assailant pulled the trigger. The smallest change in any of those variables could've led to the bullet that grazed Calvin ending up somewhere else and resulting in a far worse outcome. A direct hit to the arm would've meant a serious risk of bleeding out. If he'd been shot in the chest—

"Does it hurt when you breathe in?" Tracy asked.

Before answering he glanced over to Calvin, who'd planted himself firmly in that armchair like some kind of overprotective mother hen. "No."

Not a whole lot, anyway.

She repositioned her hands. "How about deep breaths?"

He tried taking one, hoping Calvin didn't see his wince as easily as Tracy must've felt it. Again he downplayed his answer. "I can feel that a bit."

The look on her face made it clear she saw right through him. "Of course you really should consider going in for x-rays."

"I would if it wasn't—"

"Out of network. Yeah, yeah." She reached over to grab her stethoscope. "Take a couple more deep breaths for me."

Ben took a breath each time she moved the cold metal disc. The sky-blue color of her scrubs was calming, so he tried to focus his attention on that. He could feel Calvin's piercing gaze from across the room, but he didn't risk looking. He'd probably turn into dust or something if he did.

Tracy slung the stethoscope back around her neck. "Well, it doesn't look like anything's broken, but you definitely bruised them. Wrapping doesn't help, so my advice for you is to rest, use ice to reduce the swelling, and take Tylenol or ibuprofen to help with the pain. Try to breathe normally as much as you can to reduce the risk of getting pneumonia, and if you get a fever make sure to be seen right away."

Ben started to rebutton his shirt. "I will. Thanks."

"Don't mention it," Tracy replied. She grabbed her purse from the floor and stood. "And what kind of rental car did they give you?"

"A piece of shit, apparently."

Calvin walked her to the door. "Thanks again, Trace."

"Anytime. See you guys tomorrow."

Greta watched with sorrowful eyes as Tracy walked out and the door clicked shut. She stared at the knob for a minute before moping over to Calvin, nosing his hand to solicit affection. He gave her ears a thorough rub before turning to Ben. "Let's get some sleep. We can think about our next steps in the morning."

Ben stood to give him the sofa. "You go ahead. Think I'll stay up for a bit."

"What's the matter? Too riled up to sleep?"

"I…yeah, I guess."

Calvin studied him for a moment. "That's not what you were gonna say."

"And how would you know that?"

"Because if it was, you wouldn't be guessing."

He grabbed his jacket from the end of the sofa and slung it back on. "You don't miss much, do you?"

"Not really. So might as well spill it."

Ben didn't answer right away, taking as much extra time as he reasonably could to straighten his jacket as he debated with himself. It was late, he was tired, and when it came right down to it he didn't feel like engaging in a battle of wits to hide his true thoughts. He gestured to the bandage on Calvin's arm. "I'm sorry."

"For what? It's not your fault we ran into another one of Andrew's friends."

Ben clenched his fists. He couldn't help it. Over the past year he'd had to listen to the "not your fault" crap more times than he could count, and he wasn't about to listen to it again. "If you're saying that to be nice, I don't need to hear it. You know as well as I do that none of this would've happened if it wasn't for me."

"You can't go around blaming yourself for every bad thing that happens to everyone," Calvin snapped. "I didn't go into this blind. I knew there'd be risks."

"You had no way of knowing you'd get shot—"

"It was a *graze*. I didn't get shot."

Ben pursed his lips. "Then your definition of 'shot' is quite a bit different than mine."

"Different or not, you didn't force me to be there."

"Right. Just like I didn't force Trisha to drive."

"That wasn't your fault, either."

"Really? Because it seems like the only common denominator in both of those scenarios is me."

Calvin opened his mouth to shoot off another reply but stopped short, running a hand through his hair and taking a deep breath instead. A minute of silence passed before he spoke, his tone once again calm. "I can't tell you what to think, I certainly won't tell you how to feel, and I don't need to tell you how messed up this whole thing with Andrew is. But from what I can see, if you want to accomplish anything you're gonna have to reconsider this whole go-it-alone strategy of yours."

Ben didn't answer. He knew Calvin was right. Well, partially right. He didn't need to reconsider his "go-it-alone" strategy, he needed to reinstate it.

There wasn't anything he could do to change what happened to Trisha. He knew that. He knew it and he hated himself for it. But right now, he still had the opportunity to make a different choice. A better one. He'd let Calvin stay involved up to this point, but it was time to draw the line.

"I don't need help," Ben said. "From you or anyone."

Calvin's jaw tensed. "That didn't seem to be the case when you ran into Andrew."

There it was, that brutal honesty again. Ben didn't bother filtering his answer this time, spewing the first thought that came to mind. "That wasn't your fight, Calvin. You should've stayed out of it."

"And what? Just drove off and let you get killed?"

Ben shifted his gaze to the floor as he contemplated the scenario. He'd deserved as much, that was for sure. Maybe it would've been for the best. Dixon would be spending life behind bars, Calvin wouldn't have gotten roped into some hot mess that didn't have anything to do with him, and some guy in Frontenac would still have his airplane.

"Look," Calvin said, breaking into his thoughts. "I hate to be blunt, but you don't seem to be in the greatest frame of mind right about now."

"I'm fine."

Calvin locked eyes with him defiantly. "You've been saying that a lot lately."

Ben stared him down for a minute before getting up and walking wordlessly to the kitchen, not even bothering to ask as he grabbed the keys for Calvin's truck off the counter. He shot him an ice-cold glare, the one he reserved for unruly suspects when he truly wasn't in the mood for their shit. "I'll be back in a little while."

The look was enough to persuade Calvin to keep his distance. "Where are you going?"

"I need some air," Ben said. "And time to think."

39

BEN DIDN'T KNOW WHERE he was going, and he didn't really care. Anywhere to put some distance between himself and his problems. He did know he shouldn't be going as fast as he was on a gravel road like this, given the number of deer hits lately, but he didn't slow down. As the truck's rear end started to slide from the lack of traction, he shifted into four-wheel drive.

The radio had kept cutting out from poor reception, so he'd turned it off. He made one random turn after the other, mazing his way through unfamiliar back roads as he looked for a secluded spot to park. Houses had long since given way to farms, each more derelict than the last until there was nothing left but his thoughts and the skeletal remnants of long-forgotten equipment that had been left to rot away in exile. Nightmarish, but he could handle that. His thoughts? He wasn't so sure about those.

After two more turns through the pitch-black landscape, Ben pulled to the far edge of what looked like an abandoned field. He switched off the ignition and headlights, becoming one with the deathly silence around him as he closed his eyes to contemplate his predicament.

Dixon was still running free, and his brother would be back in a day or two at most. He needed a plan and he was running out of time to come up with one. While he didn't have a lot of resources to work with, there had to be *something*. Some angle he was missing, some weakness he could exploit. Get one person arrested, that's all he was trying to do. But in the process of failing to accomplish his goal, he'd lost his badge, wrecked his brother's car, and made himself a wanted fugitive.

How the hell did he manage to screw things up this bad?

Ben ran a hand down his face, trying to snap himself out of it. Dwelling on his mistakes wasn't going to solve anything. He grabbed his phone out of his pocket and held down the power button until it vibrated, looking out the window as he gave the device a minute to boot up.

He'd never been as interested in technology as Miles had, but he was glad his brother had insisted on showing him how to use the phone's voice control feature. At the time he'd thought of it as nothing more than a gimmick, but right now it was the only thing that made it possible for Ben to see if his lead from U-Haul might've panned out.

Before he had a chance to press the home button again the phone rang, not a single pixel of light emanating from the screen. Ben stared at it, not sure why being unable to see who was calling made him hesitant to answer. He'd grown up with a landline and without caller ID, after all, so picking up the corded device that hung on the kitchen wall had always been like playing a real-life version of Guess Who.

The phone rang a second time.

At least he didn't have to worry about it being his brother. Which was good, because Miles would rain down all kinds of holy hell as soon as he found out what was going on. Not that the FBI would swoop in and take over the case from the local police. No, they'd pool their resources, which meant Ben would have twice as many badges to avoid. Twice as many badges, and one fed who knew him better than anyone.

As his phone rang a third time, Ben swiped the bottom of the screen to accept the call, seriously hoping it was the kid from U-Haul. He wasn't in the mood to listen to Calvin interrogate him about whether or not he was alright. "Hello?"

"Hey," Miles said. "Surprised you're still up."

Ben cursed himself. He'd jinxed it. Maybe if his brother laid off the coffee once in a while, he wouldn't be up every Godforsaken hour of the night. "I was about to turn in, actually."

"How'd the fishing go?"

"Not great. I didn't catch anything."

"Understandable, since your mind is on other things," Miles replied, a sudden edge to his tone. "Like that arrest warrant you conveniently forgot to mention."

Ben tapped his fingers on the seat. Fuck. "I..."

"You really thought I wouldn't find out?"

Of course he would, Ben hadn't doubted that. His only hope was that it wouldn't be before Dixon was in handcuffs. "Listen, I know how bad this looks, but I didn't try to kill anyone."

"You of all people know how this works. If that's the case, then let the courts handle this."

"If that's the case? You don't believe me, do you?"

The silence on the other end of the line gave Ben his answer.

He rubbed his eyes. He knew Miles would be upset when he found out, but the doubt of his innocence felt like a slap in the face. At the same time Ben couldn't blame him. The evidence they had against him was damning, and if Miles was calling, he'd already seen it. Running never helped anyone come across as innocent, either. Calvin could attest to that.

"You need to turn yourself in," Miles pressed.

Ben sighed. His brother was right. A decent person would turn themselves in, put their faith in the system. But he wanted to finish this. *Needed* to finish it.

If that meant he wasn't a decent person, then so be it. "I can't do that."

"You can't do that?" Miles echoed, bringing his volume up at least three notches. "What the hell are you thinking?"

Well, among other things, about how exponentially fucked he was. Again. It was shocking that no matter how bad things got, fate always managed to find yet another fun and exciting way to make it worse. He was getting damn tired of it. Maybe next time, it could spare him the torment and choose something quick and painless instead. Do everyone a favor.

Miles's tone shifted from incredulous to enraged when no reply was forthcoming. "You know what, I should've expected as much. Blatant disregard for the law, not taking responsibility for your actions, only looking out for yourself. Sound familiar?"

Ben winced. "Look, I'm—"

"And the worst part of it all? You don't even need a drink in your hand to pull it off."

"Miles, stop."

"No! Maybe you need to hear this," Miles hissed. "Maybe if you took a second to think about what you're doing—"

"Can you let me—"

"—you'd come to the same realization everyone else has. That you're no fucking better than your goddamn father!"

Silence followed the outburst, but his brother's piercing words kept playing like a broken record. It could've been seconds or even minutes before an apologetic voice on the other end of the line forced his thoughts back to the present.

"Listen, Ben. I didn't mean—"

He hung up the phone and flung it across the cab as if it had burned him.

40

MILES KEPT ONE HAND on top of the steering wheel as the speedometer crept toward ninety. He'd left Duluth immediately after talking to Ben, but that was an hour ago and it'd be at least another two before he got to Lake City. A couple of deputies had already searched the area where Ben's phone was last pinged, but he was long gone. What the hell was he doing out in the middle of nowhere, anyway? At least the property owner had called the police and given them the license plate and a description of the vehicle Ben was driving, which already had a BOLO out on it.

He hit redial and put the phone to his ear. It was probably the tenth time he'd tried calling back, and even though he knew it'd be in vain, he had to do something.

Straight to voicemail.

Miles threw the phone over to the passenger seat and cursed himself. He should've kept it civil, kept his brother talking. God damn it. He'd always envied how easily Ben could keep his emotions under control. Even in the most stressful situations, Ben kept his shit together in a way Miles barely managed to on a good day, which today certainly wasn't. He was overworked, stressed out to his wits end, and going on almost thirty-six hours without sleep. Still, he could've at least *tried* to hold it together. A fucking jalapeño could've done a better job keeping its cool.

Thanks for the temper, Dad.

And now Ben was in the wind. With his Charger impounded, Miles hadn't expected him to have a vehicle, and him having one meant they were going to have to search a far larger area. Just what he needed. But on the other hand, having the license plate meant they had something to go on. Still, Miles couldn't figure out how any of this was fitting together.

The Ford his brother was driving happened to be registered to Calvin Haggerty, the man who'd been the subject of Ben's ticket-less traffic stop. What was his involvement? The property owner had said there was only one person in the vehicle when it left, but Haggerty had to be helping him, as it didn't seem likely that by pure random chance Ben had stolen a vehicle belonging to someone he'd pulled over barely a week ago. But to be fair, Ben certainly did pull over a lot of people.

Looking back at it now, Miles wondered if his brother had been keeping busy to keep himself sane. While Ben had always taken satisfaction in his work it had never been to the point of obsession. Not until recently. But that wasn't the only thing that had changed.

After the accident, Ben had grown distant. He spent less time talking and more time thinking, something Miles felt hadn't been good for him. He gave up his hobbies, even the ones he hadn't shared with Patricia, and while he still went to the shooting range and the gym, Miles wasn't sure if that was because he enjoyed going or he was merely keeping his skills up for work. He couldn't remember the last time he'd seen Ben smile.

Other than giving a statement for the police report, Ben hadn't talked about the accident with anyone, not even him. Just flat out wouldn't. His brother wasn't the type to back down when he thought he was right, and the harder Miles had pushed him to talk to someone—*anyone*—about what he was going through, the more Ben had dug his heels in and refused. While he'd seemed to be doing better the past few months, Miles started to think he'd misread the situation. He could've simply been putting on a better facade to get Miles to back off, which he had.

Based on the footage of Ben trying to shoot someone that'd been the wrong call.

The shrill ring of Miles's phone startled him. He snatched it off the seat and looked at the screen, his frown deepening when he saw the name of his secretary and not his brother. He didn't bother attempting a pleasant voice as he answered. "What is it this time?"

"Agent Kessler, I have a call waiting for you."

Her cheerful tone shortened his already non-existent fuse. Next time they scheduled him for a week-long operation he was going to insist the office staff sit it out. "I already told you I'm not taking any calls, Gloria. Have them leave a message."

"I'm sorry, but he insists. Says it's about your brother."

He hesitated a moment. "Put him through."

A few seconds passed until Miles heard a soft beep indicating the call was connected. "Agent Kessler," he said. "With whom am I speaking?"

An agitated male voice came over the line. "You know, for a big-wig FBI guy, I still would've thought you'd answer your own damn phone."

"Calvin Haggerty, I take it."

"Cut the crap, Miles," he said. "Ben's drunk off his ass, and in all honesty, is probably gonna kill someone."

"What? No. He doesn't drink," Miles asserted. Ben had never touched alcohol, not once. It was part of the reason his circle of friends had always been small, especially in his younger years.

The reception wasn't great, but the contempt in Haggerty's voice came through clear as a bell. "Oh, yeah? Why don't you tell that to my black eye. He showed up plastered and got in my face, took the keys for my truck and smashed my phone before he left. Said he'd shoot me if I tried to follow him."

Miles took a slow breath. That sounded a lot like something their father would've done. And if Ben had already tried shooting someone, Miles couldn't put anything else past him right now, especially after what he'd said to him on the phone. "Did you call the police?"

"He doesn't need the police. He needs someone he knows to call him and talk him down."

Miles debated telling Haggerty about Ben's warrant and their phone conversation, but thought better of it. He couldn't risk giving away any information until he found out how involved Haggerty was in all of this. If he was trying to protect Ben, then he might clam up if he found out Miles fully intended to have him taken into custody. "Did he say where he was going?"

"Yeah, Larson's Point," Haggerty replied. He left his answer hanging in the air like it was supposed to mean something to him.

"I'm not familiar with that location," Miles said. "Can you elaborate?"

"It's an overlook a few miles south of Lake City, three turns off of County 4. The road going up there is treacherous as hell at night. He'll be lucky if he even makes it to the top. If he does, it's a three-hundred-foot drop straight down from the edge of the bluff."

Miles tightened his grip on the wheel. Drunk, and in his current frame of mind…that sounded like the absolute last place Ben should be right now. The three-hundred-foot drop wouldn't even matter if he hit someone head-on driving out there. "When did he leave?"

"At least an hour ago," Haggerty said. "I had to fucking walk to town to borrow a phone. He's completely unstable, you gotta get a hold of him before he does something stupid."

41

BEN SAT WITH ONE LEG over the stone barrier and looked out at the river, the can of beer chilling his hand like the others had. He had to admit, Calvin hadn't been lying when he'd said the view from Larson's Point was downright nice.

Far below him, Highway 61 was quiet, the railroad tracks its unwavering companion. The moon's glow traced the edges of the clouds while the river glittered underneath. All of it so beautiful, yet so out of reach. As the bats flitted their way through the night sky, he couldn't help but wish he could fly, too. A childhood dream he'd never accomplished.

He lowered his gaze. Even the decrepit barrier had taken on a romantic quality. It was interesting how moonlight did that, how it made everything seem more alluring.

The gun lying next to him was no exception.

A dot of light caught his attention. On the other side of the river, headlights glided north across the landscape, following the contours of the Wisconsin shoreline. Highway 35. The section he'd often driven as a teen was much farther south, but it brought him back to that part of his life all the same. Nothing but his car, the darkness, and the distant dream of being somewhere else. Leaving the past behind him.

And now, like then, he was stuck with the reality surrounding him. This one darker, literally and figuratively. The overlook's mediocre security light was too dim to illuminate the barrier he sat on. His problems had compounded to the point of being inescapable.

The wind whipped his jacket, casting a sinister howl as it snaked through the trees. Some of them creaked under the stress. The sound reminded him of the dream he'd had the night before, so similar yet so different. A different place, a different car. But this time there was no one here to keep him from leaving.

And this time, he didn't want to.

The headlights across the river disappeared, leaving nothing but an empty landscape. It darkened when the occasional wisp of a cloud drifted in front of the moon and lightened again once it passed. It probably would've been even more picturesque under different circumstances. Better ones. Story of his life as of late.

He looked to the north end of the overlook. Calvin's pickup sat at a haphazard angle in the grass, brush sticking out from the front bumper and mud caking the tires. Nothing like the pristine condition its owner kept it in. The road up here barely deserved the title and had left little margin for error. Hopefully those scratches would buff out.

The ones on the Chevelle sure hadn't. His father's Chevelle. Miles was barely thirteen when he'd decided to take it without permission. His first mistake. His second was not realizing what gear he was in and plowing its rear end into the corner of the wooden deck stairs it'd been parked in front of. To this day Ben still couldn't fathom what his brother had been thinking, but he was just grateful he'd gotten home before their father had.

Ben took the blame for that one. Had insisted on taking it. That'd led to an especially bad night for him and his car, but the Toronado had fared better. Just a baseball bat to the windshield.

What Miles said to him tonight had felt like a baseball bat to the midsection.

The wind picked up again, reminding him of its presence. Shadows in the woods moved as if the darkness itself was an entity watching, trying to spook him. He stared right back as he contemplated whether or not ghosts were real.

He hoped so. There were a lot of people he'd like to haunt.

Ben poured what was left of his beer over the abyss before crumpling the can and tossing it aside. He grabbed his phone out of his pocket and powered it on. It wouldn't surprise him if Miles had something set up to alert him it was trackable again, but that didn't matter now. He pressed the home button to activate voice control, and after a few seconds a tone indicated the device was listening. "Call Dixon," he said.

A computerized voice echoed his command. *"Calling Dixon mobile…"*

It rang five times before there was an answer. "Who is this?"

"Hey, Rudie," Ben slurred. He continued without waiting for a reply. "So I was thinking, how about we stop playing cat and mouse and settle this like men."

"You haven't answered my question," Dixon said. "Who the hell is this and how did you get this number?"

"Who the hell d'ya think it is? Oh, and next time you wanna borrow my fucking Charger, maybe you should knock on the door and ask. Save us both the hassle."

A pause. "Kessler."

"No shit, Sherlock. An' like I said, I wanna settle this. Right here, right now."

He could almost hear the smile on the other end of the line when Dixon replied. "I'm listening."

"Good, good. Right now I'm up here at, uh…hold on, wha's that damn sign say again…" Ben swung his leg over the wall and got up, taking a few steps to the plaque before running his fingers across the cold metal lettering. "Larson's Point, tha's right. Come meet me if you have the balls."

42

BEN TUCKED THE PHONE into his shirt pocket when he saw headlights nearing the top of the road. Once the car crested it he had to put a hand up to shield his eyes, the sting of the light even harsher thanks to the angle. Instead of pulling into the parking area, the Audi came to a stop lengthwise to block the narrow exit. As it did so, its high beams illuminated the side of Calvin's pickup, which looked far worse under the scrutiny of artificial lights.

Damn, no wonder bars were so poorly lit. And here Ben had always assumed they were simply being cheap.

The car's headlights went out and the driver's door opened. Ben swung his leg over to the terrestrial side of the abyss, keeping a hand on the wall to steady himself as he stood. With only one hand free, he opted to ditch his empty beer in favor of his gun.

He debated if he should stumble his way over there or wait

for Dixon to come to him. With nothing more than a plaque and security light to support himself on, he decided on the latter. "Well, well. Andrew Dixon in the flesh," Ben called over. "Didn't think you were gonna come."

Dixon's smile was as smooth as his stride. "I couldn't possibly stand you up. Not with an opportunity like this, anyway."

Behind Dixon, the Audi's doors opened in sync. Ben watched three figures get out, but his eyes hadn't fully readjusted to the darkness yet. "You brought an audience?"

Dixon shrugged, not quite managing to keep the smirk off of his face. "You didn't say to come alone."

"Damn it, I *knew* I was forgetting something. Oh, well. They can watch me kick your ass, then."

The three members of the audience stayed next to the car and out of the security light's limited range, but Ben didn't care about their identities. The only person he was interested in at this moment was standing right in front of him.

Dixon looked at the gun in Ben's hand. "So, Kessler. How do you want to do this? Quick-draw like the Wild West?"

"No, no. Like I said, jus' you and me. Let's keep our guns and our...friends out of it," Ben said as he gestured toward the Audi. "Unless you don't think you can take me by yourself."

The threesome next to the car exchanged subtle glances and not-so-subtle smirks before Dixon turned to address them. "You heard the man."

Still not satisfied, Ben gestured to Dixon's side. "You got a gun on you this time?"

Dixon lifted his jacket to reveal a compact silver handgun tucked into his waistband. "I do, but I'm a man of my word. It'll stay right here. Assuming, of course, that you put yours away."

Ben tried slipping his gun into his waistband as well but fumbled it, Dixon and his entire entourage flinching the moment it hit the ground. Thanks to the drop safety, it didn't go off.

"Shit," Ben said. He reached for it but almost fell, barely catching himself on the cold metal base of the security light. He held up a hand. "I'll grab that, just…gimme a minute."

From the fringes of the light Dixon took a step forward, offering his open palms as he smiled harmlessly. "Would you like me to hand it to you?"

"Really, man? That'd be great."

Dixon picked up the gun and immediately trained it on Ben.

"Whoa, hold on! I thought we agreed that the guns were gonna sit this one out."

Dixon shoved the muzzle against his chest to force him back. "Shut up, you fucking idiot."

"Tha's not very nice, you know. Being a poor sport an' you didn't…haven't even lost yet," Ben said. Dixon's face was nothing but menacing, but he kept rambling on anyway. "Your mother forget to teach you manners, or did the best of you run down daddy's leg?"

A knee to the midsection sent Ben to the ground. He took a moment to catch his breath before speaking again. "Like I said, not nice…"

A voice drifted over from the Audi. "Stop messing around and take care of this, Andy. I don't have all night."

"What are we thinking?" Dixon asked, stepping toward the fringes of the light. "Off the ledge?"

"No. I want it done right this time," the man said. "Use his gun. He's drunk and on the run, guilty for all anyone knows. They'll buy a suicide."

"Who's going to do the honors?"

"We wouldn't be in this mess if it wasn't for your shitty frame-job idea, so I'm thinking you should do it. Besides, if you want to move up in my organization you're going to have to prove you can handle this kind of thing."

Ben kept his eyes on the pavement as he listened to the discussion. He had to keep himself from smiling. Dixon wanted a promotion.

Yeah. Not gonna happen.

A shadow moved into view before he felt Dixon grabbing him by the front of his shirt to stand him up. He was being rougher than necessary thanks to the taunts and the audience, Ben figured, but trying to haul a drunk guy to his feet was like lifting a two-hundred-pound sack of potatoes. Ben had done the same in uniform more times than he cared to count and there was no way around it. It took two hands.

Two hands, which meant neither one had a gun in it.

When they were both upright, Ben braced for the pain and made his move. He did a one-eighty as he grabbed Dixon's arm and flipped him over his shoulder, slamming him flat on his back onto the concrete. Before he could get back on his feet, Ben came up from behind and put one arm around him in a choke hold while using the other to pull his gun from Dixon's waistband. As he stood the two of them up, he pressed the muzzle firmly against the side of Dixon's head. The already-silent landscape around them somehow got quieter as Dixon slowly raised his hands in a gesture of submission.

Ben looked over to the Audi. The three men in front of it had moved closer since he'd last glanced in their direction, and two of them—the two not in a suit and tie—had guns drawn. At least it looked like neither of them were dumb enough to pull the trigger. Or maybe they weren't dumb enough to do it unless their boss told them to. Either way, now he had the upper hand.

"Alright, boys," Ben said, his voice stone-cold sober. "You know the drill. Put your weapons down now."

43

BEN KEPT A TIGHT HOLD on Dixon as the two armed men in front of them slowly knelt down and laid their guns on the pavement. In the end, there was no better advantage than being underestimated.

As soon as he'd seen headlights coming up the road, he'd pressed the power button on his phone repeatedly, using the SOS feature to dial 911. He'd used the speakerphone enough to be able to activate it without seeing the screen, and the moment he'd heard the scripted greeting from dispatch he'd turned the speaker volume all the way down. That combined with the broken display meant Dixon and his buddies had no idea the police had been listening in this entire time on a recorded line.

Now he needed to keep them talking. "You put a lot of thought into framing me, Dixon. I'm flattered. But did you really think you'd get away with it?"

"If this was a sting we'd be in handcuffs already," Dixon spat. "Admit it. You're here alone."

"You're right, I am alone. And I lost my badge thanks to you, which means I don't have to play by quite as many rules as I used to."

"I should've killed you when I had the chance…"

Ben tightened his grip. "Hindsight's a bitch, isn't it?"

The man who hadn't pulled a gun approached, his hands up disarmingly. "Now, now. Let's calm down everyone. I'm sure we can work this out."

As he came closer to the glow of the security light, Ben was able to get a better look at him. He was tall and sharply dressed, his black hair slicked back. A match to the face on the driver's license.

Lundsford.

Ben chose his words carefully. He needed to make sure they spelled everything out for the recording. "So if my buddy Dixon here played the victim, then you must be the one who was driving my car. The shooter, am I right?"

"You're thorough, Kessler, I'll give you that. I'm still a bit disappointed you figured out my latest alias already, though. I really liked that one."

Ben tilted his head. "You seem to know who I am. Care to tell me who you are?"

A train horn from below pierced the air, the bluffs distorting the sound as it echoed between them. Ben flinched and for a split second his attention was elsewhere.

A split second was all Dixon needed.

He elbowed Ben hard in the ribs, the pain so intense he couldn't keep himself from crying out. Dixon struggled to break free and despite Ben's best efforts the pain was too much to work through. He lost his hold. As Dixon got the upper hand he landed another blow to Ben's midsection before forcing the gun out of his hand and throwing him to the ground.

The pavement was cold beneath him as Ben put a hand to his side and breathed through the pain. Footsteps approached as more shadows joined Dixon's on the ground in front of him.

Ben looked up. As the last two of Dixon's buddies came within the small area the security light covered, he was able to see their faces. Flynn the Fake, no surprise there, and…shit, wasn't that his luck. The guy he'd waved to at the marina. That's how they'd gotten his name.

The man whose real name wasn't Lundsford stared down at him with a shark's smile and his hands in his pockets. "So, where were we? Ah, your little joke about not knowing who I am."

Ben pushed himself up to a sitting position. "I know Dixon. I have no idea who you are."

"You've been a thorn in my side for the better part of six months," the man said, his face going from smug to sinister as he took a step closer. "Don't play that game with me, Miles. Can I call you Miles?"

Six months playing cat-and-mouse with his brother, multiple aliases, and a hoard of people strung around the state ready to do his bidding. Suddenly Ben knew who he was dealing with.

"You know, I would've thought the infamous Vince Leighton would be a bit more careful in his business dealings. Writing down all of your crimes in a little black book is a bit old-school, don't you think?"

Leighton smiled as he reached into his back pocket and held up the dossier in question. "Sometimes old-school tactics have their advantages. Notebooks can't be hacked, can they? And as for any pictures you might've taken of it, they're worthless without a warrant." He put the book back in his pocket. "Now, thanks to your little escapade, they won't be finding it unless they find me. So tell me, Miles. How does one of the state's best FBI agents manage to screw that up?"

"You've got the wrong guy, you know that? Miles is at least an hour away right now."

"Oh? So you've been driving his car, handing out his business cards, and introducing yourself as Agent Kessler for shits and giggles?" Leighton grabbed him by the collar of his shirt and threw him back to the ground. "Do you really think I'm that stupid?"

Ben held his side again as he processed Leighton's words. He knew about the business card, which meant TJ must've sold him out. That'd explain why Flynn was waiting for them shortly after their visit to U-Haul. Ben thought back to it. The kid froze when Ben had introduced himself as Agent Kessler and—

Fuck. Suddenly it clicked.

TJ. Thomas Joseph Hoffman. The name Dixon gave when he'd called the police to report the shooting. Ben cursed himself. He should've made the connection earlier.

Another kick brought his attention to the present, this one courtesy of Flynn. "You owe me a car."

Ben took a few seconds to catch his breath. At least having his hand already there had softened the blow a bit. "I'd say we're even," he rasped.

"So," Leighton started. "Now that everyone's had their fun. Any last words, Agent?"

Ben propped himself back up. Since Dixon's crew had the

upper hand they were taking their sweet time, but Ben didn't know how much of it he had left. He needed to tie up the only loose end that mattered to him right now.

For the past year Ben had known Dixon by nothing more than his mug shot. He'd studied him, tracked him, all the while thinking long and hard about what he'd say when he finally met him face to face. All of it revolved around the accident, Dixon's blatant disregard for the lives of others, and the fallout from that. Each sentence tirelessly practiced. Each word carefully chosen.

Ben threw all of it out the window. "You want to know why I'm here? Ask Dixon about that theft he committed at Hansen's Harbor last week."

At his mention, Dixon took a step closer. "Why? Was your shitty boat parked there or something?"

"No, but you screwed over a friend of mine when you did that."

"I did? Oh, good. I hope I left with everything he held dear."

"Is that why you need Leighton to hold your hand? Because all you're good for on your own is a quick smash-and-grab when no one's around?"

"I'll show you what I'm good for…"

Leighton put a hand out to hold him back. "Get it together, Andy. He's trying to stall."

"He's—"

"You can't be losing it in these kinds of situations," Leighton said. "And give me that gun of his before you screw something up again."

Dixon clenched his jaw but handed the weapon over.

"Good boy," Leighton said. "Now, check his phone. See if he contacted anyone."

Ben didn't resist as Dixon searched him. When he found the phone in Ben's shirt pocket he grabbed it and stood.

"Well?"

Dixon messed with the device one more time before tossing it aside. "No. Fucking thing's dead."

Leighton smiled and raised the weapon. "Just like you are, Kessler."

As Ben looked down the barrel of his own gun, he felt an immense weight lifting off his shoulders. He'd accomplished his goal. Dispatch had heard everything, which meant Dixon and his associates would do hard time—if not life—for their actions tonight, and Calvin would get off free and clear.

The rest of the chips could fall wherever the hell they wanted.

44

CALVIN WAS PACING. He'd called Miles and told him exactly what Ben had asked him to, which meant the authorities would be at the overlook any minute. Still, something was gnawing at the back of his mind as he thought about the plan.

It was risky. Clever, but risky. While Calvin had gone on a beer run, Ben had insisted on staying behind to put blanks in his gun as a fail-safe, as part of said plan likely involved Andrew trying to shoot him with his own weapon. While it wasn't a bad excuse, the fact that he'd used one at all bothered Calvin. He'd been able to tell by the tone of Ben's voice that switching out his ammo—which took all of sixty seconds—wasn't the real reason he'd wanted to stay behind. While Calvin hadn't pointed that out, he didn't understand why Ben wasn't being honest with him. He should've known Calvin wouldn't blame him for not wanting to patronize a liquor store.

Even so, the motivation behind Ben's little white lie wasn't something Calvin had to decipher right now. Ben needed to focus on clearing his name and Calvin needed to take a step back so he was able to. Let the dust settle and then he could see where the two of them stood.

They'd timed this carefully. Ben left to stage everything at the overlook and Calvin had given him a one-hour head start before calling Miles. Once Andrew showed up, Ben would only need to stall for a few minutes after the confession before the cops would arrive. How Ben had thought of the fake-drunk ploy was beyond him, but at least he was finally willing to be honest with himself and call in reinforcements. And while Calvin didn't like the plan, it was the only thing that might work. *Might*.

He sat down on the couch next to Greta, hoping that if he stopped walking in circles his thoughts would slow down as well.

And...nope, they didn't.

Maybe what bothered him the most about the plan was the fact that everything was going on over a mile away while he was sitting here at the cabin twiddling his thumbs. Ben had insisted he stay behind, said it'd be better for him if he kept himself away from the police action until everything came to light. Said he'd call once Andrew was in custody.

So far Calvin's phone hadn't made a sound.

God, he wished his truck was here. At least then he could use his scanner to find out what was happening on the police end of things. Or drive to Larson's Point if shit went south. Even if it took three different roads and five miles of backtracking to get there by car, it was a hell of a lot faster than the half hour it took to hike it as the crow flies. But his truck was the only vehicle they had, and Ben had needed it to get himself there.

And despite Calvin's protests about staying behind, Ben had insisted he'd done enough. Said he could easily manage the rest on his own, and having Calvin nearby—despite his promises to stay out of sight—would be a distraction he didn't need. While Calvin had eventually conceded, the more he thought about it, the more he began to doubt Ben's sincerity.

Things weren't adding up.

The overlook was an odd choice for someone who couldn't bring himself to stand within twenty feet of the edge. Why meet Andrew there? Sure it was secluded, but so was every other place on the outskirts of the city. And all of those were a lot easier, and quicker, for the cops to get to.

Then came the plane. Ben hadn't shown the slightest hint of anxiety during that fiasco, even during their near-crash landing. Not exactly the reaction Calvin would've expected from someone who'd said he was afraid of heights, especially considering the diminutive size of the Cessna. But then again, not getting shot was a good motivator for about anything. Catching the guy who killed his wife was probably a better one.

Dixon's going to prison if it's the last thing I do.

What if—

No, there was no way Ben meant that literally. He wouldn't have put blanks in his gun if he had a death wish.

But despite Ben's assurances, he wasn't fine. That much was obvious. What Calvin didn't know was whether or not he was getting worse. Maybe he was in more pain from the landing than he let on, or maybe the stress of everything crashing down was really starting to weigh on him. It seemed like the more help Ben needed the harder he pushed people away, and tonight he'd been particularly combative.

That wasn't your fight, Calvin. You should've stayed out of it.

And what? Just drove off and let you get killed?

At the time Ben's lack of an answer was what Calvin had found most concerning, but thinking back, the expression on his face should've been more so. He'd figured the calculating look was Ben trying to think of some snarky comeback, but that was nothing more than an assumption, one Calvin found himself starting to second guess. When Ben had returned from his solitary cruise, he was calm. Uncharacteristically so, even if you didn't take into account that his prior expression had been a glare that could freeze hell.

Calvin got up. He couldn't sit still any longer. Greta looked at him and then laid her head back on the couch, seemingly relieved that his leg was no longer jiggling it. He grabbed a Coke from the fridge as he tried to think of something he could do to occupy his overactive imagination until Ben called, which would surely be any minute now.

Maybe Tracy's book was around here somewhere. Werewolf mystery romance wasn't his usual genre, but it'd probably be a lot less dry than Ellie's A&P textbook. As he looked around, his eyes inadvertently ran across Ben's backpack, which was still sitting on the kitchen floor where he'd left it.

Slightly unzipped, as if begging him to take a look.

He stared at it, the angel on one shoulder telling him to leave it while the devil on the other promised no harm. It felt wrong to even think about going through Ben's things without asking, but Calvin had never seen blanks before and he couldn't deny he was curious about what they looked like. Were they the same shape as live rounds? Empty like empty shell casings? A strange color? He debated with himself for a minute.

No, it wouldn't hurt to take a quick peek. As long as he put everything back, Ben wouldn't even notice.

He lifted the bag onto the counter, unzipped it, and pulled out an empty gun case and the only two boxes of ammo inside. He set the half-empty box of live ammunition on the counter before turning his attention to the blue one labeled *9mm Luger Blanks*. It was heavier. He opened it and slid out the fifty-round tray inside.

Not a single one was missing.

Fuck.

Calvin sprinted to the guest room and grabbed a rifle off the wall, then turned to the closet and threw open the door. Scott kept his ammo in the safe, and Calvin's fingers hovered over the keypad. He didn't know the code. A lot of the cheaper safes used a four-digit one, but Scott's was a high-end model. It probably took a six-digit code. What would Scott choose? Something easy for him to remember. Something with meaning—

Their anniversary.

He entered the date and the safe clicked open.

★   ★   ★

Ember's hooves thundered through the otherwise silent forest. Calvin kept the reins long, pointing her in the general direction of the overlook but trusting the mare's judgment to choose sound footing. With the glow of the moon, she'd be able to see almost as well now as Calvin could in daylight.

She darted from side to side to avoid the smaller obstacles and picked up speed to leap over the ones that were too sizable to bypass. Calvin held on to a fistful of her mane each time she took flight, keeping his knees tight against her barrel. He'd had to forgo the saddle.

No time.

A distant glow of artificial light came into view between the trees, prompting him to shift his weight back and pull gently on the reins. He slowed Ember to a trot and then a walk, halting her before sliding gracefully off of her back. He patted her sweat-soaked neck, then slung the reins over a nearby branch. She made too much noise to risk taking her any further.

Calvin traversed the landscape quickly but quietly. Once he found an area with a decent line of sight, he hoisted himself up onto the thick branches of a large oak. Halfway up he positioned himself on a particularly wide limb and slung the rifle off his back. Given the angle of the branch, he had to position himself into an awkward half-sitting, half-prone position, using the crook between two smaller branches to support the fore-end of the gun. Uncomfortable as hell, but he'd shot in worse conditions.

The wind started to pick up.

He grabbed a cartridge from his pocket and opened the bolt on the rifle. He'd already loaded all four rounds into the internal magazine before leaving the cabin, and now that he was in position he quickly put a fifth into the chamber. After closing the bolt with the palm of his hand, he took his first look through the scope.

Five people, four of them standing. The overlook's security light didn't cover a wide area to begin with and the scene looked even darker thanks to the magnification from the scope's lenses. Ben was half-laying on the ground, but didn't seem to be injured. Andrew and two other men stood behind the fifth person who looked to be in charge. He seemed to be talking. In an alternate universe Calvin might've taken a hot second to consider the man's identity, but the gun in hand was pointed straight at Ben.

He aimed at the gunman's center mass and set his finger on the trigger, hesitating as he considered whether or not he'd be fast enough to take out the remaining three before any of them could get a shot off at Ben. He hadn't fired a gun in over five years, and aside from that, the man had Ben at point blank. If he missed…

Calvin readjusted his aim, quickly deciding on a better plan. He squinted from the brightness of the overlook's security light, let out a breath, and squeezed the trigger.

45

THE LAST THING BEN SAW before the shot rang out was Leighton's smug smile. After that everything went black.

Time stood still as he took an uncertain breath, not sure why the pain hadn't hit yet. Adrenaline, shock, nerve damage maybe. He'd heard the stories. People walking away from a gunfight and not realizing they'd been shot until a random bystander pointed it out. He hadn't fully believed them until now.

Why couldn't this nightmare end?

Fragments of glass rained down from above, the moonlight glinting off them like tiny shards of ice as they twinkled onto the pavement in front of him. Seeing them—seeing *anything*—felt surreal. Ben reached out and gingerly felt the ground to assure himself they were actually there, quickly pulling his fingertips away from the unexpected sting of their heat. As he looked up at the barely discernible silhouette of the overlook's light fixture, he finally registered where exactly the shot had come from—not the man in front of him, but the woods behind him.

Calvin.

Ben rolled and lashed out with his legs, unable to see but aiming for where Leighton was standing when the overlook had been plunged into darkness. A howl of pain broke the silence as Ben's heels struck what felt like kneecaps.

By the time he heard the thud of someone hitting the ground, Ben was already on his feet. His eyes hadn't fully adjusted to the darkness, but he needed to move and he needed to do it now. At least he knew the immediate area was relatively open. The shouts from Leighton and his crew gave Ben a point of reference to distance himself from, his footsteps silent as he obscured himself into the more forested area of the overlook.

As soon as he'd put some distance between himself and his assailants, Ben positioned himself behind a large tree, leaning his back against its trunk as he tried to calm himself down from the rush of adrenaline. He was shaking. Did Calvin figure out he hadn't put in blanks? He must've or he wouldn't have shot out the light. But how the hell did he get here? The time frame wasn't adding up, but the threat of being hunted down was hampering Ben's thoughts. Four against one and he wasn't even armed.

He took a minute to slow his breathing and think about the situation objectively. How Calvin had gotten here and whatever had prompted him to do so wasn't important right now. What mattered was that he was giving Ben a way out.

If he had any sense of self-preservation left, he'd take it.

46

CALVIN LISTENED FOR FOOTSTEPS, knowing that if he could hear them, they wouldn't be Ben's. The shouts that had erupted from the confusion of darkness had quickly ceased, but he wasn't about to assume anyone was down. He also had no way of knowing whether or not Ben had taken advantage of the opportunity he'd given him and gotten the hell out of Dodge, which sucked ass because taking down a group of hostiles was a hell of a lot easier when you didn't have to worry about a friendly in the mix.

The light of the moon was unreliable thanks to the shifting clouds, but the cover of darkness suited his tactics. He'd left the rifle behind. Four hostiles, close quarters. He wouldn't need it.

Footsteps prompted Calvin to put his knife away and crouch behind the Audi. His soon-to-be victim was moving quickly. Too quickly, based on the sound of ripping vegetation followed by the thud of someone hitting the ground. As he listened to the man get up, Calvin pulled a pair of gloves from his pocket and slipped them on. Black like the rest of his outfit.

The Deserter promptly got in the car and slammed the door shut. Calvin held his position behind the bumper as the engine cranked one, two, three times over without starting. He smiled. Maybe tomorrow somebody would find what was left of that wiring harness in the grass.

The man got out and shut the door, too busy cursing under his breath to notice Calvin come up from behind. In one swift move he slammed the man's head into the side of the car and watched as he crumpled to the ground. He grabbed a couple of heavy-duty zip-ties from his pocket and secured the unconscious man's wrists and ankles before dragging him off to the side and into bushes. Before leaving, he took the gun from the man's waistband and tucked it into his own.

One down, three to go.

"William? Was that you?"

The second man stage-whispered, but making any kind of sound had been a mistake. When no one answered, he raised his voice and tried again.

Silence.

Calvin circled around to the other side of the car and flung a rock into the grass several feet past where Bachelor Number Two was standing. The man immediately whirled around and pointed his gun toward the sound. As Calvin tackled his assailant from behind, the man fired an accidental shot into the air.

With practiced grace he forced the gun out of the man's hand and slung an arm around him in a choke hold, putting pressure on the side of his neck to cut off the blood supply to his brain. In under ten seconds, the man passed out and Calvin immediately released his grip. As he lowered him to the ground, distant shots fired blindly in their direction. Another hostile.

Ben wouldn't be so careless.

Calvin stayed low, securing his victim with another set of zip-ties before turning his attention to the gun on the ground next to him. He ejected the magazine and pulled the slide to expel the round in the chamber before he tossed the gun one in direction and the magazine in the other.

Two down, two to go.

The shooting stopped before a voice carried over. "William? Peter?"

No answer.

Two sets of footsteps approached as Calvin moved the other direction. Their whispers seemed that much louder in the still of the night. "If he walks away from this, we'll all do life. Circle around and find him. I'll check this side."

"On it."

"We know you're here, Kessler," someone called out. "Why don't you make this easy and give yourself up?"

Calvin skirted along the far side of his truck and reached into the open driver's side window, hoping Ben had left the keys in it. As he felt across the steering column, his fingertips brushed along their smooth metal surface.

He pulled them from the ignition.

One set of footsteps faded into the distance as the other moved closer. "Come on, Kessler. Don't be a coward."

Calvin circled around his truck and into the shadows away from it as Bachelor Number Three's silhouette came into view. Gun drawn, limping as he walked. Too tall to be Andrew, but his stance was all wrong. He didn't carry himself the way Ben did. Calvin held the fob in his hand as he watched the man sweep the area. Before he got close enough to the vehicle to see it was empty, Calvin activated the remote start.

The high-pitched whine of the starter obliterated the silence before the engine's steady purr took over. The man fired nonstop at the cab, shattering the passenger side window and riddling the windshield with holes. Calvin took advantage of the noise to sneak up behind him, waiting until he heard the telltale *click* of an empty gun before he made his next move.

"Howdy."

As the man swung around, Calvin pistol-whipped him and he hit the ground cold. He hadn't packed enough zip-ties for this many party guests, so he grabbed a discarded piece of twine from his truck and tied his catch with that instead. He disassembled the gun like he had the others, tossing the pieces far enough away that they wouldn't be easily found in the dark, but not so far that the police wouldn't find them if they searched the area.

One hostile left.

He tucked his temporary sidearm back into his waistband. Nothing suggested Ben was still here, but if he was, then there was a fifty-fifty chance the next person Calvin ran into would be a friendly. He couldn't afford to make a mistake.

★   ★   ★

Calvin's sweep of the western side of the overlook had come up empty, as had his scan of the area to the south. The surrounding forest was too extensive to search through, but that didn't mean there wasn't plenty of other ground to cover. Half-forested meant adequate cover for him, but also for an enemy.

All was quiet. Either Andrew had bailed after the last round of gunfire, or he was being very, very careful not to give away his position. Calvin watched his steps as well, but the last place he needed to clear provided virtually no cover beyond the darkness itself. He waited for the clouds to shift in front of the moon before he risked making a move in that direction.

Calvin scanned the area one last time, then left the safety of the trees and approached the wall separating the overlook from the sheer face of the bluff beneath it. He couldn't leave until he'd made sure they hadn't thrown Ben over.

"Make one move and it'll be your last."

He froze, moving his gaze in the direction of the voice until he spotted a man's silhouette in the sparsely forested area to his left. Long hair, roughly his height. The moon shed enough light to glint off of the silver surface of the pistol hanging casually at the man's side.

Andrew.

Calvin weighed his options, limited as they were. Andrew was a good twenty feet away, not nearly close enough to disarm by hand. With Calvin's gun still in his waistband there was no way he could draw faster than Andrew could raise his gun. The densely forested area surrounding the overlook was too far to make a break for. Behind him, a three-hundred-foot drop.

Yeah, great choices all around.

"Put your gun on the ground," Andrew said.

Calvin took a discreet look around, but he and Andrew were alone. He kept one hand up while slowly reaching for the gun, deciding his best course of action was stalling. He listened for sirens or anything else that might indicate backup was nearby, but the low rumble of a train was all that resonated from the base of the bluff. After setting the gun on the pavement, he carefully put his hands back up.

"Kick it away."

Calvin hesitated as long as he could before doing as he was told.

"Good. It's nice to see someone who can follow directions," Andrew said. He took a step closer. "It's a shame you won't get to again…"

As soon as Andrew raised his gun, a figure plowed into him.

Ben's silhouette blocked the muzzle flash as the shot rang out, and the two of them went sprawling onto the ground. Calvin bolted for the gun laying mere inches in front of them, reaching it a split-second before Andrew saw where it had landed. Using it was out of the question with the way he and Ben were almost on top of each other, so Calvin quickly disarmed it. As he threw it aside Andrew sprung to his feet and charged him.

The hit was harder than it should've been thanks to Calvin not having time to position himself for it. He managed to throw Andrew off-balance enough to take both of them to the ground, tucking his head for the fall. While Andrew landed gracelessly on his front, Calvin rolled off to the side and back on his feet.

Andrew got up quickly, but this time Calvin was ready for him. He knew from their earlier skirmish Andrew could hold his own in a fight, but like last time, Calvin gave better than he got. Both of them landed successful hits over the next thirty seconds, but that ended the moment Calvin glanced over Andrew's shoulder.

Ben still hadn't gotten up.

The sight kicked Calvin into a high gear he forgot he had. He landed a solid kick to Andrew's chest to put some distance between them before he backed away. Once he was in position, he took up a brawler stance and beckoned for Andrew to come and get him.

He took the bait and charged.

Right before Andrew reached him, Calvin skirted to the side and grabbed his opponent's arm, shoving him forward with his own momentum. Without the impact he'd no doubt expected, Andrew went sailing forward. Calvin braced against the wall and kept a firm hold on Andrew's arm as he went over the edge.

Andrew flailed wildly in midair as he tried unsuccessfully to find something to hold on to. Calvin kept his grip tight enough to keep from dropping him, but not so tight that Andrew would think he wouldn't.

"Come on, man! Pull me up!"

"That's a bit much to ask from a guy you just tried to shoot, don't you think?"

Andrew squirmed again to no avail. "What are you going to do, then? Let go?"

"I'm kinda leaning that way."

"Let's talk about this…"

Calvin glanced in Ben's direction, but the clouds had shifted, making it too dark to see anything. He loosened his grip. "I don't really got time to talk, Andrew."

"Please—"

He didn't hear the rest of what Andrew said, if anything. As he thought about what he should do—what he *wanted* to do—Ben's words from earlier suddenly echoed in his mind.

I just want him to face justice the way the system intended.

He hesitated. Andrew didn't deserve that level of mercy. But if anyone had the motivation to kill Andrew in cold blood, it was Ben, and he hadn't.

Wouldn't.

Calvin pulled Andrew back over the wall before throwing him head-first into the metal plaque in front of them. He slumped to the ground. With the final threat out of play, Calvin sprinted to his friend's side.

Ben was on the ground, blood seeping between his fingers as he held a hand to his left shoulder. With a groan, he rolled to his side in a completely ludicrous attempt to get up. Calvin knelt down beside him and put a hand against his chest. "Don't move. You're only gonna hurt yourself."

This time Ben didn't shy away from his touch, but whether that was from trust or distraction was anyone's guess. Sirens wailed from the bottom of the access road as the treeline started to glow with distant flashes of red and blue. Ben met his gaze, clearly trying his best to use a commanding voice despite the pain. "Get out of here."

"Like hell."

"There…there'll be an ambulance. Nothing you can do that they can't."

"Look, I'm not leav—"

"I'm fine. I—" Ben winced. He took a careful breath before looking up again. "I'll be fine. There's no reason for both of us to go to jail tonight."

"You can't possibly know you're gonna be alright," Calvin said. Even if Ben had a point about the ambulance, leaving an injured man behind screamed against everything Calvin was, had been, and ever would be.

Ben's gaze flicked to the access road. The sirens were almost on top of them now. He gestured toward the woods, his voice softening to a whisper. "Go. Please, Cal."

Calvin hesitated for a moment longer before he nodded and got up, disappearing into the tree line as the red and blue lights of the first squad car rounded the top of the hill.

47

THE AMBULANCE RIDE seemed never-ending, but at least it hadn't once crossed Ben's mind that he might be dying. The pain from the pressure they'd kept on his shoulder had been far too overwhelming to allow for such extraneous thoughts.

Those came later, when they finally rolled up to the hospital and the back doors swung open. From the looks of it, virtually every staff member who'd ever been employed there had come out of the woodwork to see what was going on. Awkward as hell, but he couldn't blame them. Twelve officers—most of them from County—escorting five suspects in handcuffs must've made for quite a sight in a town like this.

The head nurse made swift work of clearing the bystanders from the intake area. Ben hated being the center of attention, but since he was the one bleeding out while handcuffed to a gurney, there wasn't much he could do about it. Despite most people's complaints about the long wait times in an emergency room, Ben knew being first in line was never preferable. And being first in line meant the next face he saw was Tracy's.

That'd caught him off-guard, but he knew it shouldn't have. She worked here, she worked nights. As her eyes moved from the handcuffs to his shoulder, he greeted her with the only words that seemed appropriate given the circumstances. "I'm sorry."

"Ben…what happened?"

The deputy escorting him spoke up. "You know this person, ma'am?"

"Yeah. He's a friend of the family."

"Do you have any knowledge of his whereabouts recently?"

She shifted her gaze back to Ben. The look on her face was unemotional on the surface but he could see the questions in her eyes. Her words had been touching, but he still needed to think about Calvin. He didn't deserve to go down for this with him.

Ben looked at her with a subtle yet firm unspoken "no", the exact same expression he'd seen Calvin use on Mason. He could only hope Tracy would recognize it for what it was.

She held eye contact with him for a moment before turning back to the deputy. "I don't, unfortunately."

"Do you know anyone he might've been in contact with—"

"Look, I understand you have a job to do, but so do I," Tracy said. "I'd be happy to talk with you after my shift, but right now I have patients who need my attention."

*   *   *

Ben had expected to be interviewed at the hospital, but much to his surprise, he hadn't needed to stay. Just a few hours after being brought in with lights and siren, he was discharged with nothing more than painkillers, antibiotics, some stitches, and a tetanus shot.

As soon as Tracy had finished her assessment, they'd taken him straight to the radiography department to see how extensive his injuries were. Not only was the wound a through-and-through, but Dixon's gun was a small caliber. No bones, arteries, or nerves hit. According to the doctor, he'd gotten lucky.

First time in a while.

Ben ran his right hand over the cold metal table in front of him, the one belonging to the Lake City Police Department's interview room. He'd tried arguing against the sling they wanted him to wear to keep his left shoulder immobilized, but thanks to Tracy's reappearance, he'd lost that battle. Prior to discharge they'd had an officer stop at the Sunset Motel to grab him a clean shirt from his room, which he greatly appreciated since the ER nurses had cut his previous one off. Carl had handled the questioning again, but he'd long since left, leaving Ben with nothing more than his thoughts and the chill in the air.

He took in space around him. He hadn't paid any attention to his surroundings the first time. Understandable, since he'd been a complete wreck then. Now that he wasn't, he took note of every minuscule feature of the room. There weren't many, but hey, he had nothing but time.

Ben yawned, suddenly remembering he hadn't slept yet today. Or was it "tomorrow" by now? Had to be. Either way, the table started to look appealing. More or less as comfortable as the floor, but certainly a lot cleaner. Or he could put the two chairs together and lay across those.

It'd be nice. He could close his eyes, drift off…

Hold on, was he thinking of taking a nap in here? He was beyond tired, but that'd never helped rest come easy for him. For the past year sleep had been a chore, something he put off as long as possible because he dreaded it. But right now he felt surprisingly different. The formerly claustrophobic space almost seemed cozy, and he found himself looking forward to sleep. Maybe it was because for once he was relaxed, even though he knew damn well he shouldn't be. Or maybe he was so at ease because this wasn't the first time he'd been in custody.

Or maybe it was because Dixon was in custody, too.

And that made him feel…something. Satisfaction, maybe? He wouldn't go as far as calling it happiness, but whatever it was it made him feel better than he had in a long time. At least he'd have plenty of time to think about it behind bars. And oddly enough, he wasn't worried about that. Any of it. Booking, trial, prison…

There was one aspect of this whole mess that concerned him. Had concerned him, anyway. Ben had answered the questions asked of him honestly this time, but Calvin's involvement was the one thing he'd chosen to strategically omit. Everything except the part where he'd taken his pickup without consent. Which he had, technically. If you squinted really hard.

The department hadn't questioned any of Ben's statements about working alone, which meant Dixon and his cronies must not be talking. So, unless Calvin decided to contradict Ben's story when they brought him in for questioning, he'd walk away from this scot-free. Thanks to Ben's condition when he'd arrived at the ER, there was no doubt in his mind that Tracy would be calling Calvin the first chance she got. He'd have the good sense to fill her in on what was actually going on and then, hopefully, she'd cover for Calvin as well. She'd already covered for him, after all.

Good. Imagining Calvin back home, lounging on the sofa while he rubbed Greta's ears or flung scraps of food at her made Ben feel...something else. Nostalgia? Was that it?

He thought back to the first evening he'd spent at the cabin and the stories Tracy had shared. How the first time her family had gone to visit his she'd asked for a Coke and the waitress had asked her *what kind?*, since in that part of the country "coke" is synonymous with "pop". And how when Calvin was sixteen he fell into a river when he tried crossing it bareback on his uncle's new ranch horse. He'd vehemently denied it being an accident, even after she'd reminded him he had full leather chaps on when it'd happened. That'd been an interesting one.

They were good people. Ben hadn't seen a lot of those lately. He hadn't met the rest of Tracy's family, but from what little he'd heard, it was obvious she and Calvin had made a lot of good memories. With Dixon out of the picture and this mess behind them, they could get on with their lives. Calvin could get on with his life.

The more Ben thought about it, the more he felt nostalgia didn't describe what he was feeling. Nostalgia was for the past, not the future.

Maybe it *was* happiness.

The knock on the door was a clipped rapping, sudden but not unexpected. The department had more than sufficient cause to take Ben straight to jail after questioning, but they'd left him in the interview room instead. Unusual given the circumstances, but he'd had a feeling a certain someone had thrown his weight around to make that happen. Now he knew he'd been right.

As the door opened, Ben kept his gaze on the table. From the corner of his eye he watched a man in a two-piece suit step in, pocketing the badge he must've flashed to the officer who'd let him in. He walked over and pulled out the other chair with a screech before unbuttoning his jacket to sit down. The folder he slapped on the table sent a puff of wind across it.

Ben didn't look up. He didn't need to see his visitor's face. If the suit hadn't been familiar enough, the way its wearer carried himself sure was. As the room quieted, he wondered how long it would take for the man sitting across from him to break the silence. Ben sure as hell wasn't going to.

Minutes passed. As he'd expected, his visitor's patience ran out first.

"The list of charges against you," Miles said, sliding a piece of paper across the table. "It's quite extensive, if you ask me."

Ben looked at the document but didn't bother reading it. He kept his tone casual, not giving Miles the dignity of eye contact. "One thing led to another."

Vibrations rippled through the table as his brother's fist slammed into it. "You crossed the line."

Damn, that didn't take long. They must've found the Range Rover. Miles got hot-headed quickly when things didn't go his way, and as kids, Ben would use that to his advantage in their arguments. All it took to throw his brother over the edge was maintaining his own composure. The pettiness to do that had left Ben decades ago, but right now he felt like being shameless, so the poker face and laid-back tone stayed firmly in place. "If you're asking whether or not I regret it, the answer is no."

"Do you have any *idea* how much prison time you're facing?" Miles hissed.

At that Ben met his eyes, making sure his glare was ice cold. "Guess I can make up for the time Dad never served. Fitting for someone who's…how did you put that? 'No fucking better'?"

His brother's gaze faltered. "Listen, Ben. I didn't meant to—"

"Is this purely a social call? Because if you're here to read me my rights, they already did that."

"I owe you an apology."

"It's a bit late for that, if you ask me," Ben said, mirroring his brother's words as well as his earlier tone.

"Are you just feeling cocky tonight, or is that the morphine talking?"

"Does it matter?"

Miles stroked his chin, his short beard not as manicured as it usually was. "Alright, you don't want to answer that so let's move on. Did you give conscious thought to any of this before you did it?"

"You got Leighton," Ben reminded him. "Why don't you go question him for a while?"

"Speaking of which, why didn't you tell me you found him?"

"It was kind of short notice, don't you think?"

"Fair," Miles conceded. "But he's not the one who stole my car, now is he?"

"And I'm not the one who wrecked it."

Miles shot him a look before opening up his folder again. He grabbed a sheet from the back and held it in his hand. "I pulled some strings and had your blood alcohol test expedited."

"Too many pies, Miles. Why am I not surprised?"

"You know what surprised me? The results. Needless to say, I wasn't expecting zero point zero."

"No one was. That was the whole point."

He laid the paper down. "You could've told me what was going on."

"I tried that. It didn't exactly go well."

"You know, your only saving grace in this entire mess is the fact that dispatch recorded everything from that half-functioning phone of yours. Making that call is probably the only intelligent thing you've done in the last few days."

Ben leaned back and crossed his legs. "I wouldn't quite say that. I did wear my seat belt on the way up."

"Ah, that reminds me," Miles said. "Calvin Haggerty. Where is he?"

"How should I know?"

"You really expect me to believe you pulled all of this off by yourself?"

"I did, actually. But thanks for the vote of confidence."

"Alright, indulge me. If Haggerty wasn't involved, then how did you know where to find him?"

"I used to be a detective, remember? When I pulled him over he mentioned he had a cousin in town, so after I left the hospital I asked around," Ben said. "I got lucky after a few tries. This isn't exactly Minneapolis, in case you hadn't noticed."

"Why him?"

"What other options were there? I needed a vehicle, and with his warrant I knew he wouldn't report it."

"Well he did, didn't he? And he sounded concerned about your well-being when he called, I might add."

Ben leaned forward and lowered his voice. "You think we're friends? Go watch the dash cam footage from that traffic stop and then tell me what you think. Assuming you haven't already, that is."

Miles snatched his folder and stood. "This isn't over."

"I'm pretty sure it is."

"This attitude isn't like you, Ben. So, I'm going to give you the benefit of the doubt and assume it's the painkillers."

"I don't really care what you assume right now, Miles."

"You probably should, since based on what dispatch heard, it doesn't sound like you'll be doing much of any time. Assuming you get yourself a competent lawyer, and Haggerty and I both decide not to press charges."

"I can't speak for either of you."

His brother studied him a minute before turning to leave. As soon as he lifted his hand to knock on the door, Ben called over to him. "Hey, Miles."

"What?"

"Did they end up recalling Haggerty's warrant?"

Miles stepped back to the table and crossed his arms. "Oh? What's it to you?"

Ben shrugged. "I'd feel better about losing him if they did."

"You lost him either way. The fact that he's no longer wanted doesn't change a goddamn thing." With that he turned and rapped on the door, not bothering to look back as he closed it on his way out.

Ben smiled to himself.

48

Twelve Months Later

CALVIN STROLLED down the sidewalk with his hands in his pockets. The smell of rain lingered in the air, but none of it had the ambition to fall quite yet.

Cascade was a nice little town. Couldn't see the river, but it had a great view of the bluffs. Quiet, too, even for a Sunday. Population-wise it was supposedly bigger than Lake City, but it sure didn't look it. Must be the way it was laid out.

Looking ahead to the next side street, he spotted a black Explorer set back from the main road, its spotlight and steel rims a dead giveaway. The long branches of the weeping willow that graced the park behind it flowed gently in the wind.

He took a left onto the next sidewalk before crossing the street and heading toward the vehicle. He wasn't the type to walk up to a police car and hope he knew the guy or gal behind the wheel, but Ben had said he'd be the only one on duty today.

As he reached the passenger side of the Explorer, the power doors unlocked. He'd expected Ben to roll the window down, but the invitation to get in was a welcome surprise. He shimmied himself into the passenger seat and closed the door.

Space was tight thanks to all of the equipment crowding the center console and dashboard. Ben sat in the driver's seat, one hand resting leisurely on top of the steering wheel as the vehicle idled. It was the first time since they'd met in Minneapolis six years ago that Calvin had seen a genuine smile on Ben's face, and the first time he'd ever seen him in a short-sleeved uniform.

He looked good. His entire outfit was pressed and ink-black, the Cascade Police Department insignia embroidered on his shoulder done in varying shades of blue and green. The silver badge pinned to the left side of his chest almost seemed to glow against the dark backdrop of the fabric, as did the matching silver nameplate on the right that read *B. Kessler*. The scars on his arm hadn't faded, but his disapproval of them sure must've.

"Hey," Ben said. "Glad you could make it."

Calvin gestured to his uniform. "Must be nice to have your badge back."

"It is. Thank you."

"I'd say it's the jury you gotta thank."

Ben looked away. "If it wasn't for you, I probably wouldn't have been around for them to judge. You know, if we're both being honest with ourselves."

"You would've done the same for me."

He sighed and turned to the window. "When I first ran into you in Lake City, no. I wouldn't have. I'm sorry I—"

"You were going through a rough patch in your life," Calvin said. "There's no need to be sorry for that."

"Rough patch aside, that's no excuse. I shouldn't have treated you the way I did."

To be honest, Calvin hadn't held it against him. Not after Ben had opened up about the loss of his wife and the legal mess that had followed, anyway. When they'd crossed paths at Ace last year, he'd strongly felt that something in Ben's past must've been driving his behavior, so Calvin had given him the benefit of the doubt. People who seemed to be the least deserving of kindness were often the ones who needed it most, something he'd learned on his uncle's ranch. "The way I see things, that bullet you took for me more than makes up for it."

Ben flashed a brief open-palm gesture. "That did hurt like a son-of-a-bitch."

"Yeah they do. I took a couple in the service."

"You'll have to tell me the stories someday."

"You still owe me one if I remember right," Calvin reminded him.

"Damn it," Ben said, a hint of mischief in his eyes. "And here I was hoping you would've forgotten about that."

"Me? Nah. I love a good jailbreak. And I'll keep hounding you about it, too, so might as well give in."

Ben looked out the window again, not quite managing to hide his smile. "Well, maybe one day."

A female voice came over the radio. "Dispatch to 1308, just an FYI that Jim is going to be working on the chillers on top of city hall. His truck will be parked next to the building."

Ben picked up the radio. "Copy."

As he put the microphone back in its holder, Calvin gazed at the assortment of buttons and switches on the center console. He thought about asking if Ben would let him try out the lights, but decided he'd better not. He was lucky enough to be sitting in the front, felony conviction and all. "Work on any interesting cases lately?" he asked instead.

"An older one, but yeah. I have," Ben said. He pulled a sheet of paper from his pocket and unfolded it. "Have you ever heard of false confessions?"

"What, like on TV? That stuff doesn't happen in real life."

"Actually it happens more often than you might think. But you already know something about that, don't you, Cal?"

He snorted. "I don't know what you're talking about."

Ben smoothed out the paper and handed it over to him.

"What's this?"

"That'd be a police report from six years ago, the day your friend's business was robbed," Ben said. "According to that, you were cited for blowing a stop sign about twenty minutes before the break-in, which is interesting because the violation occurred in Hastings and it's a forty-minute drive from there to Paredes Fine Diamonds. Assuming you went the speed limit, of course."

That freaking stop sign, Calvin should've known it'd come back to haunt him. He wouldn't have even run it if it hadn't been for the giant shrub in front of it no one had bothered to cut down. "Look, I don't know what your game is, but you don't need to be diggin' around in things that aren't your business."

"I was the arresting detective on the case, so I'm pretty sure that makes it my business."

Calvin turned away from the cold look in Ben's eyes that reminded him of last year. He hadn't squared off with Ben very often, but the few times he had were more than enough to teach him that arguing at this point was a lost cause. "What do you want from me?"

"The truth," Ben said, his voice surprisingly soft. "You took the fall for him, didn't you?"

Calvin sighed and ran a hand through his hair. "Rodney was having money troubles, had been for a while. His wife had to quit work because of some medical condition she got during pregnancy and their health insurance left with her. Eventually the insurance on his car lapsed due to non-payment. That was a few weeks before it was stolen. Since he still had to make good on the loan, he came up with the bright idea of staging the theft so he could cash out on the business insurance while still being able to sell the jewelry through one of the...not-so-legal channels."

"So the black market."

"Pretty much, yeah. Between the two he figured he'd make enough to dig himself out of his mess."

"You didn't think to tell him what a bad idea that was?"

Calvin glared at him. "If he would've said something to me *before* he did it, you bet your ass I would've. By the time I found out, he'd already filed the report."

"And you were willing to spend five years in prison on his behalf?"

"I've known Rodney for a long time. He used to be an addict and a thief, and then he made something out of his life. Went to rehab, got an honest job, started a family. It took him years to save up enough to open his own business. I couldn't let him throw all that away over one bad decision."

"A lot of people have money problems at some point or another," Ben said. "He could've made a better choice."

"He could've, but he didn't, and he was about to get busted for it. I'd just gotten back from deployment, and it's not like there was anyone waiting for me at home."

"So you confessed to a crime you didn't commit, fabricated testimony, and lied to the police. Lied to me, specifically."

"It was the right thing to do," Calvin said, trying to keep the frustration out of his voice. "Even you gotta be able to see that."

"Why would you—"

"If you're gonna judge me, Ben, then answer this first. Have you ever been there? Taken the fall for someone else's mistake because that hurt less than watching them pay the price for it?"

A pained look crossed Ben's face. "A long time ago, yes."

"Then you know where I'm coming from."

For several minutes the soft idle of the Explorer was the only sound. As the wind picked up, a handful of narrow leaves from the weeping willow fell onto the windshield, lingering for only a moment until the next gust had them flitting across the glass and onto the street below. Ben watched them absently as he spoke. "If this comes to light in court, you can get your felony conviction overturned. Get your right to carry a gun back."

"I appreciate the thought, but if you wanna do me a favor then keep this quiet. Rodney did something stupid. We all have. He doesn't need this coming back around to haunt him."

Calvin tried to give the report back, but Ben refused. "Keep it. I already submitted the official paperwork to the court."

"What the hell, Ben? He could be looking at ten years!"

He put his hand up in a reassuring gesture. "The statute of limitations for insurance fraud is five years, so Rodney won't be facing any charges."

"You knew that?"

Ben smiled. "I made a point of finding out."

Calvin was quiet for a moment. There was no way Ben had dug into his conviction for shits and giggles. Something must've tipped him off. "How long have you known it wasn't me? The spare key under that statue…I didn't lie about that."

"I know, I checked. And you were right. It was a Chihuahua."

"How long, then?"

"Since Red Wing."

"What?"

"Like I said, my father had a gambling habit. And drinks are free at a casino, which you would've known if you'd ever been in one."

Calvin thought back to their conversation that night. It'd struck him as an odd topic for Ben to bring up, but he hadn't given it any more thought. He should've known he was fishing, trying to catch Calvin in his lie without him even realizing it. Damn cop tactics. "No, don't give me that crap. The way you set me up, you had to have known something before then."

"Well, my first clue was the ring you stole from the boat. Stole back, I should say."

"You saw that?"

"It's my job to see it," Ben said. "Rodney's, I assume?"

"No, his late grandmother's. He was going to restore it at work, so it was in the glove box the morning his car was stolen."

"Damn, what an unlucky guy."

"It takes one to know one," Calvin said.

Ben smiled. "I have a feeling that's going to change."

A car drove past and Ben glanced at the radar on the dash, but the reading must've been acceptable.

"So how's life been treatin' you?" Calvin asked. "Outside of work, I mean."

Ben dropped his gaze, tapping his fingers on the console for a few seconds before he answered. "I'm, uh…seeing someone."

Calvin looked up sharply. "Oh? Who's the lucky lady?"

The corners of Ben's mouth turned up in a faint smile as the nervousness left his face. "No, I mean a psychiatrist."

"Ah. Maybe not so lucky then," he teased.

"To be fair, she is getting paid."

Calvin laughed. "It better be a whole lot."

"How about you? Anything new and exciting in your life?"

"Nothing much. Ellie's pretty active with 4-H so Tracy and Scott and I hit quite a few of the county fairs this summer. She loves having an audience when she competes."

"Riding, I assume?"

"Equitation, mostly," Calvin elaborated. "She's good, too. The fairs are more or less done for this year, but it'd make her day if you went with us to one of her shows next summer."

Ben smiled. "Tell her I'd love to."

Two more cars passed, and he kept quiet as Ben scrutinized them. Afterwards, Calvin decided to bring up a less-distant plan they'd already made. "Are we still on for fishing next weekend?"

Ben looked at the floor. "Yeah, about that…"

"What? Don't tell me you got called in or something."

"No, but, you know…wouldn't you have a better time if you went with someone who's gone fishing before?"

"Who said you have to know how to fish to enjoy nature? It's about the company as much as the catch, anyhow."

Ben sighed. "Alright, I'll be there. But if Greta flips the boat over or anything I—"

A female voice cut him off. "1308, I have a report of a hole in the fence near the southern entrance of the old manufacturing building. The caller is advising that it looks like someone cut it."

He picked up the radio. "1308, copy. I'll be en route."

"Guess I better leave you to it," Calvin said. He opened the door and stepped out. "Thanks for this. It was nice to sit in the front for a change."

Ben leaned over to talk to him through the open door. "Once your paperwork goes through I can take you on a proper ride-along. If you're interested, that is."

"I'll take you up on that. And thanks, Ben. For everything. With my record clean and all…well, you gave me my life back."

He smiled. "I'd say we're even."

Calvin shut the door, then walked behind the Explorer and over to the sidewalk. The pond near the center of the park had caught his eye, and with the rest of the afternoon to kill he figured he might as well check it out. He barely made it five steps before rain started dotting the sidewalk in front of him.

He glanced over his shoulder. Ben's brake lights were on but he hadn't pulled out yet, taking a moment to put his hand out the window to feel the rain instead. Calvin shoved his hands back in his pockets and turned around to continue his walk. As he cut diagonally across the grass, the Explorer drove past him along the tree-lined main thoroughfare and Calvin smiled at the sight.

Ben was gonna be just fine. They both were.

ACKNOWLEDGMENTS

THERE ARE A LOT OF PEOPLE who contributed in some way to the writing of *Twist of Fate*. First and foremost would be my sister for her expertise and endless encouragement, which gave me the confidence to take the leap and consider writing a novel in the first place.

Thank you to everyone who gave insight and advice from their respective fields. Assistant District Attorney Passe, Detective Meyer, Officer Dahl, Deputy Rakes, and Dispatcher Shelby. All of you played a huge part in making the details of this book far more realistic than my internet research would've on its own, and your stories were too good not to be included in a novel. Any and all deviations from actual police, legal, or medical procedure are purely mine, and were done for narrative effect.

The story itself wouldn't be everything it is now if it wasn't for my amazing editor Rachael Waldburger. Your suggestions took my manuscript to the next level, and your fantastic writing skills always encourage me to keep improving. I'd also like to thank my lovely beta reader, M. L. Ferrer, for all of her feedback. You helped me refine the story into the best version of itself.

And last but not least, a special thanks to writer Paul Guyot. If it wasn't for your explanation of "write what you know", this book would've never existed.

ABOUT THE AUTHOR

WHILE ALENA has dabbled in writing for almost as long as she can remember, it was the entertaining and unbelievable stories told by her law enforcement family members that inspired her to begin penning her debut novel *Twist of Fate*. A Driftless Area native, her hobbies include reading, writing, painting, hunting for rainbows, and exploring  the great outdoors with her husband and two endlessly energetic children. If time allows she also likes to sleep.

If you'd like to learn more about Alena's work or see what went into the writing of *Twist of Fate*, be sure to visit her website at alena-mcpherson.weebly.com.